Steps to Heaven

Soldiers murdering their children.
Then committing suicide.
An SIB detective determined to stop the killings
A British Army soldier on Arborfield Garrison
deliberately kills his wife, his 6 year old son and
then himself. He cuts their throats and then his
own. But this is not an isolated incident. There are
similar crimes on other Garrisons. Sergeant Major
Crane, a Branch detective with the Royal Military
Police must deal with one of the most horrific cases
of his career. He is convinced the link is a local
church But is the church offering salvation - or
slaughter? How many more innocent children must
die before Crane catches the man responsible?
"A dark and twisted thriller" **Indie Book Spot**

Steps to Heaven

by

Wendy Cartmell

Costa Press

DEDICATION

For Ed, without whom this book would not
have been possible.

SOLOMON 15:30 HOURS
16TH AUGUST

Solomon knew that people described him as a quiet and unassuming man. A family man, a member of the local church, a Christian. But he was more than that. He was a Christian who had been chosen.

His first born was the key to that choosing. Not everyone could father a son, especially not their first child. It was a sign. He had studied the scriptures long into the night and knew that the ultimate sacrifice was the way to eternal salvation. Ensuring that he and his son would climb the steps to heaven.

Now it was a matter of timing. He had his instructions and intended to follow them to the letter, like a good soldier. A soldier of Christ. It was God's will.

Solomon decided to check the house once more. The mirror in the hall caught images of him, clad in his battle fatigues, as he closed and locked the doors to the front and back of the house, leaving the internal door to the garage open. That was the way they would come in. He knew their routine.

Mentally going over his check list, he realised he had one more task. Fishing the house keys out of his pocket he carefully locked the windows downstairs and then upstairs, before returning to his base.

Once there, he settled down to wait, crossed legged on the floor, his back against the kitchen door. After adjusting the beret on his shaven head Solomon began to slowly, rhythmically sharpen his knife. There was no other sound in the house, save the grinding of the blade against the pumice stone. Death given a voice. Rising and falling. Ebbing and flowing. Marching steadily closer.

Solomon repeated his mantra as he worked: "Follow the will of the Lord. Follow the steps to Heaven. Follow the will of the Lord. Follow the steps to Heaven."

CHAPTER 1

03:00 hours. Unable to sleep, Sergeant Major Tom Crane counted cases not sheep, as he stared at the ceiling. The sounds of the night rolled over him; a barrage of barking in the distance, cats fighting nearby. As the headlights of a car washed the bedroom in a pale silvery light, he slid out of bed. Picking his way across the bedroom around unseen but familiar obstacles, he grabbed his bathrobe and reached the door without disturbing Tina.

Once downstairs in the kitchen, Crane shrugged on his robe and tied the belt around his thickening waist. Resolving to lose weight yet again, he carefully put two sugars in the mug of tea he was making, instead of his usual three and made a mental note to up the mileage on his weekend run.

He passed his hand over his short dark beard, still not entirely comfortable with it. He had gained permission to grow it, in an attempt to hide the scar running across his cheek to his chin. A souvenir from shrapnel, during his last tour in Afghanistan. The scar itself still red and angry, as though an outward reflection of his inner feelings.

The beard grown not for vanity, but to stop his disfigurement being a distraction.

Waiting for the kettle to boil, Crane stared out of the window into the black void of his garden. The click of the kettle boiling sounded unusually loud in the stillness of the house and Crane shivered, looking forward to the warmth of the tea.

He collected his briefcase, which he kept strategically placed by the kitchen door and pulled out a thin buff folder. Unable to resist, he also collected his packet of cigarettes and lighter from the bottom of the case. Squaring everything on the table, he sat down, lighting up before he opened the folder, as if to give him courage to face the contents.

Squinting through the smoke, he read the British Army Special Investigation Branch (SIB) file on Lance Corporal Solomon Crooks. Aged 26, with six years' service, Solomon had returned from Afghanistan a couple of months ago. A routine tour. Or so it seemed on the surface. Crane noted down the name of Solomon's commanding officer on the pad by his elbow. He had an appointment with Colonel Pearson later that morning. Perhaps he could shed some light as to why an exemplary soldier would be involved in a domestic argument, resulting in three deaths.

Returning to the front of the file, Crane read the report by Staff Sergeant Jones of the 3rd Battalion Royal Military Police (RMP). Jones was the poor sod who was first on the scene yesterday. Glancing at the pine clock on the wall, Crane realised it was nearly 04:00 hours, so rather than face the crime scene photographs, he opted for trying to sleep. Tomorrow, or rather today, was going to be a long one.

After replacing Solomon's file in his briefcase, Crane stood and stretched, his spine clicking, reminding him of his age. At least he didn't have to worry about hair loss, he smiled to himself. He still had a good head of hair, even though the army required it to be short and smart. In fact short and smart kind of summed him up, he decided, as he tidied up the kitchen. Totally belying his name. Under six foot and stocky, smart in both appearance and intellect. Proud of his military service, Geordie roots and candour, which even he had to admit, sometimes bordered on rudeness.

Turning off the kitchen light, Crane once more felt his way through the darkened house to the bedroom, hoping to dispel the despair of the night by curling into his wife's body.

***

Crane realised he had made a mistake driving through town to Aldershot Garrison the next morning, rather than using the back road from Ash. God, what a depressing place, he thought, as he crawled through the traffic. Grey summed up Aldershot. The murky sky was dark and oppressive, despite it being August. Pedestrians hurried along, clad in dark coloured clothing. Their heads down and shoulders hunched, bowed under the weight of the greyness. He passed filthy Victorian terraces, complete with a jungle of domestic detritus that served as front gardens. An air of seediness pervaded the area, that he couldn't remember having been there a few years ago.

At last Crane pulled onto Queens Avenue, driving along the main thoroughfare of the garrison. He strictly obeyed the 30 mile an hour speed limit for nearly a mile, before turning into Provost Barracks. An un-modernised building more or less slap bang in the middle of the garrison that it policed. Slowing to a halt in front of the barrier, Crane lifted the ID hanging around his neck, ready for the young private on guard duty. After parking the car, he collected his briefcase and locked the door. Looking up he saw Staff Sergeant Jones waiting for him on the entrance steps.

Pleasantries complete, they settled themselves in the Sergeant's office. A small square room. A study in grey. Crane felt as though he was still driving through oppressive Aldershot.

"Nasty business this, sir," Jones said. 'I don't really know where to start."

"At the beginning." Crane folded his arms. "I want to hear from you what happened and what you found. You were the first on the scene. We'll discuss theories later, for now I just want facts."

"But it was in my report and you were on the scene yourself!" objected Jones, and then hesitated. "Oh, you want me to go over it again, don't you?" he asked. "To re-live it, to describe it for you, so you can feel it too."

"Sorry," Crane bent forwards focusing his sharp blue eyes on Jones, "but it really could help tease out things that you may have forgotten."

Running one hand over his nearly bald head, Jones said, "I tell you what, I'd rather forget the whole bloody thing if I had my way, but here goes."

CHAPTER 2

Crane watched Sergeant Jones pace his small office, as he relived the horrific events of yesterday. Jones told Crane that a panic 999 call was made at 16:00 hours, by a distraught neighbour, (who by rights should have called the guard room) on the afternoon of the 16th August. The neighbour reported shouting and then screaming, soon after a mother and young boy returned home from the school run. As per procedure, the police called the RMPs, as it concerned an incident at a house on Aldershot Garrison.

Arriving a few minutes behind the police, Jones and his assistant Lance Corporal Steve Tomlinson parked their vehicle and made to enter the house. At that stage they thought it was a domestic violence call. Thinking they would simply have to cart the solider back to the guard room while he cooled down, Jones and Tomlinson were unconcerned. After all, incidents such as this were a common occurrence on the garrison.

Jones was heading for the front door, when Detective Inspector Derek Anderson of the

Aldershot Police appeared in the doorway of the house. His face bleached so white, that Jones thought Anderson was going to faint. Leaning against the doorframe for support, Anderson looked at Jones, with haunted eyes that barely registered him. "It's bad," he whispered, "really bad this one. You might want to leave the young lad out here," jerking his head towards Tomlinson. With that Anderson walked to the end of the drive. After ordering Tomlinson to stay where he was, Jones made his way inside.

Interrupting the recount, Crane said, "Okay, first of all describe your entry into the house. What could you see? What was the atmosphere?"

Pausing for a moment, Jones returned to his seat and leaned back. "I walked into an entrance hall. I could see the stairs on my left and a door on my right, with a further door in front of me at the end of the hall."

"Open or closed?"

"I'm sure the door on my right was closed, but the door at the end of the hall was half open."

"And the atmosphere?" Crane asked.

"Very quiet and still, deathly quiet, if you'll excuse the pun." Neither man smiled. "It seemed stuffy in there, shut up, if you know what I mean."

"Good, so then what did you do?"

Jones rose once more. He stopped by the window and leant against the wall. "I went to the end of the hall and pushed the door to the kitchen open with my elbow as I wasn't wearing gloves. The smell hit me first, bitter and coppery, so I knew even before I looked down that there must be a lot of blood. And there was. Everywhere. Pools on the floor and arterial splatter on the walls and doors."

Crane waited patiently, not wanting to interrupt. Afraid that if he did, Jones won't be able to continue.

"I saw a woman. She was lying on the floor, with her arms stretched towards a door to my left, which I presumed was the door to the garage. There were drag marks in the blood by her feet, as though she had tried to get to the garage, but hadn't made it."

Jones looked down at his trembling hands. Stuffing them into the trouser pockets of his uniform he cleared his throat and continued.

"Raising my head, I saw a glass door to the garden in front of me, with a sink and kitchen units next to it. On the right hand side of the room more units ran along the wall." Jones bowed his head and Crane had to strain to hear his next words. "They were all covered in blood. The units I mean. It was as though someone had splattered red paint from a brush in an artistic frenzy. Living art, or rather deadly art in this case."

As the silence stretched, Crane worried at the scar under his beard. "What about the windows and doors?"

"Sorry?" Jones turned and looked at Crane.

"Windows and doors in the kitchen," Crane repeated. "Open or closed?"

"Closed, all of them," Jones replied.

Jones stared blankly out of the window, as if seeing the scene painted on the panes. "I looked down…and there they were…a soldier in battle fatigues sitting on the floor with his back against the kitchen units, cradling his son on his lap. The boy had a football strip on, but his white shirt had turned pink. His dark curly hair had red streaks in it, probably from his father's blood. He couldn't have been more than about six years old. They were both dead. The soldier still had the knife in his right hand, which had fallen on the floor next to him. His left arm was around his son's chest, pulling him close. Both had their throats cut."

After a pause, allowing Jones to collect himself and return to his seat, Crane questioned him about his actions following the gruesome discovery.

"I followed procedure, sir," was Jones' curt response. "I vacated the scene without touching anything and then called the Adjutant, who in turn called you lot, the Branch." Jones used the euphemism for the SIB.

"So who opened the door to the garden?"

"What? What the bloody hell are you talking about?"

Leaning forward across the desk, Crane explained. "When I arrived, just after the Pathologist, I felt fresh air blowing through the house. I understand that we had the front door open, but I noticed the back door to the garden was also open, allowing through a draught." Jones made to speak, but Crane persisted. "And you've just told me that when you entered the house, all the doors and windows were shut in the hall and in the kitchen. That's why the smell of death was so strong."

Pushing back into his chair, recoiling from the force of Crane's words, Jones thought for a moment. "Shit. I think Tomlinson must have done it then. Opened the door to the garden. He slipped past me to look when I called the Adjutant. But what difference does it make? It didn't interfere with any evidence surely?"

Levering himself out of his chair, Crane looked down at Jones. "That's a matter of opinion, Staff. Think about it. If the door to the garden had been open when Solomon and his wife were having a row and in the heat of the moment he went for her, she would have escaped into the garden. And anyway, the boy wouldn't have been there."

"Well, yes," agreed Jones. "If you're having an argument, you tend to send the kids out of the room."

"Exactly. So with the house locked down tight, maybe Solomon planned it. Maybe it wasn't a domestic argument gone wrong as we all thought, but a deliberate, pre-meditated attack on his wife and son. Solomon always meant to kill them and then commit suicide. So put that stupid bastard Tomlinson on report."

"Dear God," whispered Jones, putting his head in his hands as Crane left the office.

CHAPTER 3

Due to see Solomon's commanding officer, Crane made his way to his car. As he drove, he mulled over his knowledge of the garrison. Aldershot Garrison had a fine military history and was split into two Camps, North Camp (which became known as the Marlborough Lines) and South Camp (the Stanhope Lines). It was first conceived in 1854 as a large scale space for the concentration and training of troops. Over the years the garrison had become known as 'The Home of the British Army' and was the home of the Parachute Regiment. But when the Paras left in 1999, it became the base of the 12 (Mechanised) Brigade. Crane believed the relocation of the Paras was Aldershot town's downfall. A once vibrant place, reduced to a ghost town by comparison.

A five minute drive up Queens Avenue, towards North Camp, brought Crane to Lille Barracks, the new home of the 145 (South) Brigade. The difference between the RMP headquarters and the shiny new buildings was startling. After passing through the guard post and entering the barracks,

Crane gazed around. Here new floors caused boots to squeak and records of the regiments' achievements decorated the eggshell coloured walls. Through double doors at the end of the main corridor, Crane could just glimpse the new mess hall, resplendent with its gleaming stainless steel fittings. Walking with his head held high and his arms swinging, marching as though he were in uniform instead of dark suit and white shirt, Crane followed the directions given to him yesterday and found his way to the Colonel Pearson's office. The Adjutant showed him through to the great man's domain.

Crane saw the Colonel standing by a large window which dominated a room furnished in an old fashioned style, redolent of an officers' mess. A large mahogany desk, empty of papers, filled one half of the space, complete with a large leather office chair and two smaller visitors' chairs. A conference table with seating for six took up the remaining space. The beige carpeted floor was covered by a large rug that Crane imagined had some fancy name and an equally fancy price tag.

Colonel Pearson gazed down on the parade ground, which was filled with marching, wheeling soldiers. A sight that still had the ability to fill Crane with pride. He may be SIB, he thought, but was first and foremost a soldier. The Colonel pulled down his tunic, which seemed rather large on his shrunken frame and turned his rocky, weather beaten face towards Crane. Crane stood silently to attention until asked to sit. Once seated,

Crane began, "Thank you for seeing me, sir".

"No problem, Crane. I just wish it was under better circumstances. Nasty business this."

"Indeed, sir, a view that many of us share. But it's my unfortunate duty to investigate it."

"Investigate?" queried the Colonel, the bushy eyebrows that dominated his face arching. "Sorry, but what's to investigate? I was led to believe by the Adjutant that it was a domestic argument that got out of hand. A young soldier murdered his family and then killed himself, unable to face the consequence of his actions."

"Maybe, sir," said Crane. "But even if that turns out to be correct, I want to find out why."

Rising, the Colonel resumed his position gazing out over the parade ground. Without turning round he said, "Then investigate his private life. Find out what his wife had been up to."

"Of course, sir …but…" Crane subconsciously scratched at his beard.

"Spit it out, man, can't abide a ditherer," called Colonel Pearson, raising himself to his full height and once more turning to look at Crane.

"I also need to investigate what happened during his tour in Afghanistan." Expanding on his thinking, Crane continued, "Could any incident in particular have affected Solomon badly? What was his mental state whilst he was in Afghanistan? What was his mental state when he returned? Did he ask for counselling? Did he-"

"Alright, alright, I get the picture." Returning to sit at his desk the Colonel leaned back in his chair, the leather squeaking in protest. "I suppose you want permission to interview my men, never mind the disruption you'll cause and the bad feeling you'll spread throughout the regiment."

"Sorry, sir, but I really feel it's necessary."

"Why? What have you found?" Colonel Pearson narrowed his eyes, his forest of grey splattered eyebrows all but obscuring the lids.

"I'd rather not say at this stage, sir." Crane folded his arms.

After a short silence Colonel Pearson barked, "Very well. See the Adjutant. Keep me posted through Captain Edwards."

Rising to his feet before the Colonel changed his mind, Crane replied with an equally curt, "Sir," and a nod of his head.

***

On one of the newer housing estates on the garrison, Crane found Newton Avenue. Aldershot Garrison boasted a range of accommodation for its soldiers and their families. The newer barracks incorporated brand new single men's quarters, whilst houses for officers and other ranks, some old and some new, sprawled across the garrison, like clutches of Lego land buildings, hugging each barracks.

As Crane drove through the estate, he saw the comings and goings of a suburban street. Mothers with babies resplendent in their smart new strollers; small children playing on the swings, under the watchful eye of a parent or child minder; wives staggering under the weight of their shopping bags as they emerged from a local store. Crane was acutely aware of such normal, everyday scenes, juxtaposed with the horrific murder of a child.

Drawing up opposite number 13 Crane stopped the car, turned off the engine and looked at the outside of the house. It was one of a number of newer terraced houses, each with their own driveway and integral garage. They looked quite small and had just two bedrooms. But still, the sort of house that anyone in 'Civvy Street' would be proud to live in with their family. Crane supposed that the other members of his team attached to the investigation would still be in the house and went to join them.

Inside the living room he found Staff Sergeant Billy Williams looking through a desk, which at first glance seemed to contain household bills and other such correspondence. Raising his head from the paperwork, Billy made to stand, but Crane waved him back down.

"Anything interesting, Billy?"

"No, sir, just the normal stuff everyone has. Lance Corporal Crooks had a laptop, which the techies have taken away to look at. Better than me trying and messing up, eh, sir?" he finished with a grin. His youthful face had an openness that was appealing, with a shock of blond hair that constantly fell into his eyes.

Billy was not technically minded and had messed up on more than one occasion, so now Crane kept him away from computers that may hold potential evidence. Strange for a young man not to be good at that sort of stuff, but Billy was more the physical type, forever in the gym, playing football or out with the lads. Crane knew he wouldn't find him holed up in a room with a PlayStation or computer. Fresh air and exercise were his mantras and he had a well-muscled, fit body to show for it.

"Okay. What about scene of crime?" nodding his head in the direction of the kitchen. Normally SIB investigators collected their own forensic evidence, but as this was such a large crime scene Crane had called in a specialist.

"All finished, sir. Sergeant Smith said he'll be ready to report tomorrow morning at 09:00 hours. If that's alright with you, of course."

"Yes, fine. We're not up against time on this one."

"No, sir," the younger man agreed. "Major Martin said he'll be ready with the post mortem results by then as well. DI Anderson agreed to the meeting being held here on the garrison and will be in attendance."

"Fair enough. Now, what about friends, relatives, neighbours? Who's handling the interviews?"

"Kim is. She's gone back to the office to write up her reports. She said to let you know that she'll meet you there."

"Good choice, Billy," Crane said. "A bit sexist I know, but people have enough trouble talking to the Branch as it is. Maybe the wives will open up to Sergeant Weston." Turning to leave Crane instructed, "Finish up here, then chase the techies and while you're waiting fully investigate Lance Corporal Crooks' finances. I need to know if he had money problems."

"Sir," Billy acknowledged, pushing his hair out of his eyes and going back to the paperwork.

Leaving the room, Crane avoided the kitchen and went upstairs. There were three doors. The first one Crane chose revealed the child's room. It remained frozen in time. The bed was unmade and books tumbled across the small desk in the corner. Aeroplanes were strung from the ceiling, still and silent in the dead air and pictures of Aldershot football team adorned the walls. Crane picked up a small photo frame from next to the bed. A picture of the boy, grinning for the camera, with his arms around his father's neck. Crane paused and closed his eyes for a moment, reflecting on the utter waste of a young innocent life, before replacing the photograph and backing out of the room.

In the hall, Crane pushed open the second door revealing a neat bathroom and then turned to the final room. The master bedroom, if you could call it that, was at the front of the house, over the garage. A small double containing a bed, bedside cabinets, double wardrobe and small dressing table. The few pieces of cheap pine furniture seemed to dominate the room and Crane immediately found it claustrophobic.

Moving to one side of the bed, he opened the drawer to the bedside cabinet, finding women's magazines and a couple of paperback books. Going around the bed to the other side, he found a drawer filled with pamphlets. Fishing them out, Crane laid them on the bed.

The religious tracts seemed to be the kind of thing Mormons or Seventh Day Adventists pushed through doors, or handed out to anyone willing to take them. Just about to dismiss them, Crane found one from a local church. 'Jesus is King!' hailed the banner headline and skimming the text Crane found an invitation to those who were feeling lost to go along and be saved. Had Solomon gone to the church and if so, what did he feel he needed saving from? Pondering these questions, Crane gathered up the pamphlets, put them in his pocket, ran down the stairs and left the house.

CHAPTER 4

Chewing on a sandwich that tasted of the plastic wrapping it had come in; Crane sat at his desk looking at the pamphlets from Solomon's house. Spread before him the innocuous pieces of paper seemed to offer no threat, merely salvation. He pushed them away, as he couldn't make any sense of them, dumped his half eaten BLT in the bin and went through to the main office.

"Sergeant Weston," he called. "I was told you'd have a report on the interviews with Lance Corporal Crooks' neighbours ready after lunch."

"That's right, sir," confirmed Kim, rising from behind her desk in a corner of the room.

"Well, as it's after my lunch, my office. Now!" Turning away, Crane returned to his office and sat watching the newly promoted young Sergeant.

Kim Weston was an asset to the team. A fact that he would share with her in due course, he decided. She was collating the paperwork strewn across her desk, to carry into Crane's office but he knew that once she settled herself, her report would be clear and concise. Her work reflected her appearance, or was it the other way round? Smart, tidy and organised described them both. Her blond hair was scraped into a tight bun and her uniform pristine. In fact she was so focused that sometimes Crane wondered if she ever relaxed, even when off duty.

"So," he said once Kim was settled in the chair opposite him. "What have you got for me?"

Kim opened her ever present notebook. "Well, sir, first I interviewed the immediate neighbours. It seemed the family were well liked. No history of marital problems, so as a result everyone was pretty stunned."

"Any gossip about the wife?" asked Crane, leaning back in his chair, pursuing the line of enquiry instructed by Colonel Pearson.

"What sort of gossip? Are you suggesting this could have been her fault, sir?"

"Come on, Kim, you know the score. Solomon had been away for six months. Did she get lonely? Turn to someone else to keep her warm at night? Maybe Solomon found out and lost it?"

"There's no evidence to suggest that, sir," said Kim bristling. Crane could hear the lining of her skirt crackling. "If there was, I would have found it."

"Look, there's no place for sensitivities here, Kim. We're dealing with murder and then suicide. Something triggered it. It's our job to find out what. Go back and interview the neighbours again. This time I want facts not feelings. And don't forget to interview Mrs Crooks' family. I want reports on interviews from them as well."

"Sir." Kim snapped her pad closed.

"Have everything ready for a full briefing at 09:00 hours tomorrow. Well off you go then," barked Crane at the still seated Kim.

"Sorry, sir, just one more thing."

"Yes?"

"I've been getting press calls. Specifically from Diane Chambers of the Aldershot Mail."

"Refer her to the press office and the Aldershot police."

"I've tried that, sir, but she won't go away."

"Then make her, Sergeant. The Branch doesn't talk to the press. Now off you go."

With his team fully occupied, Crane left the office and went looking for the army chaplain for Aldershot Garrison.

***

Padre Francis Symonds was the Senior Chaplain of the Royal Garrison Church, he was assisted by two other chaplains and between them they covered the large garrison and surrounding barracks. Crane found him in the Officers' Mess, just finishing lunch and they met in an empty conference room. Padre Symonds had the type of soft rounded features that meant it was hard to accurately guess his age. Crane put him in his mid 30's. He was dressed casually, wearing uniform trousers and a black clerical shirt with a dog collar. Simply furnished, the room had a circular meeting table and six chairs and Crane and the Padre took seats opposite each other.

Crane explained that there had been a murder/suicide on the garrison, perpetrated by Lance Corporal Crooks and that Crane was in charge of the investigation. At first the Chaplain was reluctant to comment on the matter. As far as the he could remember, no one of Crooks' name or description had ever approached him for help or advice. However, Crane pressed the mild mannered, courteous Chaplain, wanting to know about local churches in the Aldershot area.

"Well, of course, a range, as you would expect," was the non-committal answer.

"Could you be more specific, sir?"

"Oh, I suppose, Church of England, Roman Catholic, Baptist, Methodist…"

"Do any of them actively recruit in the area?"

"Actively recruit?" Symonds stared at Crane as though he was some sort of simpleton. "Well, of course, we all actively recruit in our own way."

"Yes, but are any of them more persistent than others?"

"More persistent? Sergeant Major I really don't grasp what you're trying to imply. I rather think you're the one that's being persistent."

Exasperated, Crane fished the pamphlets from the Church of Jesus is King out of his pocket. Realising he would have to be rather more direct, Crane pushed the papers across the table towards the Chaplain.

"I found these pamphlets in Lance Corporal Crooks' bedroom," he explained and then leant back in his chair. "I wondered what you knew about this church and their methods."

"Ahhh…" said the Chaplain after looking at the papers for a few moments and then adopting a reflective position with his chin resting on clasped hands.

"Ahhh, sir?"

"Yes, well, this is a little delicate."

"Let me spell this out for you, Padre. There is nothing delicate about a murder and suicide by one of our lads. Not the crime and not the investigation that follows. I need answers and I need them now. So let's forget sensibilities and diplomacy and tell me about this church."

"Really, Sergeant Major, there's no need for that kind of attitude," rebuked the Padre, standing and folding his arms.

"Really, Padre, there is." Crane refused to be bullied, even by a superior officer. "I've been tasked by Colonel Pearson to find out what happened to one of his boys and I intend to follow orders. I'm sure he doesn't want to hear that you were unwilling to assist in that investigation."

After a moment's reflection, the Padre sat down again and began to talk.

"If I may be frank."

Resisting a more sarcastic reply, Crane inclined his head and said, "Please do, Padre."

"The Church of Jesus is King in Aldershot had concerned me a little I must admit. Their methods are, well, a trifle over enthusiastic, when it comes to persuading people to join their church."

"Over enthusiastic?" Crane leant forward.

"Yes. It seems that once you attend the church for a service, they are, shall we say, reluctant to let you go. They pile on the pressure to make you keep going. Ensnare you with invisible threads as it were. Also it's a very evangelical type of worship."

"Meaning?" Crane was more than a little perplexed by the description.

"Well, the congregation are encouraged to, ah, let themselves go. You know, fully join in, shout out when the need takes them and," continued the Chaplain dropping his voice to a whisper, although there was no one else in the room, "I've heard reports of members of the congregation speaking in tongues."

Not liking what he was hearing, Crane wanted to know if members of the Church of Jesus is King were actively recruiting on the garrison.

"Not as far as I'm aware, but I couldn't say for certain."

Crane stood and paced the room for a moment, before turning back to address Symonds. "Thank you for your frankness, Padre, but I need to know if this church is active on the garrison. If our soldiers have been attending and getting ensnared by invisible threads, as you put it. Also, more specifically, if Lance Corporal Crooks was a regular attendee."

"But, Crane, I can't just go along and start accusing them of what I deem to be inappropriate religious behaviour!" The Chaplain looked at Crane as though he had just suggested that God was the devil in disguise.

Crane remained standing but placed his arms on the desk, closing the space between himself and the Padre. "Of course not, sir. But you could go and meet with the leader of the Church, as a result of the tragic events here on the garrison. Ask for any help and information on the Lance Corporal that he may be able to give. You know the drill, I'm sure. All in the spirit and love of Jesus and mutual co-operation in the community. That sort of thing." Crane tried hard to keep the sarcasm out of his voice.

A gleam appeared in the Padre's eyes and he smiled. "Of course, I see now. Very clever, Sergeant Major."

Sitting back down, Crane said, "Not really, sir, just standard investigative procedure. But much better coming from you, don't you think? And of course I'm sure the Colonel will look favourably on your co-operation."

Hesitantly, the Chaplain finally nodded his agreement. "I'll see what I can find out for you by tomorrow."

"Thank you, sir," a relieved Crane replied.

CHAPTER 5

That night at home, Crane was preoccupied. It was troubling him deeply that something as awful as the murders had happened on his garrison. He was aware things like this happen in 'Civvy Street', but he had always thought soldiers more disciplined. Fair enough, most of them flare up at one point or another, Crane had to admit it was almost a given. But to go as far as murdering your family? He was having a hard time getting the whole business out of his head.

Unfortunately Tina hadn't picked up on his mood. "Tom..." she began over dinner at their large farmhouse table in the kitchen, which was far too big for just the two of them.

"Yes, love?" he replied, looking up from his plate. The sight of her made him smile. She had changed from the business suit she wore for work at the bank into what he called a track suit and his wife called a leisure suit. Her long dark straight hair was loose, framing her face and most of her makeup had worn off. That was how he liked her best. Natural and relaxed, her arched eyebrows giving her a slightly quizzical look. Her eyes were searching his, as if trying to decide whether to speak or not.

"Well, I've been thinking about our future," she said, dropping her eyes to look at her food instead of him, pushing around the vegetables on her plate, studying them as if they were suddenly foreign to her.

Crane groaned inwardly, whilst keeping the smile plastered on his face. "Oh yes?" he tried to inject enthusiasm into his voice.

"You know, wondering if the time was right. What do you think?" Tina raised her head and looked at him, with eyes like a timid dog. Soft, liquid and trusting.

What Crane thought was that she couldn't have picked a worse time to want a discussion about having children, when all Crane could see when he closed his eyes was the young boy dead in his father's arms, by his father's hand. But of course he couldn't tell her that.

"What about your career at the bank?" He answered a question with a question.

"I know, I know," Tina replied turning her wine glass round and round. After pausing to take a sip of the blood red liquid, she continued, "But I figured that I could take maternity leave and then see where we go from there."

Dragging his eyes away from the wine she was drinking, Crane took a long draught of his beer. Placing the glass back on the table, he got out of his chair and began to clear the debris of their meal.

Another avoidance tactic, he knew that, but he couldn't seem to help it.

"What about the finances though?" he called over his shoulder from the sink.

"Well, I was thinking that if I look into that first, taking into account my maternity pay and all the benefits you seem to get these days when you have a child, I was wondering if we could just manage, even if I don't go back to work."

Crane slumped against the sink, thanking whatever God there might be up there for the reprieve.

"Why don't you do that then?" This time his enthusiasm was genuine. "We could talk about it again next week and go over the figures."

Moving over to the sink, Tina placed her arms around his chest and her head against his back. "Thanks, love, I knew you'd understand."

Crane dropped the plate he was holding, turned in her arms, kissed her and then whispered in her ear. "No, thank you."

"What for?"

"For being just the kind of wife I need right now."

"And what kind of wife is that?" she teased.

"The kind that doesn't care if the washing up doesn't get done tonight."

***

Crane awoke refreshed the next morning and was in the office by 08.00 studying the incident board. As he requested, everyone was in place by 09.00 hours ready to go through the reports.

Major Martin, an army officer who had taken up a position as pathologist at the nearby Frimley Park Hospital on his retirement from the forces, gave his report first. He was greatly respected by Crane and other members of the Branch, who did everything they could to ensure the Major dealt with any post mortems they had an interest in.

"Right, well," the Major began. "I can confirm that all three died by knife wound to the throat, made by a right handed man and that the cuts were consistent with the blade found in Solomon's hand. The times of death, although very close together, indicate that Mrs Crooks died first, followed by her son and then Solomon. All this is consistent with murder and then suicide. None of the three had any health problems and the initial toxicology reports are clean. There was no alcohol in either Lance Corporal Crooks' blood, or his wife's. None had any fatal illnesses. Crooks was healthy, as one would expect."

"So you found nothing physical that could have caused Crooks to behave in such a way?" Crane asked.

"What do you mean?"

"Oh, I don't know, a brain tumour or something, anything." Crane rubbed his scar.

"Sorry, Crane, I can't help you there. You're clutching at straws. If there was an illness behind this behaviour, I would have to say it was psychological not physical and even though I'm good, I'm not God. I can't see from his brain what his last thoughts were."

Amid good natured chuckling, Crane said, "Thank you for your report and for coming along to give it personally, sir. Right then, let's hear from Sergeant Smith."

The room stilled as Smith moved to the front of the room. "Well, sir," he addressed Crane, "the Major's opinion of murder and then suicide is borne out by the forensic evidence. The blood splatter is consistent with arterial spray and the finger prints found in the kitchen match all three victims. Other prints found in the house are too smudged to be identified, the house having been recently cleaned. The blood at the scene has been identified as belonging to all three victims. No other blood type has been found. Solomon had blood on his clothes from his wife and also his son. Only the boy had Solomon's blood on him, consistent with Solomon killing his wife first, and then the boy and finally committing suicide. From the drag marks in the blood near Mrs Crooks, it is presumed she tried to reach the garage door, but failed. The footprints found in her blood match the boots worn by Lance Corporal Crooks." Smith paused and shuffled his papers before continuing. "All the rooms in the house have been examined and we found that all the windows in the house had been locked, together with the front door. The door to the garage was closed and locked. The door to the garden was open when I arrived on the scene."

"Anything else we should know about?"

"Only trace evidence, sir. We found something

on his trousers. But I'm not sure what it is yet. I'm still waiting to hear from the lab."

"What sort of trace?" Crane was impatient. He hated having to wait for the results of forensic tests. Any trace evidence could be highly important and give them further leads, but the trouble was that it took several days for the findings to be analysed. Crane fantasised about the labs in the American CSI programmes, but knew that in reality, results took days or weeks, not hours.

"Small grains of two different substances," Sergeant Smith explained. "I'll let you know as soon as we get the results."

"DI Anderson, anything you want to add?"

The policeman shook his head. "Not at this stage, Crane. It looks as if it's fairly clear cut. So unless there is anything else, I'll see you at the inquest." Anderson stood and collected his jacket and briefcase, both of which looked as tired and beaten as he did. After the three men left, Kim and Billy stayed on for a team discussion.

"Okay, thoughts," invited Crane, sitting on the edge of a desk.

"Clear murder and then suicide," said Billy, leaning back in his chair and locking his hands behind his head.

"Well, of course it was. But why? Why in God's name would Crooks kill his wife and son and then kill himself?" asked Crane.

Kim and Billy failed to reply.

"Come on, come on, you must have some theories," said Crane raising his voice in frustration at their lack of initiative.

"Okay, boss, how about his wife playing around?"

"Good, Billy. Kim, what did you find out?"

"Absolutely no evidence to suggest that, sir," replied Kim, as formal as ever. "I spoke to the neighbours. Mrs Crooks was particularly friendly with Jean Byrd next door, so I talked to her at length. She said that Mrs Crooks told her most things and had never mentioned a love interest. She also claims she would have known if 'something had been up', as she put it."

"And family?"

"I spoke to Mrs Crooks' mother and sister. Again both said that she had a happy marriage. They believed she had loved her husband and enjoyed being in the army community. They also stressed that she was very proud of Solomon and his achievements. So it looks like that theory is a dead end. Crooks had no immediate family. His mother and father died a few years ago and he was an only child."

"Billy, what did you find out about their financial affairs?"

"Well, as with most soldiers, they sailed pretty close to the wind, but were basically alright, just about keeping their heads above water," said Billy as he consulted his notes.

"Anything unusual? Any regular withdrawals? Maybe the one playing away was Crooks himself. If he was he'd need to finance it, either paying a prostitute or taking a mistress out for a meal?"

"Not really, sir. The only thing was that he used to take out money every Sunday morning, regular as clockwork, at about 10am. £50 each time. Could have just been his weekly spending money I suppose."

Crane's interest was piqued. He cocked his head and scratched at his beard. "Every Sunday at the same time?"

"Yes, sir."

"The same cash point machine each time?"

Again Billy consulted his notes. "Yes, sir. The Santander on the High Street. Just across the road from his quarters on the garrison. So I guess that was his nearest one. Maybe you're right and he had an assignation every Sunday," grinned Billy. "You know the sort he didn't want his wife to know about." Billy stopped short of winking, but gave Crane a knowing look.

"Is that all you ever think about?" snapped Kim, her voice dripping venom.

"Just exploring possibilities," said Billy, putting his hands in his pockets and stretching in his seat.

After a brief pause, Crane stood and said, "Alright, dismissed for now. Billy, let me know when the computer boys come back on the Lance Corporal's laptop. Kim, check with welfare to see if there have been any visits there by Solomon or his wife. Oh and fix me up a meeting with Padre Symonds and Crooks' Sergeant Major. Both for some time today."

"Yes, sir," Billy and Kim replied in unison.

Just then the phone rang. Kim answered,

listened and then replied, "Certainly, sir." Replacing the receiver she looked at Crane, "The Captain is waiting in his office for you, sir."

CHAPTER 6

Captain James Edwards had been in command of the SIB in Aldershot for the past year. That made him a newbie as far as Crane was concerned, having himself served there, between his posting in Afghanistan, for over two. A fact that Crane had been known to needle Captain Edwards with, citing superior knowledge of the garrison and the men stationed there. This time though, neither Crane nor the Captain had ever dealt with a murder/suicide before, so it was new ground for them both.

Captain Edwards was sitting at his desk as Crane entered the room, which was not nearly as opulent as the Colonel's office. Basic furniture including a small desk, were crowded into the small space. There was not enough room for a conference table. Looking at his Captain, Crane saw a man with regulation short black hair and the kind of aristocratic features that came from years of family inbreeding – long aquiline nose and a weak chin. His eyes were a startling blue and he had the natural haughty expression of someone used to being obeyed, either because of his money or his rank.

"Sir," Crane said, remaining standing, before being invited to sit.

"Right, what's your update on the Crooks case?" Captain Edwards began.

Crane proceeded to go over the reports presented at the meeting by Sergeant Smith and Major Martin, finishing with the team discussion and their proposed way forward.

"Sorry, Crane, but isn't this case closed?" said his superior officer in his most superior voice.

"Yes, in terms of what happened, it is, sir."

"Well then, that's all there is to it," replied Captain Edwards, closing the file on his desk.

"Sir?"

"Case closed, Sergeant Major, don't you agree?"

"Not at all, sir…with respect," Crane added.

"What do you mean, Crane? It's as plain as the nose on my face what happened," the Captain said in exasperation, tapping the file in front of him to make his point.

"But don't you want to know why?"

"Why?" queried Edwards.

"Yes, sir. Why did he do it?"

"Is that relevant?"

Breathing deeply to calm himself down, Crane began to speak, choosing his words carefully. "It's certainly relevant, sir. Perhaps there are lessons to be learned from what happened, so we can at least try and make sure it doesn't happen again."

Clearly not looking favourably on Crane, or his

opinions, Edwards rose from his chair, as though the increased height would give him back some of the advantage that his rank should have afforded him, and began prowling around the small space.

"Is this the mamby pamby, new age shit I keep hearing about? Where we should wrap our men in cotton wool, instead of making soldiers of them? Generations of my family have served in the armed forces and in our experience men have to put up and shut up."

Suppressing a smile and keeping his face blank, Crane clarified things for Captain Edwards. "I don't know about that, sir. What I do know is that Colonel Pearson has given me permission to investigate the matter from a personal angle."

"A personal angle? Are you sure?" The mention of Colonel Pearson made Edwards stand still.

"Yes indeed, sir. Crooks could have been affected by family problems, financial problems, or even problems he faced in Afghanistan or that have developed since he returned."

Going back to his desk, Captain Edwards said, "Colonel Pearson's given his permission you say?" ,

"Rather willingly in fact," said Crane, stretching the truth somewhat.

"Oh very well, but make it snappy. Let's get this one wrapped up quickly. Dismissed."

"Thank you, sir," said Crane, smiling inside. His face, his usual mask of respect.

As Crane was leaving Captain Edward's office, he received a call from Kim.

"Lance Corporal Crooks' Sergeant Major can see

you in 15 minutes, sir."

"Good. Give me the details."

***

Crane arrived at Lille Barracks and followed Kim's instructions, finding his way to Sergeant Major Phil Tomlinson. Tomlinson was just finishing up on the parade ground and Crane watched with interest as he put the soldiers through their paces. His voice rang loud and true, bouncing off the walls of the buildings covering three sides of the large space. As a result, his instructions were barely intelligible to an untrained ear. But the soldiers under his command seemed to have no problem understanding and responded immediately to his every bark and shout. Once the officer commanding gave the order, Tomlinson dismissed the troops and marched towards Crane, his barrel chest pushed forward. Standing stiffly to attention in front of Crane for a few seconds, his face then relaxed and crumpled into a less formal arrangement of features, before holding his hand out to Crane.

"Crane, good to see you."

"And you, Phil." Crane shook his old friend's hand. Crane and Phil Tomlinson had joined up at the same time and went through basic training together, managing to keep in touch irregularly over the years as they passed through various locations on their way up the career ladder.

"Come away to my office." Phil indicated the building opposite. As they walked, the two friends caught up with each other's recent postings and asked after their respective wives.

Upon reaching the privacy of Phil's office, they sat in a couple of chairs to discuss the subject that both of them had been avoiding. Crane wanted to know about Solomon.

"Good soldier, showing leadership potential. What else is there to know?" asked Phil.

"Come on, don't give me that bullshit," countered Crane, leaning forward with his hands on his knees. "I know you too well for that. I need to know what was behind this whole sorry business. A man doesn't just up and kill his family and then commit suicide."

"Fair enough, but I don't have exclusive access to all the men's thoughts and feelings you know. It's more of do they jump high enough and fast enough as far as I'm concerned and Solomon certainly did that."

"How was he in Afghanistan?"

"Seemed alright on the surface."

"Meaning?"

"He did his job."

"Any signs of fear, questioning why he was there, that sort of thing?"

"Not that I saw."

"Who would have seen? Who was he closest to? Come on, Phil, work with me on this," Crane implored, standing and pacing around yet another small grey room, failing to hide his frustration with the ping pong of the questions and answers. It was becoming clear that Phil wasn't opening up as much as he had hoped he would. Tomlinson remained seated and stared at Crane, refusing to answer the last question. Given no choice Crane returned to his own chair and changed tack.

"Had an interesting conversation with Colonel Pearson yesterday," he said casually.

Phil made no comment but raised his eyebrows.

"He was very concerned that this should have happened to someone in his regiment." As the silence from Phil continued, Crane said, "He was most insistent that I investigate this matter from all angles. Obviously from the personal one – his family life – but also from a professional angle. For instance, he was particularly interested to find out if anything had happened in Afghanistan that had affected him and could have been an underlying cause."

Leaning back and folding his arms, resisting the temptation to finger his scar, Crane waited for Phil to respond. A range of emotions had crossed Tomlinson's face during Crane's last words; widening of the eyes at the mention of his Commanding Officer; a slight wry smile at the mention of the personal angle; to finally a hardening of his eyes at the mention of Afghanistan.

After a short pause, Phil grabbed a pad and pen from his desk and scribbled two names on it. Tearing off the paper and thrusting it at Crane he said, "Try these two, perhaps they can give you more of an insight into the man than I can. You'll find them in the Mess Hall."

Pushing his chair back, Crane rose and after

placing the paper in his pocket said, "Thanks, Phil, appreciate it."

***

Walking through the mess, Crane caused quite a stir. In the same way a policeman is easily marked out even when in plain clothes, SIB personnel seem to have a neon sign on their foreheads, particularly as Crane was in civvies not uniform amongst a sea of khaki. He was holding a piece of paper and scanning the tables looking for stripes on arms.

Approaching two corporals leaning against a side wall, Crane asked them to find the men named on his piece of paper. Within minutes the two men in question met Crane at the door of the mess and he made arrangements to interview them in his office later that day.

As he left the barracks he phoned Kim, demanding to know if she had contacted the Padre. Pleased by her response, he made his way over to the church.

The Royal Garrison Church of All Saints stood in its own grounds, with brick pillared sentries guarding the entrance to the driveway. Not a tall building, it sat low and squat, reassuringly nestled by the hedging and flowering shrubs on either side of it. The front was covered by an ivy creeper that had settled itself around the building like a warm blanket.

The ivy had been kept clear of a large mullioned stained glass window that dominated the eye. This grand window was protected on one side by a tall steeple and on the other by a smaller version of itself. Crosses were littered around the uneven roof line, warning possible invaders from every vantage point.

Opening the door and entering the gloom of the church, Crane took a few minutes to let his eyes adjust. As he looked around the cavernous space, the light from the arched stained glass windows seemed muted, causing shadows in every nook and cranny. The layout was very traditional. Down the centre of the church were wide rows of highly polished wooden pews, facing the large high altar at the end, with the pulpit placed between it and the congregation. Bisecting the pews on either side, were large pillared arches, pointed at the tops, echoing the shape of the large stained glass window that rose majestically above the high altar. Flags and standards hung from both sides of the arches proudly announcing the regiments and battalions that had served at the garrison over the years. Crane spotted the Padre on his knees before the altar rail. Walking towards the front of the church, Crane's footsteps heralded his arrival, no matter how hard he tried to be unobtrusive. The Padre turned at the disturbance and stood to meet Crane.

"Sergeant Major," he called. "I believe I told your office that I wouldn't be available until later today."

"Oh, really, sir? Sorry, I didn't know that. I just called in on the off chance, as I was passing. If it's not convenient?" Crane let the question hang in the air, without turning to leave.

"Oh very well, as you're here now, follow me."

CHAPTER 7

Padre Symonds had a small office behind the vestry and he ushered Crane inside. The room smelled musty and faintly damp, with only a very small window set high on the wall offering any sort of illumination. The room resembled a cave rather than an office. Book shelves were crammed with religious tomes. Richly coloured, textured robes hung in a wardrobe, peeping through the slightly open doors. The Padre's desk was lit by a small desk lamp and full of papers and books, which he pushed out of the way.

"Just working on my next sermon," he explained, moving to sit behind the desk, indicating that Crane should sit in front of it.

"Sorry to interrupt, Padre."

"Actually, it's not going too well at the moment. I was seeking divine intervention when you came in, but that wasn't helping either, so maybe a break was a better idea. I was trying to explore how faith in Jesus could help our serving soldiers when they are on tour in a war zone."

"Why was that proving difficult to write?" Crane

was interested to know. He crossed his legs and leaned his head to one side.

"Probably because I haven't experienced service in a war zone," the Padre sighed. "I must admit I'm finding it difficult to deal with the problems soldiers face in these situations, in relation to their faith, because I haven't actually been there myself. It's all very well to talk about the love and support Jesus could provide to the individual in general terms, but I wish I could draw on relevant personal experience and then cross reference that with the scriptures. Somehow it would ring more true, don't you think?"

"I see your point, sir, although I'm not a religious man myself. Even when I served in the most hellish places on earth I personally found it difficult to turn to God, although I know many who did. It seemed to me that in order to try to make some sort of sense out of what they had seen and been subjected to, they needed help and guidance from the Padre."

"Exactly, Sergeant Major, so I want to make what I say relevant to their experiences."

"Do you think you will ever serve in a war zone, Padre?"

"I think that's a discussion for another day, Sergeant Major," said the Padre, starting to tidy up the mess of his desk.

After a short silence, Crane changed the subject. "So, do you have any information for me on the Church of Jesus is King?"

Before responding to Crane's question, the

Padre pulled out several leaflets from his top drawer. "I had a meeting yesterday afternoon with Elias Montgomery, the Church Elder of Jesus is King, who gave me these pamphlets. He said he had no personal knowledge of Solomon, but would ask around the congregation to see if anyone knew him. Elias was very concerned that we felt there could be a link between the murders and his Church, but I did my best to reassure him that we didn't think any such thing. I told him that it was just that Special Investigations Branch wanted to leave no stone unturned and he seemed to accept that."

"What was his general demeanour?"

"Well, he was concerned, but not overly embarrassed or nervous. He didn't seem to mind that I'd gone to see him. In fact he understood it was logical, as you'd found the literature at Solomon's house."

"Mmm," Crane thought for a moment and then asked, "Do you think he'll take your request seriously?"

"I think so, but he did say it might take some time, maybe a few days or even a week. He wanted time to talk to people naturally, you know, not in an accusatory way. If you can understand that?"

Rising from his seat, but not to the bait, Crane thanked Padre Symonds for his efforts and asked to be kept up to date, leaving the Padre to grapple with his sermon. He needed to get back to the office to interview Solomon's fellow soldiers.

***

Sergeant Bullen and Corporal Palmer were both waiting at Provost Barracks when he walked in, even though they had separate appointment times.

"What's this, safety in numbers?" he joked to the two men standing awkwardly to attention in front of him, before assuring them they could stand at ease. But his efforts at light hearted humour seem to have made them even more nervous, as their hands fidgeted and eyes roamed around the open plan office. Neither man seemingly brave enough to look at Crane's face.

Giving up on the humour he said, "I need to speak to you separately," causing two sets of eyes to widen in fright. "Sergeant Bullen first and then Corporal Palmer." After pointing to a chair where Palmer could wait, he barked, "Follow me," to the Sergeant.

The interview room Crane was using did nothing to put an interviewee at ease. Plain walls were painted army green and the only furniture was a metal table with two hard chairs placed on either side of it. Nothing else. No papers, no telephone. Two small windows were high up on one wall, grey light from the outside fighting with the gloom of the inside and losing. As a result the room seemed dim, confined and claustrophobic. Seating himself on one of the chairs Crane gestured for Sergeant Bullen to sit opposite him, as Billy slipped in through the door and leaned against the wall.

"Right, Sergeant," Crane began. "I understand from Sergeant Major Tomlinson that you are in command of Solomon's platoon."

"Sir," was the extremely brief reply.

"How well did you know him?"

"Well, you know…" the Sergeant spread his hands and hunched his shoulders.

"No I don't, so tell me."

"He was just another solider. Normal, like everyone else." Bullen began to study his hands as though he had never seen them before.

"Since when have soldiers been normal, Bullen?"

"Come on, sir, you know what I mean," he replied, head down, still looking at his hands.

"No I bloody don't – so explain."

As the silence stretched, Crane left his chair, leant against the wall next to Billy, folded his arms and stared at the Sergeant. "Are you a good sergeant?"

Bullen seemed confused by the change of subject, his eyes flicking from Crane to Billy and back.

"Sir?"

"If I was to look at your record, would it say that you were a good leader, understood your men and got the best out of them?"

"I would hope so, sir," was the immediate response. Bullen sat up in his chair as though sitting to attention.

"Then bloody well prove it and tell me about Lance Corporal Crooks."

Crane pushed off the wall and returned to his seat. Bullen looked around the room, glancing once again at Billy, who still hadn't moved and was managing to make his open friendly face look menacing. Clearly finding no help from that quarter, Bullen looked at Crane and began to speak.

"He was a good soldier, you know, followed orders, tried hard, and worked to the best of his ability. But..."

"But?"

"Well, sir, he could be a bit odd at times."

"What does odd mean?" Crane masked the urgency in his voice with a gruff tone.

"Well, when we were on our last tour, he started disappearing out to a far corner of the camp when off duty, instead of mucking around and relaxing with the other lads. You know how it is, sir, we all keep each other's spirits up, combat the boredom by playing cards, having a cup of tea, that sort of thing."

"So, a bit of a loner then?"

"Yes, but he didn't used to be, if you see what I mean. Just on this last tour," Bullen shook his head sadly. "I don't know - the pressure seemed to get to him somehow. Changed him."

"Was there any incident in particular that seemed to spark off this behaviour?"

After moment's consideration Bullen said, "I couldn't say, sir. Corporal Palmer may be able to help there. He's obviously closer to the lads than I am."

"Fair enough, Sergeant. Thanks. "

Walking across the room and opening the door, Crane indicated the office outside with his head. "Hang around for a bit please, in case I need to speak to you again before you make your statement and send Corporal Palmer in."

Palmer entered the room and sat in the seat Crane silently pointed to. Closing the door, Crane saw Palmer jump at the noise and then start again when he saw the implacable Billy leaning against the wall.

"Why so jumpy, Corporal?"

"Sorry, sir," Palmer replied, clearing his throat after speaking.

"Solomon." Crane said nothing else, merely waited, standing beside Billy, and leaning against the wall.

After once more clearing his throat, Palmer said, "Nasty business that, sir."

"Yes, yes." Crane was exasperated by the term that many people had already used to describe such horrific and saddening murders. "What can you tell me about him?"

"Umm, he was a good soldier, sir."

"For God's sake man, I know that already!" exploded Crane, as he pushed off the wall. Still standing, he leant on his arms, which straddled the table. Putting his face right up to Palmer he said, "Look, I've talked to Colonel Pearson, Sergeant Major Tomlinson and just now, Sergeant Bullen. This is serious and everyone is helping as much as they can. So, now it's your turn to spill the beans – or do you want me to report back up the chain that you're impeding my investigation?" Crane stopped talking, but stayed in the intimidating position, banking on the young man's fear of his chain of command being greater than his fear of the Branch.

Slumping in his chair as if realising there was no alternative, Palmer mumbled, "What do you want to know?"

Getting out of Palmer's face and sitting down, Crane said, "I want to know everything you know, from the beginning, from when you first met him."

CHAPTER 8

Arriving home that night Crane slammed the car door and then the front door, threw his briefcase down and kicked off his shoes. Barely managing to grunt hello to Tina he went into the living room, turning on the television and surfing the channels. Finding nothing to watch he shut it off again, throwing the remote control onto the settee. After hurrying through his meal, he changed into loose comfortable track suit bottoms and a t-shirt. Leaving Tina to watch a particularly banal reality TV show and taking a few cans of beer, he climbed the steep stairs and shut himself in the spare bedroom that they used as an office. His computer and desk were surrounded by book shelves and filled with his and hers reading material, Tina's shelves being much fuller than his.

Crane settled in the swivel chair behind his desk and went through Solomon's file, methodically going back over all his notes and the statements taken from the men in Solomon's regiment. Working his way through the cans of beer, he poured over the scene of crime and pathologist's reports and examined the crime scene photos meticulously. As he went to bed he knew there was something there, an explanation for Solomon's behaviour, but it was just beyond his grasp.

The weather outside was stormy and Crane could hear the wind rushing through the trees, occasionally howling around the corners of the house as he fell into a troubled sleep.

But there was no escape in sleep for Crane. His dreams were plagued with images of sand storms. Flashbacks from Afghanistan and Iraq. Choking sand was filling his eyes, ears, nose and mouth, rendering him blind and deaf. He felt as if a million iron filings were wearing away his skin. As the wind continued outside, so it continued in his dream, filling his head with an unholy noise from which there was no relief. He was lost and alone, fighting to get over the next sand dune where he was sure he would find his fellow soldiers. But no sign of life in any direction left him disorientated, not knowing which way to turn.

***

Morning did nothing to lift Crane's mood, even though the stormy skies had cleared. Later in the day the team gathered for a briefing, Crane, Kim, Billy and Captain Edwards. They all sat around an oval conference table partitioned off in the main SIB office, ready to debate the evidence, or rather lack of it, Crane thought.

"Good afternoon, everyone," Edwards intoned. "Would you begin please, Sergeant Major?"

"Thank you, sir. Well, first of all there is

irrefutable evidence from forensics and the post mortems that Solomon killed first his wife, then his son and finally committed suicide. But, if that wasn't enough, I believe it wasn't a domestic argument that went wrong, but a deliberate and premeditated act, as all the windows and doors of the house were locked. Aldershot Police had to break down the front door to gain access. Lance Corporal Tomlinson is on report for tampering with evidence, as he had opened the back door, having found the keys in Solomon's pocket. Also, we are still awaiting the results of the analysis of the trace evidence, which could prove to be significant. So," he finished, "if the act was indeed deliberate and premeditated, the question is, why?"

Captain Edwards ignored the question and nodded to Kim.

"Thank you, sir. Well, with regard to the family relationships there is no evidence to suggest marital difficulties from conversations with close friends, neighbours and family. Neither Solomon nor his wife have ever been to welfare with any problems."

"Billy?"

"Well, sir, the techies haven't yet managed to come up with anything on the computer. They send their apologies, but it's due to a backlog of work, not helped by their recent move to temporary premises. I'm afraid they are yet another departmental casualty of the garrison's upgrading."

"Yes, yes, Sergeant, get on with it please."

"Sorry, sir. Um, the only strange thing in the family finances is Solomon taking £50 from his local cash point every Sunday."

This led Crane nicely into his suspicions about the Church of Jesus is King, based in an old cinema on Aldershot High Street. He stood and passed around the religious pamphlets he found in Solomon's bedside drawers.

"Right, everyone, take a look at these. I think that perhaps Solomon withdrew the money every Sunday morning to place at least some of it in the church offering."

"So?" asked Captain Edwards.

"Sorry, sir?" Crane looked up from his pile of pamphlets.

"So what, Sergeant Major? Is there anything wrong with that? Surely you can't think there is something disturbing in a young soldier turning to the church? Or is it that you think there's something wrong with this particular Church?"

"Well, no, sir. I mean, there's nothing at the moment to suggest there is anything untoward about the Church of Jesus is King."

"So by that, I take it the Padre hasn't been able to help."

"The Padre has advised that at this moment in time it appears there isn't a connection between Solomon and the Church of Jesus is King, after speaking to the Church Elder," Crane had to admit. "But—"

"Right then, let's move along."

Crane's eyes widen at the rebuff from Captain Edwards, but he made no comment.

Billy then reviewed the statements of Sergeant

Bullen and Lance Corporal Palmer. "Sergeant Bullen had nothing much to say apart from the fact that Solomon was a bit of a loner towards the end of their last tour in Afghanistan, but he doesn't know the cause. Palmer's statement is more interesting. He reported that Solomon had begun to question why they were there and what it was they were achieving, if anything, in Afghanistan. He'd become more and more disillusioned. Palmer didn't feel it was any one incident in particular that caused this questioning, but a combination of things."

"Such as?" Crane interrupted. He wanted to make sure Captain Edwards heard the reasons.

"Palmer talked about the daily fear every time they went on patrol. As he put it, 'not knowing if today was the day you would die'. He talked about how difficult it was being away from family and friends for such a long time. A six month tour really takes it out of them all. Palmer also said that they were well aware that when they went home, all they had to look forward to, after an all too short respite, was another six month tour in Afghanistan. But Palmer felt Solomon was more depressed about it than the other lads. He also described Solomon as very much a family man," Billy continued. "According to Palmer, he particularly doted on his child, talked about him all the time. Therefore the cold blooded killing shocked Palmer and the rest of the men. So much so that no one wants to talk about it, as if by ignoring it, they can pretend it hasn't happened."

After Billy finished, no one spoke.

Crane eventually broke the silence. "Well, I'm afraid we can't ignore it and pretend it hasn't happen."

Clearing his throat, Captain Edwards addressed the group, "No, quite, but we have investigated and to me the conclusions are clear."

"Really, sir?"

"Really, Sergeant Major. A clear cut case of murder and then suicide. Very unfortunate but there it is. Cased closed." Edwards closed his file to make his point.

"For God's sake!" exploded Crane. "You couldn't seriously close the file."

"Sergeant Major, I know you're upset by this case, but—"

"Upset!" Crane cut in, his head jerking upwards, yet he remained seated, "Of course I'm bloody upset."

"Sergeant Major!" Edwards shouted, which had the desired effect of shutting Crane up. After dismissing Kim and Billy, the Captain turned on Crane. "Don't you ever do that to me again and certainly not in front of the rest of the team."

"Sorry, sir," conceded Crane, as he struggled to put a lid on his temper for the moment. "It's just that I really want to find out why. I need to make sure this doesn't happen again on our garrison."

"Crane, it's just a one off. So put the file away and get on with the rest of the cases that need your attention." Edwards gathered his papers, left the table and turned towards the open office.

"Don't you care, sir?" Crane called to Edward's back.

Wheeling round, Edwards insisted, "Of course I bloody care, man. But you have no real evidence to support any theory you've come up with. So case closed."

With that, the Captain left the room. Crane followed, intending to pursue Edwards, but as he glanced around the office, he saw Billy shake his head. Heeding the warning, Crane changed direction and went outside, intent on taking out his frustration on the nearest wall.

Walking around the car park at the front of the Barracks, Crane simmered with rage and frustration. Drawing deeply on a cigarette, he tried to calm down. He understood his Captain's attitude, but just couldn't let the case go. The question 'why' echoed through his thoughts, but he had no answer.

Just then his mobile rang. Looking at the screen he saw it was Tina. It was unusual for her to ring during the day.

"Yes, love?" he answered.

"Hi, Tom, how's things?"

"Fine, fine, what's the matter?"

"Nothing at all, in fact it's good news." Crane could hear the happiness bubbling in her voice.

"What good news?" asked Crane, trying hard to ignore the fear building in the pit of his stomach.

"I've just had a meeting with personnel. The maternity pay and benefits are great and they've assured me maternity leave won't hinder my future promotion prospects – isn't that fabulous?"

Crane looked around the car park, hoping for someone to come and call for him. But no one appeared. He was alone, being forced to face his fears. He realised he was holding his breath.

"Tom?"

"Sorry, love, someone was trying to attract my attention," he lied. "I can't really talk now. But yes, it's great news," he continued, trying his best to inject a lighter tone into his voice. "We'll talk about it tonight."

Clearly deflated, Tina's voice dropped to a whisper, "Oh, okay then. Sorry to have disturbed you."

Shit, now look what I've done, Crane thought and tried to retrieve the situation by saying, "Sorry, Tina, it really is good news. Let's have a good talk tonight and make some plans together. Love you."

"Love you too," Tina said, her flat tone devoid of emotion, belying the words. "Bye."

And with that she broke the connection. Leaving Crane alone in the car park. Leaning his back against the wall, he closed his eyes and tried to calm himself. Sliding down to sit on the floor, he put his elbows on his knees and his head in his hands.

CHAPTER 9

Crane's mobile phone rang again, stopping any further wallowing in self-pity as he listened to the voice of his Captain.

"Crane, there's a problem. Fire at 26 Mason Street. Possible arson and we've a missing person. As you haven't got anything more pressing on at the moment, I want you to go over there and check it out."

"Sir," Crane acknowledged the order, ignoring the jibe. He closed the phone and returned to the office to find Billy. He didn't like it one bit, but an order was an order and the Crooks case was clearly out of bounds.

Entering the office he called, "Fire at a house on the garrison, come on, Billy," and they both ran to Crane's car.

Aldershot Garrison was slowly being enveloped in mist coming off the low lying playing fields as Crane and Billy drove along Queens Avenue. Fingers of grey grasped at their car as they turned right and drove into the housing estate located at the top edge of the garrison, near North Camp.

The gathering gloom of early evening was split by the glow of the fire coming from a nearby street.

Abandoning the car at the top of Mason Street, Crane and Billy threaded their way past RMP cars, fire engines and snaking hoses. A cluster of uniformed men were talking at a safe distance from the burning house and at their approach, one of them detached himself from the group.

"Sir." Staff Sergeant Jones acknowledged Crane and nodded at Billy. Jones was in uniform, but minus his cap, so his nearly bald head gleamed in the light of the fire.

"What's up here then?" Crane pointed in the direction of the house fire. "How come the Adjutant called us out?"

"Because we believe Sergeant Barnes is in there," Jones replied. "At least according to his hysterical wife he is. She had to be pulled away before she plunged into the house to find him. She'd just got back from a visit to her sister and found the house ablaze. We've evacuated the adjoining houses and the fire brigade reckon they have it under control."

Crane shivered in the damp of the early evening, rubbing the mist out of his short dark hair and then his short dark beard.

He turned to look at the house, where indeed the firemen seemed to have the blaze under control. The flames had subsided and firemen in breathing apparatus were preparing to go inside. The damage didn't look too bad from the front of the house and Crane saw that the street contained a neat row of semi-detached houses. There were no driveways, just small front gardens with short pathways leading to the front doors. He knew there were garages at the rear of the houses, with access through the back gardens.

Turning to look at Jones he asked, "So what do we know about Sergeant Barnes?"

"Career soldier, done over 12 years so far. Been at Aldershot for the past two. Responsible for the St Omer Barracks Stores. In his late 30's, married but no children."

"And he can't be found?"

"No, looks like the silly sod must be inside. He finished work around 17:00 hours. Apparently he wasn't known for frequenting the mess after work, so it's probable he followed his normal routine and went straight home."

"The firemen are coming back out, sir," Billy interrupted.

As they waited for the fire officer to come and brief them, Crane lit up.

"Bad for you, those, sir," murmured Billy. As Crane turned to look at him, he saw Billy's open boyish features crease into a grin, his shock of blond hair falling over his forehead as usual.

"Don't think they'll do me much harm tonight, not with all this smoke around," laughed Crane. His laughter was also tinged with relief. He was glad to be investigating again after what he perceived as a failure with the Crooks case.

Their mood became more sombre as the fire officer approached.

"Found a body," he confirmed. "At the back of the house in the kitchen. Looks like that was the seat of the fire. Sorry but I can't tell you anymore until the house is safe and we can do a proper investigation and get a pathologist in there. That might not be until tomorrow morning."

"Fair enough," said Crane. Effectively dismissing the fire officer by turning his back on him, he turned his attention to Staff Sergeant Jones.

"Make sure the scene is secure and keep the rest of the houses evacuated. Alert the local police," he ordered, "because of the body. I'll be back tomorrow morning when I can enter the house."

Crane dismissed Billy and went home to face Tina, cold fingers of guilt over their telephone conversation still playing across the back of his neck. He hoped telling her about his new case would avoid any more discussion about having children. All he wanted was to get out of his smoke filled clothes and have a hot bath.

***

The next day saw Crane back at the scene. His plan last night had worked and Tina had been solicitous and caring, agreeing that it would be best to put their conversation about children and their finances on hold, conceding that she hadn't had time to put the information from the Personnel Department into their budget forecasts yet. With that domestic matter dealt with, Crane pushed it to the back of his mind and concentrated on the case in hand.

He met the pathologist coming out of the front

door of the Barnes' house. "Morning, Major. What have you got for me, sir?"

"Well, one body inside, pretty certain it's Sergeant Barnes, but as you can appreciate, the fire damage to the body is considerable." The Major pealed the latex gloves off each hand, managing to make the snapping of the rubber sound professional.

"Where is he?"

"Where the firemen found him yesterday. Still in the kitchen, at the back of the house. We're just about to move him."

"Give me a minute in there," Crane said, more of a statement than a request.

"Be my guest," replied the Major, turning away to get the body bag and stretcher organised. "You can't go upstairs though, it's not safe," he called over his shoulder.

Crane entered the house. Before investigating the kitchen and inspecting the body, he walked into the lounge, which was immediately on his right. Despite the smoke and water damage, the furniture and fittings were mostly intact. A couple of paintings still hung on the wall, although a bit crisp at the edges. They were nothing to write home about, just something to put on the walls rather than well chosen artistic pieces, even to Crane's untrained eye. The three piece suite was old fashioned, large and chunky, a mixture of wood and fabric, with a coffee table and side tables dotted alongside the sofa and two chairs. A large writing bureau stood under the front window, the top filled with pictures. Crane walked over to scrutinise them and found they were all of Sergeant Barnes at various stages in his army career. There were no pictures of Mrs Barnes, he noted with some surprise. Looking through other people's homes made Crane feel like a voyeur. A ghost-like figure, intruding into private spaces, stealing impressions of their lives.

Crane walked back through the hall into the large kitchen/diner, to see what remained of Sergeant Barnes. The body was on the floor, close to the door that opened into the back garden. The smell, which had been present in the front room, was now cloying, draping over him like a blanket. Crane put a handkerchief to his mouth and nose as the stench stabbed at him, stifling his breathing and blurring his vision.

Barnes was unrecognisable from his photographs. Facial features had melted away leaving a prominent jaw and teeth, frozen in an agonised scream. He was lying on his back, with arms raised and bent across his body. There were only small fragments of clothing left. Melted flesh and fat had long since congealed and become solid again, in all the wrong places. A horrible death. Crane had heard stories from older colleagues about men melting into the metal of the Sir Galahad, in front of their eyes, during the Falkland's War. Now he understood that they only kept such images at bay through sheer willpower. Employing that tactic himself, he ripped his gaze from the body.

Looking around the kitchen, Crane was struck by the greyness. The units that hadn't been burned and turned into grey ash were coated with it, leaving the kitchen looking as if Vesuvius had recently erupted in the vicinity. The walls and floor were black with smoke damage. The door to the garden was partially destroyed by the fire and partially by the fire brigade, similarly the windows. Turning away, Crane left the house and met Major Martin returning to retrieve the body.

"When will you be able to do the post mortem?" Crane realised he still had his handkerchief clenched in his fist, but couldn't seem to uncurl it.

"Oh, tomorrow morning, first thing."

"Good. Briefing at 12:00 hours tomorrow, in the SIB office...sir."

Ignoring the quizzical look on the Major's face, caused by his habit of effectively giving a superior officer an order, Crane left the scene, trying not to run, anxious to put the horror behind him. Returning to Provost Barracks he spoke to Staff Sergeant Jones and telephoned the fire officer and DI Anderson, directing them to be present at the meeting as well.

CHAPTER 10

The following day Crane waited whilst everyone settled themselves at the briefing. He asked the Fire Officer to give his report first. He confirmed the initial suspicion that the seat of the fire was Sergeant Barnes himself. Evidence of an accelerant, most probably petrol was found. Crane wanted to know why the body was so badly charred. The Fire Officer explained that when a body burns, first the thin outer layers of skin fry and begin to peel off, as the flames dance across the surface. After a few minutes, the thicker dermal layer of skin shrinks and begins to split. This allows the underlying yellow fat to leak out. The clothes Sergeant Barnes was wearing then acted as a wick. This meant that the small pieces of cloth absorbed the fat and pulled it into the flames, where it vaporised and burned. In his opinion, for the body to be that badly burned in such a short period of time, the accelerant was most likely on the body itself, rather than close to it.

Major Martin was next. He confirmed the body they found was that of Sergeant Barnes and his death had been caused by the fire. After a couple of low sniggers from somewhere in the room, which he completely ignored, he went on to explain that there was no evidence of gunshot wounds or stab wounds on the body. However, there was smoke damage to the throat and lungs indicating that Sergeant Barnes was alive when he was set on fire. His arms were raised and bent, most probably because the heat of the fire caused muscles to dry out and contract. This made the limbs move and adopt characteristic postures, such as the position they found Sergeant Barnes in.

Crane broke the silence that followed by thanking the Fire Officer and the Major for their reports and they both left the meeting.

"Bloody hell," mumbled Billy, as he ran his hand through his hair.

"Bloody hell indeed, lad," agreed Jones.

"Right, what else have we got, Jones?" Crane was determined they should get on with the job and not dwell on the horror of Sergeant Barnes' death.

"Two possible leads. Local kids on the garrison have been making a bit of a nuisance of themselves. Riding around on bikes and being a bit lippy. Sergeant Barnes was very upset about it and the more he tried to stop them, the more the kids took pleasure in winding him up."

"How do you know about this?"

"Barnes made a couple of complaints to the RMPs, but to be honest we didn't take him too seriously. Thought he was over reacting."

"And the second one?"

"As you know, Barnes was in charge of the stores at St Omar Barracks. He had suspicions about a couple of lads pilfering stuff. Nothing major, but again it wound him up. He gave us the nod, but without any evidence there wasn't much we could do."

"Barnes seemed to get wound up a lot, wouldn't you say?" observed Billy.

"Looks that way," agreed Crane. "Leave the details of those two cases with me would you, Jones?"

"But…" Jones blustered, "is that really necessary? The lads and I can follow them up."

"We'll look into them," Crane said, emphasising each word as though Jones was either deaf or stupid. "This is a Branch investigation now."

Mumbling something under his breath, Jones left.

"If I need you, I'll let you know," Crane called to Jones' retreating back.

"I'll be off then as well," DI Anderson said, attempting to control his flyaway hair by running a hand through it. "These two leads are about incidents on the garrison, so I'm happy to leave things with you, Crane." Anderson stood. "But don't forget to keep me in the loop. A charge of arson and possibly even murder could be the outcome of your investigation, which will put the responsibility firmly back with the police."

"Understood, Derek."

Crane and Billy then spent the rest of the day setting up their investigation and making sure everyone, including Staff Sergeant Jones, was fully briefed.

***

Crane decided to take the second allegation first, so the next morning they went to St Omer Barracks Stores at the appointed time of 10:00 hours. Looking through the glass in the large double entrance doors, they observed two men lounging around inside, chatting away and at times laughing out loud. Books and papers were scattered over the counter, but being studiously ignored. Both men looked untidy with creased uniforms, their hair just a bit too long. Crane put them both in their early 20's.

"While the cat's away, eh?" said Crane as he opened the green swing doors.

The two men jumped to attention, their faces suffused with embarrassment. By the fear on their faces, they had realised it was a visit from the Branch.

"Sir" they called in unison.

"Tweedle dum and tweedle dee, I take it?"

"Corporal Potts, sir."

"Lance Corporal Mathews, sir."

"That's what I thought. Billy stay here and talk to the Corporal would you whilst Lance Corporal Matthews and I have a chat outside."

Crane turned and walked out of the room without bothering to see if he was being followed. Once in the corridor, he turned on the young man.

"Right, son, you know why we're here I take it."

"Sergeant Barnes, sir?"

"You catch on quick. But we're also here about rumours of pilfering from the stores. Got a good business going on the side have you?" Crane nodded towards the closed doors of the Stores. "A bit here and a bit there, hoping no one would notice and then selling the stuff on."

The young Lance Corporal remained silent.

"That's what I thought," said Crane, pulling his hands out of his coat pockets and rubbing his beard. Mathews' eyes were riveted to the beard and the livid red gash just visible beneath the hairs. "Barnes had rumbled you, hadn't he? So what did you decide to do about it? Maybe you just meant to frighten him by setting the back door on fire? Perhaps it was a warning that went wrong?"

Crane was enjoying seeing Matthews looking uncomfortable. From being red in the face, his colour drained to grey, and his skin turned clammy as beads of sweat broke out on his forehead and he wiped his hands on his trousers.

"Sir...no, sir..." stammered Matthews. "I mean yes...to the pilfering, but not to anything else."

"Well, we'll see. Staff Sergeant Jones and the RMP are just around the corner, waiting to take you into custody on suspicion of murder."

"Jesus," Matthews whispered, forgetting about standing to attention and leaning against the painted wall for support, his voice rising as he blabbed, "I swear we never did it, you've got to believe me!"

They both turned as Billy emerged from the stores, holding Corporal Potts by the arm. The young man's wild eyes were swivelling around in their sockets, jumping from Crane to Matthews and back to Billy. He was also unable to stand and was leaning on Billy. Crane and Billy frogmarched the two young men outside, straight into the arms of the RMP, who wasted no time in cuffing them and bundling the two unfortunates into separate cars. Billy waved goodbye as they were driven away.

With the first part of their plan complete, Crane and Billy then made their way to Lille Barracks, to speak to the father of the kids causing trouble in the street. Aiming for maximum drama, they watched from the fringes of the parade ground for a moment, leaning against Crane's Ford Focus, as Sergeant Hollins put his men through their paces. The air was still and heavy with thunderous clouds gathering high in the sky, the men's boots on tarmac imitating the sound of the approaching storm. In the middle of a complicated wheeling routine, Billy slipped up to the officer in charge and had a quiet word in his ear. The Captain's voice rang out across the parade ground and the men came to a confused, straggling stop. Crane and Billy pulled Sergeant Hollins away, to the gaping astonishment of his men, to interview him in an empty office.

"What the hell's this all about," Hollins demanded in a deep growling voice, his anger crackling like electricity, charging the air. He had a large frame and barrel chest and at over six foot, towered above Crane. "How dare you pull me off the parade ground."

"Sit down, Hollins," barked Crane, wanting to gain the height advantage.

"No need, I won't be here that long. You lot don't frighten me. I've done nothing to warrant an interview by the Branch," he finished, glaring at them.

"Maybe not, but your kids have," began Crane.

"What? What the hell are you talking about?"

"Heard the news about Sergeant Barnes dying in a fire?"

Hollins nodded. "It's all over the garrison. But what's that got to do with my kids?" Barnes tried to look nonchalant by sitting on the edge of the desk.

"They seem to have known Barnes from what we hear."

"Oh that. Nothing but kids messing around." Brown dismissed the remark with a shrug of his shoulders.

"Really? Is that what you call setting fire to his house and burning him to death? Messing around?" Now it was Crane's turn to get angry.

At that point the Sergeant slithered off the desk and fell into the nearest chair.

"You can't seriously think that?" he cried, wide eyed in his horror.

"We can and we do," said Crane, "and you'll do well to remember that you are responsible for your children, Sergeant. If they've done anything wrong, it's you that gets busted as well. This isn't 'Civvy Street' where parents can let their kids do whatever the hell they want."

Sergeant Hollins sank further in his chair,

bewildered and crushed. Gone was the bluster and anger.

"So I'll tell you what we're going to do," said Crane leaning over the table towards Hollins. "Have a nice little meeting later on today at your house. Say 17:00 hours. Make sure your kids are there and your wife if you like."

"You can't do that!" Hollins started to spring from his chair but Crane's next words stopped him.

"I can do what the bloody hell I want. Remember your Commanding Officer knows we're speaking to you, as do your men. Do you want them all to know how uncooperative you're being? That you're impeding a murder investigation?"

Slowly Hollins shook his drooping head.

"Well done, right answer," said Crane straightening up. "I intend to get to the bottom of this, Hollins," he warned.

They left the Sergeant staring blankly at the wall.

JOHN 22:55 HOURS
23RD SEPTEMBER

John took one last look around the house before he climbed the stairs to join his family. It wasn't much to show for the last 10 years but, nevertheless, neat and clean as a new pin, just as he always insisted. Joan fought back of course, from time to time, but he soon kept her in check. Let her rebel while he was away, as long as she toed the line on his return from a posting.

Anyway, now was the time to really show her who was master in this house. Nothing and nobody - certainly not Joan - was going to keep him from his destiny. Because it wasn't just his destiny, it was also his son's.

In the past he'd dreamed of his son following in his father's footsteps. Joining the army. Where John would be the proudest father of them all at the passing out parade. But after his experiences in Afghanistan, John was no longer convinced that it was the right path for his son. Visions of him dying in Afghanistan or any other God forsaken country, for a cause most people don't believe in, flashed through his mind. What would that achieve? No, he had found a better way, a better future for them both. For his mentor had opened his eyes, his heart and his soul.

Squaring his shoulders, he stood to attention in front of the full length mirror in the hall, looking carefully at his reflection. Sergeant John Sergeant. The butt of many a joke. But he had shown them, shown them all, by attaining the rank that equalled his name. Front line man, not afraid of dying. Not then and not now. A soldier of Christ, ready to go into battle.

He had already spent some time preparing. Sharpening his knife whilst repeating his mantra. Over and over again, methodically, rhythmically, hypnotically. 'Follow the will of the Lord. Follow the steps to Heaven.' Now he was ready.

With resolute steps he mounted the stairs and halted at the door to the bedroom he shared with his wife. After drawing his knife he checked his watch. Three minutes to 23:00 hours.

One minute later he was back in the hall, not bothering to wipe the dripping blood off the knife. It didn't matter, his son wouldn't see it in the dark. In fact the only thing he would be seeing shortly would be the steps that they will both be climbing. The steps to eternal salvation. The steps to Heaven. In just two minutes.

CHAPTER 11

Crane and Captain Edwards were having their weekly review of his open cases. Crane explained he was still in the middle of the house fire case, but had to admit they had hit something of a brick wall. Potts and Mathews checked out. Solid alibis for the afternoon of the fire. The only good thing was that they'd confessed to the thefts. As for the kids, Crane was pretty sure they were telling the truth about having nothing to do with it. Eight and ten year olds couldn't lie that effectively, he surmised. One of them would have burst into tears and admitted they had started the fire. Crane and Edwards agreed that, if nothing else, it would keep them off the streets in future and stop them annoying the neighbours. But as a result, they hadn't much else to go on in terms of motive or opportunity, but Crane intended to keep digging.

Thinking their business was concluded, Crane started to collect his files and made to rise from his chair.

"One more thing."

The Captain's voice halted Crane and he sat

back in his chair, trying not to mumble out loud – 'what does the stupid bastard want now?'

"Sir?" queried Crane instead.

"It's been, what, six weeks or so since that nasty business with Solomon?"

"About that, yes, sir."

"How are we doing with that one?"

Crane thought his Captain had finally fallen off the edge of the cliff called rationality. "We're not, sir. If you remember the file is on the back burner. Or to be more precise 'in the deep freeze' as you put it the last time I raised the case. I told you then that the forensic tests showed Solomon had spent some time sharpening his knife that afternoon. Trace evidence of metal shavings and pumice stone suggesting an element of pre-meditation to his actions. Coupling that with the fact that all the windows and doors in the house were locked, it was a deliberate murder and then suicide, not a domestic argument gone wrong." Crane hadn't been able to resist the dig and sat staring at his Captain, defiance clear in his eyes.

"Mmm, that's what I thought." But the Captain wasn't meeting Crane's glare, choosing instead to rise and fiddle with something behind his desk, turning his back on Crane.

"The thing is, we may have been a bit premature on that," Edwards said to both the wall and Crane.

"We?"

"This is no time for splitting hairs," was the curt reply from Edwards, his back still to Crane.

"Something's happened hasn't it, sir?" Crane put

his files on Edwards' desk and sat forward on the edge of his chair.

Returning to his seat, Captain Edwards eventually faced Crane, opened his desk drawer and retrieved a thin file.

"It would appear so." The Captain's voice was grave. He spoke in the tone that Crane knew his Captain reserved for informing families that their loved one had been found dead. "As you know we now get updates from the computer system about cases that are being dealt with by other Special Investigation and Royal Military Police Branches.'

"Yes, sir." Crane knew all about it. The Special Investigations Branch were still able to work with paper files, as it was a procedure everyone knew and loved, but certain members of the team were now tasked with putting reports and details of crimes, offenders and victims onto the new computerised system. It was a pain in the arse, but the powers that be said it could help in current and future investigations and maybe even help solve cold crimes. It was the result of the recommendations of a Report written in 2006 after a voluntary inspection of the SIB.

Clearing his throat, the Captain continued with his explanation. "It would appear there has been a murder followed by suicide in somewhat similar circumstances on another garrison."

"What the?" Crane exploded from his chair, nearly knocking it over. He paced the office, unable to keep still. Wheeling around he asked, "Where, when, how?"

"Colchester. A week ago. A soldier named John Sergeant killed his wife and five year old son by cutting their throats and then committed suicide."

"Jesus." This piece of news made Crane sit down. "Jesus," he repeated, running a hand through his hair down to his neck, where he tried to massage away the shock and horror.

"Exactly, Sergeant Major." Edwards looked washed out; all the colour drained from his arrogant face, which didn't look haughty anymore. "Here's a copy of the file. I think it may be worth you taking a trip to Colchester, don't you?" Edwards pushed the file across the desk to Crane. "In there are all the details we have at present. I'll leave the arrangements to you. Report to me when you get back."

"Yes, of course, sir. Thank you, sir."

Crane left the office at a run.

***

He was on the road within the hour, after calling Colchester, Tina and then collecting an overnight bag. When he left the M3 and joined the M25 he settled into the journey. Showers of rain mean the wipers were on intermittent and their regular rhythm and the hiss of tyres on wet tarmac soothed him, allowing his mind to process the little information he had at present. He knew that by the time he got to Colchester he would have to be focused, thorough and professional. He couldn't afford to let emotions get in the way.

Crane recognised that under normal circumstances, dealing with a murder case wouldn't touch him so personally. He was a soldier after all, trained to follow orders and not question or react to situations, merely do his job. As he went through the Dartford Tunnel, his thoughts turned darker. Crane was disturbed by the fact that children were involved. As far as he was concerned, innocent children should never be subjected to that kind of horror. He was now very angry that another child had suffered a similar death. As he drove out of the tunnel, into bright sunlight, he sharpened that anger into a determination to solve the murders. He hoped that the two cases combined might reveal clues otherwise hidden, so he could make sure no other child, wife or soldier, lost their lives.

Skirting the city of Colchester, he made his way to the garrison. From his knowledge of military history, Crane knew that Colchester had long had a military presence, starting with the Romans who built the first military garrison there in 43AD. Since then various factions had fortified the town and it was extensively used in both world wars. Previously located in the centre of the town, the garrison had moved to a brown field site just outside the city. The new modern purpose built complex was completed in 2008, and was still the home of the 16th Air Assault Brigade.

Crane navigated his way around a garrison that he thought looked more like Farnborough Airfield than a military barracks. The new low buildings were constructed on a grid system and from the air look like giant aircraft hangars assembled around long airstrips. If Crane thought Aldershot Garrison was large, Colchester was equally so, having more than 110 buildings across a 185 hectare site. Crane finally found Goojerat Barracks, home of the Royal Military Police. His contact was Sergeant Major Brown, an experienced Special Investigations Branch man who had spent much of his time on tour abroad.

Crane met Brown in his modern office and shook hands with a man who would have been far more suited to the name Crane. Brown was tall and lanky, with long arms and legs and a slim body that seemed incapable of supporting them. His equally long and lanky face was topped with sandy hair. The complete antithesis of Crane himself. Brown ushered Crane into a bright neutrally painted office devoid of frills, but furnished in the same simple fashion as the other parts of the building Crane had seen since his arrival. Crane figured that the sales director of a national office furniture company somewhere, must have rubbed his hands in glee when he got the contract to furnish the garrison.

Brown was welcoming but initially unhelpful.

"So," he began, "you rushed down here as soon as you found out about our case. A bit hasty don't you think? You could have just phoned."

"Hasty? No, why would you think that?"

"Well, I don't really see what you can do here." Brown's tone was dismissive.

"I need to see for myself the similarities and differences between this case and mine. Then maybe I can establish a link," Crane explained folding his arms across his chest in an attempt to keep his anger under control.

"Why on earth would there be a link?" Brown leant towards Crane across the desk. "The two barracks are miles apart."

"I know, but don't you think it's strange there are now two cases of murder and then suicide within two months of each other. Something unheard of in the British Army before now." Crane leant forward to meet Brown.

"True," Brown conceded, backing off. "But surely the link is Afghanistan? Both soldiers served there, albeit separately. As far as we know they never met." Brown was warming to his theory, his voice sounding as if he was giving a lecture, confident in his information and his interpretation. "Perhaps they were both so badly affected by their experiences they decided they just couldn't take anymore. I can understand that, having served there myself," he finished rather pompously.

"Okay, fair enough," agreed Crane, unwilling to be pulled into a pissing contest about who had served when, where and for how long. "That theory is fine, as far as it goes."

"As far as it goes? For God's sake, Crane, what more of an explanation do you want?"

"I want to know why two unconnected men killed their families and then committed suicide. In the same way. How on earth would they both come up with that idea?"

"Perhaps Sergeant heard about Crooks and decided to follow his example," countered Brown.

"How would he have done that? The publicity was only local to Aldershot and you know how the army likes to keep things quiet. So I've brought with me a copy of my file on Crooks for you to go over," Crane placed his briefcase on his knee, snapped open the catches and slapped a thick file down in front of Barnes. "I need a full copy of yours as soon as possible please, delivered to the Sergeants' Mess. I may find something when I go over your case tonight. I also need to see the crime scene tomorrow."

"Okay, if you think it's necessary." Brown was beaten into submission by Crane's determination and refusal to back down.

"I do," was Crane's firm reply and he left the office to find the Sergeants' Mess, where he had been booked in for the night.

Housed in the prison, or to use its correct term, the Military Corrective Training Centre, the Mess had recently been extended to provide further bed sitting rooms and it was in one of these vacant rooms that Crane found himself. Looking around, he decided he may as well be in the room of a national hotel chain anywhere in England. Once again the banality of the room echoed across the new garrison and Crane wistfully remembered the old Sergeants' Mess in the centre of Colchester. A fine brick building built in 1875, with tall windows and high ceilings, standing as proud as a Georgian terrace in Bath. Whilst he realised the modern army had to have modern, practical barracks, he fervently hoped that its history, tradition and architecturally unique buildings would not be lost in the process.

Once settled in, he gave Tina a quick call. He was conscious of the spectre of the 'great decision' still lying between them. During the past few weeks they hadn't made much progress towards reaching a point where they were both in favour of trying for a family. He almost expected her to be cool towards him, having rushed off at short notice, but to his surprise she seemed happy and relaxed.

"I'm going to have a bit of quality 'me' time," she giggled. "You know a lovely relaxing bath, do my nails, that sort of stuff."

"Good for you," enthused Crane, sitting at the small desk in the corner of the room, surrounded by his papers. "You deserve a bit of pampering. I do love you, you know," he said. "It's just that…."

As if understanding he couldn't finish the sentence, Tina cut in, "And I love you too, so just do what you have to do and I'll see you when you get back. Don't worry about me, I'm fine. If you're not back tomorrow, a couple of the girls from work are going to see the latest rom com, so I'll probably go with them. I know how you hate that sort of thing anyway."

"Yes, definitely not my scene at all," agreed Crane, laughing. "You do that, love. I'll keep in touch and let you know when I'll be back. Now off you go and have your bath."

After he ended the call, Crane moved to lie on the bed and closed his eyes, a picture of Tina in his mind in her bubble bath. He could almost smell the fragrance of jasmine scented candles strategically placed around the bathroom. As he began to imagine parts of his wife's naked body peeking above the level of the creamy water, half hidden by wisps of steam, his phone rang, dispelling the image and bringing him back to reality.

It was a message to say that Sergeant Major Brown had been as good as his word and there was a full copy of the file on John Sergeant waiting for him. As Crane collected it from the young corporal waiting at the front desk, he decided to eat before going over the file, while he still had the stomach for food.

CHAPTER 12

The next day saw Crane standing outside the Sergeant family home, steeling himself to go in. The house was still a protected crime scene, with tape all around it. The attractive modern semi complete with garage, bound up. Sealing its secrets inside. In his hand he held large crime scene photographs, to help him place the bodies in their exact location in the bedrooms, the Sergeant family having been taken to the mortuary for autopsy days ago. Brown had offered to accompany him, but Crane preferred to be alone, to absorb the atmosphere without any distractions.

The downstairs of the three bedroom semi-detached house was untouched by the murders. He toured the rooms anyway, trying to get a feel for the family. His first impression was that the house was immaculate. The downstairs toilet still smelled of bleach. In the lounge he could see the linear marks of a vacuum cleaner in the thick beige carpet. All the surfaces gleamed. The sofa was a work of art with the plethora of cushions plumped and strategically placed. Too neat and tidy for a home that housed a five year old boy, in Crane's opinion. But then again, not having children, maybe that opinion wasn't worth much. He found it surreal to be yet again walking through a house that only a few days ago, had been the secure refuge of a happy family. Traces of them were everywhere, despite the neatness. Family photographs were displayed to their best advantage, books adorned the shelves with a selection of DVDs - albeit regimentally straight and alphabetically arranged.

Passing through to the kitchen, Crane found it once again spotless. Not even any dishes from the family's last evening meal drying on the drainer. As he turned to leave the room, he saw a large fridge freezer in the corner. Here was the only evidence of a more normal family life, Crane realised. Pinned on the front by magnets were letters from the boy's school. They included forms to be filled in and notices of forthcoming events and a child's picture. The normal type of stuff all kids did at school, he guessed. It was entitled "My Family" written in wobbly letters, each one a different colour. Under the heading were pictures of a house and three people. Each was carefully labelled by a teacher, with the words painstakingly copied underneath in a child's handwriting. My house. Mum. Dad. Me. Crane felt the weight of the deaths on his chest and had trouble breathing.

Turning away, Crane ventured up the stairs. The first room he entered was the double bedroom occupied by Sergeant and his wife. Crane spent some time looking at the bed, which had been stripped bare of linen and compared it with the crime scene photos. The blood on the mattress was concentrated on one side of the bed in a large pool near the headboard. The photographs in his hands showed an attractive brunette lying on her back. She was clad in a thin nightdress, which could just be seen above the bedclothes. Her face was unlined, her skin smooth and perfect. Her long slender neck now permanently disfigured by a deep red slash.

The second room he went in was the child's room. Again the bed had been stripped. Crane referred to the photographs. These showed Sergeant lying on his back on the bed, propped up against the small headboard with his son cradled in his arms. Being a large man, he took up much of the narrow bed. The bed, headboard, Spiderman bed linen and the boy were all covered in massive amounts of blood. The boy's eyes were closed. Sergeants were still open. He was dressed in his army uniform. He was also wearing a smile that mimicked the cut in his throat and that of his son.

Having seen enough, Crane left the house, hoping to leave the images behind, sealed inside the house. But they followed him anyway. Deciding to skip lunch, he returned to the Special Investigation Branch office intent on spending the afternoon going through the case with Brown.

"So, have you come up with any theories linking the two incidents yet?" Brown asked sarcastically, as Crane arrived.

Unperturbed by Brown's attitude, Crane made him go through the file in some detail, all the time looking for connections. There weren't any.

"Right," Crane said, draining his third cup of coffee.

"Right what?"

"Let's look at what we haven't got."

"For God's sake, Crane, there's nothing there. Can't you just leave it alone?" Brown's anger which had been simmering all afternoon finally erupted. He pushed his chair away from the desk and stood up.

"Not until there's been a full investigation."

"How dare you!" roared Brown, his fists tightly clenched. "You can't just bloody well come down here onto my patch and accuse me of not doing my job properly."

"Sit down, Brown. I'm not doing that," Crane said his voice low, counteracting Brown's shout. "I'm just helping you to finish up."

"Finish up, finish up, what the bloody hell are you talking about?" But the volume was fading and he dropped back into his chair.

Continuing in the same flat voice, Crane said, "I just wondered if you had thought of looking into Sergeant's religious views?"

"What?" Brown's head snapped up.

"You know, did he go to church? Believe in eternal salvation? That sort of thing."

"How the bloody hell should I know?" the volume rising once again.

"By asking neighbours, friends, family, the

garrison padre?" suggested Crane.

"But why in God's name should I do that?"

"Trust me on this one, Brown. Just find out will you. Then just maybe you'll get me out of your hair and out of your barracks. Unless you want me to make the enquiries?" Seeing the look on Brown's face he smiled and added, "I thought not." Putting all the files back in his briefcase he stood. "I'll be in the Mess."

***

Later that evening, Crane was annoyed, having still not heard from Brown. He was just about to leave the Mess, where he'd been enjoying a quiet drink to go outside, have a smoke and phone Brown, when he saw him striding through the room.

"What are you drinking?" Brown asked Crane without any preamble.

"John Smiths thanks."

Crane watched as a dour Brown ordered and paid for the drinks. Once back at the table, Brown sat down in the easy chair opposite Crane and took a large gulp of his lager. "Why did you want to know about Sergeant's religious inclinations?" he demanded, placing the half-drunk pint on the small low table between them.

"Just a hunch," shrugged Crane, looking at Brown over the top of his glass.

"Yeah, right."

"Why, what have you found?" Crane placed his drink next to Brown's and leant forward across the table.

"These," Brown pulled some leaflets from his pocket and threw them across the table.

'Jesus our Savour!' screamed the banner headlines. As Crane picked them up and glanced through them, cold fingers of dread crept across his shoulders and down his arms, hugging him in their icy embrace.

"Jesus Christ," he whispered.

"Now will you tell me what's going on?"

"We found similar pamphlets at Lance Corporal Crooks' house."

Crane saw Brown close his eyes for a moment.

"And?"

"And, I don't know," Crane replied honestly. "But there has to be a connection somewhere, between the two men and the two churches."

"But they're hundreds of miles apart!" Brown couldn't contain his astonishment.

"Yes, I know, but," after a moment, Crane continued, "what do you know about this place, this Church of Jesus our Savour?"

"Nothing. I've only just found the leaflets," Brown had to admit.

"Only just found them? What do you mean?"

"They were in a pile of papers still being sorted through. Because of that they hadn't been logged."

"Bloody hell, Brown."

"Look, there was no hurry on this one. A straightforward murder and then suicide. We would have got to them eventually."

"Eventually?" Crane's tone suggested he was seriously unimpressed.

Taking a moment to finish his drink, Brown retorted, "Alright, give it a rest. I went through all the papers myself after you left the office and that's how I found them. To be honest if you hadn't said anything earlier, I don't think I would have taken any notice of them. In fact I still don't really know why we should. Couldn't this just be a coincidence?"

"Maybe, but then again maybe not. Can you make some enquiries about this lot?" he asked Brown, indicating the pamphlets.

"Sure, but don't hold your breath, Crane. It'll take some time. I'll have to ask the chaplain for help. It's going to have to be a favour. Let's face it, there's no evidence to suggest a pile of innocuous leaflets have anything to do with anything."

"Understood. I'm pretty much in the same boat over in Aldershot. The Padre made some enquiries about the pamphlets Crooks had in his bedroom but, on the surface at least, everything seemed normal. It's just that now finding another similar type of church... Oh I don't know," he finished in exasperation. "Still, I'd like copies of these. I'll take them back with me to Aldershot tomorrow."

"No worries, I'll do them now," replied Brown, rising from his seat.

"Oh, Brown," Crane called him back, waving his beer glass in the air.

"Yes, Crane?" Brown's indignation was still evident in the clipped tone and rigid posture. He remained standing.

"Could you get forensics to do some tests on

Sergeant's clothes? Particularly his trousers."

"What?" As recognition dawned, Brown held the back of the chair he had just vacated with two hands. Leaning heavily on them, he looked at Crane. "What have I missed now?"

"I think you might find traces of steel and stone. He would have sharpened his knife before he killed them, don't you think?"

CHAPTER 13

The next few days brought no good news in the murder/suicide cases. In fact, no news at all. Crane became dispirited and frustrated and his days merged into one another, as he went about his work like an automaton, before he turned his attention back to the fire case.

Sitting down and brainstorming one afternoon in Crane's office over a cup of tea, Billy said, "You don't suppose he did it to himself, sir?"

"What?" Crane spluttered, choking on the tea that he'd just started to drink.

"Sergeant Barnes. Maybe it was suicide. Turned himself into a human torch."

"A bit bloody extreme," was Crane's reaction as he mopped up the spilt tea from his face and his tie. "And anyway, why would he do it?" he asked, dropping the tissues into the bin under his desk.

"Who knows?" Billy shrugged his shoulders. "Medical reasons perhaps? Maybe he was ill?"

After a pause, Crane said, "Alright, follow it up. Get his medical records from the health centre. We've nothing else, so look into it."

"Sir," agreed Billy as he left the office, taking one of Crane's biscuits with him.

It was some time later when Crane realised Billy hadn't come back with the medical records, so he went into the open plan office in search of him. He found him at his desk going through some papers.

"Billy, what the hell are you doing? Where are Sergeant Barnes' medical records?"

"Well, sir, I... um... was just about to come and see you about those."

"Well come and see me then," called Crane striding back to his office.

Billy sat opposite Crane, looking like a mouse facing a snake. After swallowing he said, "Well, sir, it's just that I've cocked up."

"Jesus Christ, what have you done this time?"

"Well, you know you asked me to get Sergeant Barnes' medical records?" Billy played with the brown paper envelope in his hand.

"Of course, where are they?"

"Still in the medical centre."

A confused Crane asked, "So what's in your hand?"

"Mrs Barnes' medical records, sir."

"What the hell! How did that happen? No, don't tell me," Crane held out his palm to stop Billy replying. "A pretty young receptionist?"

Nodding in agreement, Billy looked abashed. "She was really sweet, boss, with big you know what's. Anyway we got chatting. So she was a bit distracted when she gave me the records for A. Barnes. I just took them and when I got back I realised she had given me Mrs Barnes' medical records. Alice, that is, not Adrian."

"You bloody idiot. How could you be so stupid?"

"I know, boss, but, it could be a good thing."

"Enlighten me."

"It seems Mrs Barnes has had several 'accidents' over the past few years." Billy began taking out papers from the brown lined packet from the medical centre.

"Oh yes," Crane leant over his desk to take the papers from Billy.

"Yes. See here, firstly broken ribs, then injured knees, and finally a broken wrist. And that's just in the past year. All plausibly explained… but…"

"Domestic violence," Crane said shaking his head, leafing through the computer printed sheets, "probably over a prolonged period."

"Looks that way, sir," Billy agreed.

Crane paused to think, stroking his scar as he did so, his eyes looking inwards.

"Right," Crane came to a decision. "Get those bloody medical records out of my sight and back where they belong, before anyone notices they're gone. Then we better talk to DI Anderson of the Aldershot Police. Don't forget Mrs Barnes is a civilian and as her husband is dead, she is effectively outside of army jurisdiction. Especially if she's suspected of murder, a charge in the civilian court."

***

DI Anderson was drinking tea in his office at

Aldershot Police Station and enjoying a sweet sticky cake when they arrived. He was wilting in his chair and looked as crumpled and tired as his office. His dark tie and tweed jacket were full of cake crumbs. His thinning dark hair was unruly, as though he had just been out in the wind. After talking to Crane and Billy he pushed away the cake and picked up the phone.

It only took an hour for Anderson to bring in Mrs Barnes for questioning and during that time Crane had Staff Sergeant Jones and his lads search the garage at the bottom of the Barnes' garden. They reported their findings to Crane by phone, just as Mrs Barnes arrived at the police station.

DI Anderson and Crane interviewed Mrs Barnes together, with Billy listening in from an adjoining office. Mrs Barnes refused legal representation and sat down. She didn't fidget, just sat with her hands clasped in her lap, shoulders hunched and head down. She was in her mid-thirties and very thin. Skeletal even, Crane thought. She looked very small sat at a metal table that was screwed to the floor.

At first Mrs Barnes denied killing her husband. She stuck to her story about being at her sister's for the day and finding the fire on her return.

It was only when they started asking questions about the rumours of her having a lot of 'accidents' that she became agitated. She asked for some water and sat without speaking until it was brought in. After a few gulps, she admitted that her husband had physically abused her throughout their marriage. She explained that he usually hit her so that any bruises or injuries weren't noticeable, but every now and again he got it wrong. Once he had thrown her down the stairs and her wrist had become caught in the banister and broken. Mrs Barnes hugged herself and rocked slowly from side to side.

Crane had to ignore her distress and press on, confronting her with what the RMP had found in her garage. After that, she was ready to tell them what had really happened.

Hiding behind her curtain of long dark hair, Mrs Barnes admitted to feelings of dread as she returned from a lovely day out with her sister. The freedom she had enjoyed for just one day had been liberating. No violence, no shouting, no one putting her down. As she got closer to home she decided, on impulse, to try to free herself from her tyrannical husband. She parked her car on the edge of North Camp and managed to walk to the back of her house and slip into the garden without being seen by the neighbours.

"I could see him in the kitchen, making a cup of tea," she explained. "I went into the garage, poured some petrol into a jug and walked up the garden path. When I opened the back door, he looked at me and demanded to know where I'd been. He wanted to know why I wasn't at home preparing his dinner. He called me a lazy slut and told me I'd get what I deserved later. I... I..." Mrs Barnes faltered and fell silent for a moment. No one spoke. Into the silence she whispered, "If only he'd been nice to me, asked me if I'd had a good time, wanted to know what we'd done."

"So what did you do?" Crane asked, no longer the demanding investigator, finding some sympathy within him for the woman and her plight.

"I threw the jug of petrol in his face. While he was recovering from the shock I pulled a box of matches from my pocket and went to light one. He looked at me in horror and wanted to know what the bloody hell I thought I was doing. He told me to stop being so bloody stupid and to pull myself together."

Pausing to take a deep breath, she then continued. "You can't imagine the feeling of power I got from holding that box of matches," she confessed. "For once I was in charge, not him."

Raising her head and looking straight at Crane she said, "He fell to his knees and begged for mercy, but I decided he didn't deserve it. So I struck the match and threw it at him."

CHAPTER 14

Crane's latest call to Brown in Colchester provided little in the way of encouragement. He had sent Sergeant's clothes to forensics as promised and was still awaiting the results. However, there seemed to be no connection between John Sergeant and the local church in the pamphlets. No one had any idea where he got them from or when. If he had attended the Church, no one was admitting it.

Even though Captain Edwards was extremely pleased with Crane and Billy for solving the mystery of the fire on the garrison and the death of Sgt Barnes, he told Crane to once more keep the case of Lance Corporal Crooks on the back burner. Determined to continue with the investigation, albeit not in a direct way, Crane tried again to enlist the help of the Chaplain.

Padre Symonds was happy to meet, but as he explained on the telephone, he could shed no new light on the matter. They met on the playing fields, where the Padre was taking his 'morning constitutional'. The weather was sunny, but blustery and cold, with gusts of wind tugging at their clothes and hair.

"I really have tried, Sergeant Major," Symonds told Crane. "But Elias assures me there's no connection between the Church of Jesus is King and Lance Corporal Crooks."

"I know, sir, but just because he said so, doesn't mean it is so, if you get my meaning."

"Quite. But I really don't think it's my place to interfere further."

Crane ambled alongside the Padre, alternating between kicking the ground in frustration and looking up at the wide expanse of sky for inspiration. The playing fields were quiet. All Crane could see was the odd dog walker and a solitary kite flyer, trying desperately to keep his convoluted contraption in the air when the wind was up. But the blustery gusts caused the kite to crash to earth in a tangled heap. Crane wondered whatever happened to the old fashioned simple triangular kites with bows on their tails.

"It's just so... oh I don't know. There's something there, a connection of some sort. I just can't see it yet. It's those children. It shouldn't have happened," Crane said.

Symonds remained silent.

"I just wish I could find a way to infiltrate the Church somehow. Find out what's really going on."

"That's your military training coming to the fore," Symonds said with a smile, stopping and looking at Crane. "Why are you so suspicious of it?"

"Must be in my nature, I suppose," Crane

replied after mulling the question over for a few moments. "Maybe that's why I'm in SIB and not in a tank regiment. I like a good puzzle. But I have to win, you know?"

Taking a seat on a bench overlooking the rugby ground and the main road beyond, Symonds gestured for Crane to join him. After a few moments of reflection, the Padre asked, "Is that what is most important to you, Crane, winning?"

"No, I don't think so, sir. Justice is equally important. I want whoever is behind these killings to pay." Crane stuck his hands in his trouser pockets and stretched his legs out, thinking about Mrs Barnes. She'd clearly felt her husband had to pay for what he'd done to her and meted out her own particular brand of justice. But in turn, she would have to pay for what she did to him.

"Always assuming there is somebody."

The Padre's words broke into Crane's thoughts.

"Oh, I'm sure there is," Crane replied. "It's too much of a coincidence, two murder/suicides within a few weeks of each other, both with connections to evangelical churches." Sitting up and turning sideway to face the Padre he continued, "You see, broadly speaking, there are two different reasons for murder and then suicide. Firstly, revenge borne out of anger and secondly, altruistic which is a result of misplaced love."

"You sound very knowledgeable on the subject, Sergeant Major."

Laughing, Crane had to admit, "No, sir, not really, just a bit of research on the internet."

"So, which category do these murders fit into?"

"Well, I believe they are altruistic. There is absolutely no evidence to suggest that they were done out of anger. Neither family had a history of unfaithfulness by any party. There were no financial difficulties or history of gambling or alcoholism. Ergo, nothing to get angry about. That leaves the altruistic path. Misplaced love of some sort."

"Umm, saving the family from some shame that could befall them in the future you mean?" the Padre's round features creased in thought.

"Well, saving them from something. Which is where the religious angle comes in. But at the moment it's all going round and round in my head with nothing concrete to fix my thoughts to."

The two men stood and Crane held out his hand.

"Thanks for your time, Padre. Sorry to disturb your walk, but I just wanted an opinion from a religious expert."

Padre Symonds replied, "No problem, Crane. I was glad of the company. I'm just sorry I can't be of any help."

"So am I, sir, so am I."

Crane turned and left the Padre to continue his constitutional and walked back to his car, jamming his hands in his trouser pockets, keeping his head down and allowing his jacket to flap around in the gusts. Just before getting into the Focus he looked over at the playing fields. Symonds was still walking, looking pensive, oblivious to his surroundings. Suddenly, the Padre looked up and seeing Crane, waved and ran across the field.

Pleased, Crane waited by the car.

"Glad I caught you," Symonds puffed, as he struggled to take in air. "Not as fit as I should be," he conceded placing his hands on his bent knees and taking a few moments before straightening up and speaking again.

"Cults," he finally managed to gasp.

"Cults, sir?"

"Yes, what if the soldiers were involved in some sort of religious cult?"

"But there's no evidence to suggest they were involved in any religion, apart from a few pamphlets, let alone a cult. Also they lived hundreds of miles apart," Crane said, for once playing devil's advocate.

"Maybe not, but that would be an explanation for the murder/suicide." Symonds' face was animated.

"You mean brainwashing?"

"Well, some people think cult leaders use brainwashing techniques, whilst others think the leaders are just plain mad, who attract followers that are just plain mad as well."

"Sorry, but this isn't my field at all."

"No, but I was thinking it might be more mine, as I'm supposed to be a religious expert." Symonds laughed at the label. "Let me see what I can find out."

"Pleased be careful, sir," Crane was beginning to doubt the wisdom of manipulating the Padre, albeit ever so subtly.

"Of what, Sergeant Major? Anyway what harm can a little research do?"

"I don't know. But remember there are two families dead already. I don't want anyone else added to the list."

"Don't worry, Sergeant Major. Just leave it with me," Symonds said as he turned and walked away down Queens Avenue, in the direction of his Church. A new purpose in his stride. At the sound of his mobile phone, Crane pulled his attention away from the Padre and back to more pressing cases.

***

The next morning Crane was surprised to find an email in his inbox from the Padre.

TO: tcrane@sib.org.uk
FROM: padresymonds@mod.org.uk
SUBJECT: Research
Sergeant Major,

I thought I would follow your example and do a bit of research on the internet. It appears there have been many cases of cults forming since the early 1990s across Europe and America, some of which have practised murder/suicide. These include the obvious one of WACO, but interestingly there are others including:

The Order of the Solar Temple, spanning France, Switzerland and Quebec, a new religious movement drawing on the Western esoteric tradition.

Aum Shinryi Kyo, a new Japanese religious

order, an idiosyncratic Buddhist movement.

Heaven's Gate, a UFO religious movement based in California.

The Movement for the Restoration of the Ten Commandments of God, a fringe Catholic group in Uganda.

Therefore the cult tradition is still alive and well in our times. As I explained yesterday there are differing theories for people joining cults and the persuasiveness of cult leaders. Firstly, brainwashing and secondly, out and out madness of both the leader and his followers.

I don't believe our soldiers are out and out mad, despite the awful duties that befall our brave men these days, so I am erring on the side of brainwashing. The questions are, who was brainwashing them and why?

I am delighted to be of some service in my so called 'area of expertise' and will continue my investigations this end.

Regards
Padre Symonds

"Bloody hell," was Crane's reaction to the email.

"Sir?" asked Billy, as he was passing the door.

"Come and look at this, Billy," Crane swivelled the monitor to face the other side of the desk. "Looks like the Padre thinks he's some sort of religious detective now, after not wanting to get involved."

Billy leant over the desk to get closer to the monitor. After a few moments of reading in silence, Billy wanted to know why the Padre was off on this tack. Crane realised he had kept the Padre's involvement quiet, so he recounted their meeting yesterday.

"Surely no harm can come of it, though, sir," Billy said, taking a seat in front of Crane's desk. "After all he'll probably just approach it from an academic point of view, rather than a 'hands on' one. It seems to me he's relishing the thought of doing some research to help, that's all. And let's face it, it may mean something to him, but to be honest phrases like 'the esoteric Western tradition'," Billy placed air quote marks around the words, "don't exactly mean a lot to me. How about you?" he grinned at Crane.

"No."

"So there you go, this is probably just appealing to his academic side."

"I hope you're right, Billy. And I hope I'm wrong,"

"About what, sir?"

"I hope I'm wrong about there being a darker side to these murders."

PETER 08:55 HOURS
9TH OCTOBER

It was nearly time. Just five minutes to go. Peter could hardly contain his excitement. His wife had left about half an hour ago for work, leaving him alone in the house with his son, Ryan. He was glad he had persuaded her to take the Sunday job at the local supermarket a few months ago, after he returned from his posting in Afghanistan. Since then it had just been the two of them every Sunday, free to worship without interference. Oh and how she would interfere. He knew that. That's what she was, an interfering old cow. It was always the same whenever he came back from a posting. He felt an outsider in his own home. 'That's not the way we do it,' she said constantly. Or, 'I've had to manage without you all this time, so leave things alone. Let me do it.' Even worse was, 'Ryan has his routine, we can't change things just because you've come home.' Well, he was in charge now and leaving her out of it for a change.

He thanked the Lord every day that he'd found the church. And thanked him even more that he was encouraged to take his son along, forging a new bond with the boy that he'd never had before.

And now he was going to forge the strongest bond of all,

for he was going to save his son. Save him from the awfulness of this world, from the senseless fighting, misery and poverty. Give him a better future than he'd ever thought possible.

After making sure the house was secure, he took a few minutes to prepare himself. Sitting at the bottom of the stairs, he removed his knife from the sheath clipped to his belt and the pumice stone from his pocket. Wetting the stone with spit, he began to sharpen the knife. Repeating his mantra, "Follow the will of the Lord. Follow the steps to Heaven. Follow the will of the Lord. Follow the steps to Heaven."

Caught up in his hypnotic chant, his body moved backwards and forwards as he sharpened the knife. The grating cadence filled the air as the stone ran along the blade. First one side, then the other. Swoosh, swoosh, swoosh. Long drawn out strokes, dipping and swooping like a bird of prey.

Prepared, he climbed the stairs to Ryan's bedroom. Pausing at the door he looked down at his sleeping son. Earlier he'd slipped a sedative into the boy's breakfast orange juice, so Ryan wouldn't panic at the last minute. He didn't want the glorious moment spoiled.

After removing the knife from his pocket and placing it on the floor, he lifted the boy from his bed. Holding him in his arms he sat on the floor, propped up against the side of the bed, with his son in his lap. Ryan stirred in his sleep, his arms winding themselves around his father's neck before he settled once more.

Peter reached for the knife and pulled his son's head to one side exposing the delicate white skin of his neck, where his pulse was visible. With a swift left handed movement, he slit the innocent throat. A small smile played across his lips, as he lifted the blade to his own neck.

111

CHAPTER 15

When Crane returned home that night, he found the lights down low, soft music playing and the table in the kitchen laid for dinner, compete with candles.

"I've poured you a beer," called Tina from the kitchen. "Settle yourself down on the settee while I finish up in here."

Inwardly groaning, Crane realised he had forgotten that tonight was the night of their 'big talk'. The one he had been successfully avoiding for the past few weeks. Shrugging out of his jacket and hanging it in the hallway, he took off his shoes and swapped them for slippers. Tina always teased him about the old fashioned image of slippers, but after a day pounding around the garrison, it was bliss to get out of his shoes or boots and let his feet breath and move around in the comfort of a well-worn pair of slippers. He just hoped that piece of information wouldn't find itself widely known in the barracks.

He sat down on the black leather settee and took a long draught of the beer, whilst wiggling his toes and stretching his feet. Emerging from the kitchen with a glass of red wine in her hand, Tina kissed him hello and settled down beside him, leaning in against his arm. Just then, the Grover Washington Jnr CD changed tracks to 'Just the two of us', which Crane found rather ironic.

"So, you want to talk about changing from 'Just the two of us', to 'Just the three or more of us'," he quipped.

Smiling, she nodded. "Oh, Tom, I don't know, maybe it's just my biological clock. You know, I must start to have kids now before it's too late. At other times I just want company when you're away. Then again, I want lots of little Cranes running around. A continuation of us, maybe. Someone to prove that we were here, after we're long gone."

He could see the raw emotion on her face and he said softly, smoothing her hair down with his hand, "I do understand, sweetheart, but you mustn't look at this with rose tinted glasses." As she stiffened against him, he continued speaking and stroking her hair. "What about how hard it could get if you were alone with a small baby for prolonged periods of time? You know I could get posted overseas again. How would you cope then?"

Shrugging away from his hand and uncurling from the settee, she said, "Come through to the kitchen, dinner's ready."

Crane followed her in silence, knowing better than to pursue his line of thinking until she'd spoken again and sat down on his side of the table. As she placed his plate in front of him, Tina said,

"Lots of people cope with that, look at all the army wives with kids."

"Okay, but there's one big difference." Crane shook salt on his food.

"What's that? Are they better mothers than I would be?" She stabbed at the meat on her plate with her fork.

"No, they live on the garrison. That way they have a support network."

Tina fell silent. That was her worst fear, he knew. Living on the garrison. She was proud of the fact that they'd managed to buy their own home, courtesy of his increasing rank and her job at the bank.

They ate in silence, Crane finding it harder and harder to swallow each mouthful, as his stomach tightened. Her carefully prepared meal mocked him. Were those tears he saw glistening in her eyes, or just the reflected candlelight? He had no difficulty with awkward conversations at work, yet when it came to his wife he always seemed to put his foot in it. Realising it was because of the emotionally charged subject matter, he decided to change tack. Placing his knife and fork in the middle of his plate he said, "Okay, Tina, let's look at the facts." Ignoring her rolling eyes, he pushed on. "Go and get the budget forecast you've prepared. Go on, let's look at this properly," he urged.

Whilst Tina was getting the paperwork from their bedroom-come-office, he cleared the table of their half-eaten food, as he for one wasn't able to eat another mouthful. His clenched stomach had still not relaxed. He also took the opportunity to refill their glasses and dowse the candles, putting on the overhead light so they could read more easily.

They spread the budget sheets across the table and sat side by side to examine them.

"See, I get good maternity pay," said Tina, running her finger down the income column.

"Mmm," Crane agreed, "but what about this column?" His finger was placed on the expenditure column, where the figures gradually increased to take into account the extra costs incurred with a baby in the house. "As the outgoings increase, the income decreases – see? Once your maternity pay stops there's only my salary left."

"Well, it does get a bit tight, I suppose."

"Tight doesn't begin to describe it."

"Look, I've spent hours going over these figures, Tom." Tina crossed her arms and sat up straight. "The other alternative is that I go back to work after maternity leave and put the baby in a nursery.

"And how much is that going to cost? Most of your salary probably."

"So what's your solution then?"

"The only way I can see it working, is that we either sell up, or rent out this house to cover the mortgage and move back onto the garrison. That way we at least halve our outgoings. You know how much cheaper it is to rent an army quarter."

"No!" As Tina stood, her chair rocked and then tipped over.

Ignoring the interruption, Crane continued, "You'd also have the support network, other wives, welfare, crèche…."

"But," Tina tried again, flustered now as she straightened the chair.

"And you won't be so isolated when I'm away." Crane wouldn't stop. "I won't need to worry about you so much, knowing you'll be safe within the army machine."

"I can't do it," Tina protested, finally getting the chair in front of the table again and sitting on it. "I'd go mad." She gulped at her wine. "Remember how much I hated living on the garrison when we first got married. All the nosy neighbours wanting to know what you're up to. The rank system, where I wasn't supposed to mix with the wives of lower ranks, or the wives of officers."

"Of course, you'll also lose your independence," Crane countered, keeping his voice level, and refusing to be drawn into an argument.

"What?" Tina looked at him, half way through pouring more wine into her glass.

"At the moment," he patiently explained, leaning back in his chair, "you pretty much do what you want, when you want. See your girlfriends, go to the pictures, have the odd weekend away at the Spa, take an impulsive shopping trip to London."

"Oh," a small sound in the silent room.

"You won't be able to do any of that with a baby. Anyway, let's face it, you won't have the money."

Tina stared at him without speaking. Before

either of them could say any more the phone rang.

Returning to the kitchen five minutes later he found her still sat at the table, fiddling with her wine glass. Joining her, he fell into his chair and dropped his bent arms onto the table.

"Tom?"

"That was Captain Edwards on the phone. There's been another murder and suicide. This time in Catterick. There's a meeting tomorrow afternoon up there and I've got to go, as well as Brown from Colchester. We're going to compare the cases, see if we could find any similarities between the three. Apart from the obvious one that is."

"Oh, Tom, I'm so sorry. Was it another boy?" Tina covered his hands with hers.

Crane nodded, grateful for her touch. But he couldn't keep still and rose to pace the kitchen. His mind already elsewhere. Suddenly realising Tina was still in the room, he turned to her and asked, "What will you do? I'll probably be away over the weekend."

"Go to the Spa," she said. "I've a lot to think about."

CHAPTER 16

Crane nodded to Sergeant Major Brown, who had driven up from Colchester to Catterick and his appearance showed the wear and tear of the journey. His once crisp white shirt was wrinkled down the front and along the sleeves, where they had clearly been rolled up. Tom was sure he looked in the same dishevelled state. The journey north had taken over six hours with stops the majority of the time on, joy of joys, the M1. That motorway never got any better, no matter how many times Crane drove up or down it. Choked with lorries and traffic, populated by overcrowded, overpriced, filthy service areas that charge over £2 for a bottle of water and nearly £3 for a simple cup of coffee. It was no wonder Crane and Brown looked as exhausted as they felt.

The office was in Beachhead Lines Barracks, named after the World War II Normandy Landings. Most of the other barracks on Catterick Garrison were named after historical British Army battles, many of which took place in northern France during the First World War. The garrison itself was basically a group of barracks situated in a wider area that had in effect grown into a town in its own right. It was recognised as such when it first sported a Tesco supermarket and then a McDonalds. Yet more nuggets of army history Crane had found in his thirst for knowledge.

Crane and Brown looked at Sergeant Major Keane who was moving to sit behind his desk. Crane put Keane in his late forties, his weary face showing every twenty or so years of his service. His suit jacket was slung over the back of his chair and Keane's white shirt was losing its sheen. As he settled in his chair his tie went the same way as his jacket.

"Right," he said his tone as weary as if he himself had just driven over 200 miles to the meeting. "Where do you want to start?"

"I think the first thing Brown and I need to do is to familiarise ourselves with your case and you with ours, of course." Crane rummaged in his briefcase, produced his file on Solomon Crooks and Brown did the same with the file on John Sergeant.

Looking at the still immobile Keane and placing his file on the desk, Crane prodded, "You do have copies of your file for us, detailing your investigation so far on the murder/suicide by Corporal Fisher?"

"What, oh yes, it's just being copied now. Ready in a few minutes I expect." Keane washed his face with his hands, but the motion did nothing to refresh the man.

"Okay," said Crane still in charge. "Then I suggest Brown and I go to the scene and then go over the file in the Sergeants' Mess, while you read ours. First thing tomorrow we can go through similarities and differences."

"If you really want to, I suppose that's alright." At the quizzical look from the two men, Keane hastily added, "Look at the scene, I mean."

"I think so," Brown chipped in. "Crane here has been to the previous two, so it makes sense for him to see the third as well. He'll be the only one of us who has seen all three."

There was a knock at the door and after being invited in, a young sergeant appeared with copies of the file. Keane ordered him to take the two SIB investigators to the scene of the crime and they agreed to meet again at 08:00 hours the following morning.

***

Corporal Peter Fisher's house was in a four storey building that looked like a block of flats, but was actually a two storey maisonette on the ground floor with a garden and another two storey maisonette above. The Fisher's was the ground floor property and the small garden was crammed full of children's toys, a swing and small slide. The first thing Crane noticed as he went in was the muddle and confusion. The kitchen was located at the front of the property and was a symphony of disorder, with dishes in the sink and on the drainer. It seemed that every piece of work surface in the small room was covered with clutter.

The small lounge cum dining room wasn't much better, with toys all over the floor and magazines on the furniture. The throw over the settee was askew and wrinkled.

"Who's in charge here would you say?" Crane asked Brown.

"The wife. What a bloody mess." Brown looked around the room, frowning in disgust. "But is that relevant?"

"Could be. At least this time we've got a wife to interview. Come on," Crane called.

The two men climbed the stairs that led from the living room to the two bedrooms and bathroom. The main bedroom was at the back, overlooking the garden and was large, running the width of the property. One half was a mess with clothes strewn on a chair, on the floor and in an overflowing wardrobe. The other half was neat and tidy and when Crane opened the wardrobe door he found what he suspected. Peter Fisher's wardrobe was the complete antithesis of his wife's.

The child's bedroom was at the front of the property, half the size of the main bedroom, as it shared the remaining space with the bathroom.

Pushing open the door with his foot, Crane entered the bedroom, leaning against the open door, so Brown could see in from the doorway.

"Jesus," Brown whispered as he looked at the blood stains on the carpet by the side of the bed and those on the mattress. "The amount of blood, you know?"

"Mmm," agreed Crane, distracted by papers

lying on the floor under the window. Stepping further into the room, he picked them up. It was a colouring booklet, with images of Jesus smiling down on little children. It was partly complete.

"Let's go and see Mrs Fisher," said Crane, putting the booklet into his jacket pocket.

Carol Fisher was staying with friends further along the street. She raised no objection to seeing them and it was soon clear why.

"What do you lot want this time?" she demanded not rising from the settee, where she was surrounded by magazines, cigarettes, lighter and a full ashtray.

"Just a few questions, Mrs Fisher, and then we'll leave you in peace." Crane motioned for Brown to sit at the nearby dining table, while he took the easy chair in front of her. "We're very sorry for your loss," he said.

"Yeah, right. The only thing you lot are sorry for was that it happened on your bloody garrison." The hard words matched the hardness in the woman's face. There were mascara stains under her dull eyes and her dried pinched lips had traces of red lipstick still sticking to them. Her jet black hair was tied back but gave the appearance of a bird's nest perched on the back of her head. She sucked loudly on a lit cigarette and deliberately blew the smoke into Crane's face.

"I can assure you," Brown began but was cut off by a hysterical laugh.

"Assure me, assure me." Mrs Fisher's hand waved in the air. "The only thing you can assure me of is that the army will get me out of here as soon as they can. They've already told me they plan to issue an eviction order to get me out of my quarters and my boy's only been dead a few days." Her eyes glinted, but with rage not tears. "Not that I could ever go back in there again," she added looking from one man to the other, "but they're making me bloody homeless!" she finished.

"I'm sure it's just standard procedure," Brown tried.

Before Mrs Fisher could blow up again, Crane decided to intervene, having had enough of, what to him, was a pointless conversation.

"Have you seen this before?" he asked Mrs Fisher, handing her the colouring booklet.

"Of course, he was obsessed with it," she handed back the booklet as though it had scorched her fingers.

"Sorry?"

"My boy got that from the local Sunday school. He insisted on taking it with him every week so they could do the next page."

"Did you take him?"

"Not bloody likely," Mrs Fisher replied. "I don't hold with that sort of stuff myself. His dad took him every Sunday while I was at work."

"So who was obsessed?" Crane wants to know.

"Both of them, as bad as each other. Now if there's nothing else, I need to get on."

Unsure as to what she had to 'get on' with, Crane and Brown nevertheless left.

When they arrived at the Sergeants' Mess at

Cambrai Barracks, Crane and Brown decided to have a nose around first, as both were keen to see the newly built premises. The official blurb said the intention was to create a 'modern but not austere residence with sufficient formality to accommodate traditional mess activities without compromising on comfort for the occupants'. Crane personally thought that was a load of PR bollocks, but admitted that the mess was light, bright and comfortable, yet with traditional features such as wooden panelling, reproduction furniture and a range of large comfortable sofas and armchairs. Sinking gratefully into the pair of well plumped feather filled armchairs nearest to them, they ordered a beer and studied the menu. The agreed plan was to eat together first, then go their separate ways to study the files before meeting again the following morning. They didn't discuss the case until they were sitting in the dining room.

"Thoughts?" Crane asked Brown as they ate.

"The obvious initial one of a religious connection."

"Exactly. It'll be interesting to see how far Keane has investigated that. What did you make of Mrs Fisher?"

"Hard cow."

Crane agreed. "Looks like they were as different as chalk and cheese, Fisher and his wife."

"The worst type of army wife that one. Just along for the free ride if you ask me." Brown finished his food, placing his knife and fork together in the centre of the plate.

"Maybe. Either way he'd not have got very far up the ladder with her."

"Thank God for decent army wives, that's what I say," and the two men raised their glasses in a silent toast to their wives.

Crane phoned Tina later that evening, but got the answer machine and guessed she'd been as good as her word and gone away to think.

CHAPTER 17

At the meeting the following morning, Crane still couldn't decide whether Keane was an ineffective investigator, just biding his time until he'd completed his 22 years, or if it was because he was badly affected by the case. Either way, Crane had to take the lead, as he had yesterday. The three men agreed to Crane's proposal that each take their own case and report under various headings to compare each with the other.

"Okay, let's start with the most obvious, religious activity," Crane began after they settled in Keane's office. "We know that Solomon was drawn to the Church of Jesus is King in Aldershot, but we don't have any evidence to put him inside the church yet, only that he was in possession of the pamphlets."

"The same here," agreed Brown. "Sergeant was in possession of religious tracts, but again we found no evidence of him actually attending the church. In both cases the wives were also killed, so we don't have any evidence from them to support this theory."

"Keane?" enquired Crane.

"Oh, what? No, nothing here." Keane absently leafed through a few pieces of paper. Keane looked worse today than yesterday, with the air of a man who needed a cold shower to wake him up. His complexion was grey and his eyelids drooped, almost completely covering his eyes.

"Sorry?"

Crane and Brown looked at each other in astonishment, Brown going rather pink around the ears, as though remembering his earlier blunder when up against Crane in Colchester.

"No mention in the file of Fisher going to a local church," Keane clarified, closing the file to make his point.

Crane looked at the older man and made the decision that he was a pathetic excuse for a SIB investigator after all and not a man badly affected by the horrors of the case. Therefore his initial reaction was anger.

"Bloody hell man, didn't you examine the scene yourself?" Crane exploded as Brown hid behind his paperwork, raising the file in front of his face as if to shield himself from Crane's diatribe.

"No, I sent a couple of the lads," was the weary response, muffled by the hand Keane placed over his face.

"Well then, they were clearly following in the ineffectual footsteps of their Sergeant Major then weren't they? Because they missed this!" Crane threw the colouring book onto Keane's desk.

Lowering his hand, Keane's face crumpled as he

looked at the front cover of the booklet, which had the words, 'Christ our Savour' emblazoned across the top.

Unable to sit still, Crane stood and paced up and down the width of the office, waiting for a reply from Keane, which never came.

"Have you interviewed Mrs Fisher?" Crane pointed a finger at Keane, although he knew full well what the answer would be.

"Not personally, no," Keane had to admit, seeming to shrink, as he hunched down into his chair.

"So you didn't ask her what her son and husband got up to on Sunday mornings?"

"Obviously not." Keane put his head in his hands, unable to face either Crane or Brown.

Taking a deep breath, Crane continued with his attack. "What about forensics?"

"What about them?" Keane mumbled.

"Have you done forensic tests on his clothes?"

"No, I didn't think it was necessary." Keane's failure was now complete.

"Jesus Christ man, that's standard procedure. I ought to bust you from here to kingdom come," said Crane, moving to lean his hands against the chair he had just vacated.

"Crane," warned Brown.

"Bloody pathetic."

"This isn't getting us anywhere, Crane," said Brown as he stood. "Let's take a break and then start again, eh?"

Crane looked at both men and stalked out of the

room, intent on finding a quiet corner outside where he could have a smoke.

The nicotine, fresh air and movement calmed him. The day had turned bright and sunny and was one of those typical English Indian summer days, when you want to stay outside for as long as possible, as it could be your only chance until next year. Crane turned his face to the sun and closed his eyes. When a cloud obscured the warming beams, he went back inside. He found Keane gone, replaced by the young Sergeant who had escorted them to the crime scene yesterday.

"It seems Sergeant Major Keane is indisposed at the moment," murmured Brown, "so Sergeant Harris here has stepped in."

"Very well, let's get on with it then." Crane sat down and picked up his file.

For the next few hours the three men went backwards and forwards through each case, with only a short break for lunch.

***

Before leaving the garrison the next morning, Brown and Crane took one last opportunity to see Mrs Fisher, with Sergeant Harris deciding to go along and observe.

They found Mrs Fisher once more ensconced on the settee in her friend's house, watching morning television. She refused to turn it off, but after some persuasion turned the volume down. As soon as the three men sat, she started on again about how badly the army was treating her. After letting off some steam, Mrs Fisher began to calm down.

As she did, Brown turned the conversation to the relationship between husband and wife. "How well did you get on?" he wanted to know.

"Okay I suppose," was the dull response.

"Is that a good okay, or a bad okay?"

"Just okay," Mrs Fisher replied with a shrug of her shoulders.

"Was it difficult when Peter was away?"

"Not really no. To be honest it was more difficult when he was here. Ryan and I tended to have our routine, you know? And Peter kind of disrupted it when he came back. So it took a bit of adjustment that's all." Mrs Fisher began a minute examination of her badly painted nails.

"Was it harder this time, after he came back from Afghanistan?"

"I guess, but no not really. He was a bit quieter this time maybe, wandering around, lost somehow. Got under my feet he did. Wouldn't talk much, just sat staring at the TV but not really watching it, you know?" she lifted her head to look at Brown.

"Mmm…did it get any better?"

"Well I don't know about better. He got religion. Was always off at that Church on the other side of town, couldn't be doing with it myself. Not that I was invited," she concluded, resentment making her stiffen and fold her arms.

"Did he ever say what happened there?" Crane asked, unable to keep quiet any longer.

Turning to look at him she said, "I asked, but he wouldn't talk about it, said it was none of my business."

"How often did he go?"

"Let me see," Mrs Fisher looked up at the ceiling, "once a week on a Wednesday night and then all of Sunday morning. He took Ryan with him then. Insisted he had to go every Sunday, but Ryan was keen enough." Talking about her son, Mrs Fisher's eyes filled with tears and she scrabbled through the mess on the settee for tissues.

Despite further probing Mrs Fisher knew nothing more, other than the Church was called Christ our Savour and that services were held in a disused school. As the three men left the house Crane asked Sergeant Harris to see what he could find out about the Church and specifically what happened there on a Wednesday night and to keep him informed.

**

Crane drove home later that morning, mentally comparing and contrasting each case. The cases from Aldershot and Colchester were both deemed premeditated. Forensic evidence in both cases showed the knives were recently sharpened, with residue steel and stone on the men's clothing. Also both houses had been secured. All windows and doors closed and locked.

The other link was definitely religious and at least this time they had a more substantial lead, thanks to the information provided by Mrs Fisher. He resolved to try to find out more about his own local church link, with the help of the Padre.

As far as other information went, Brown said

that John Sergeant took out money each week for the household expenses, the same amount each time. When John was not there, if he had gone on exercise for a couple of weeks say, Mrs Sergeant continued with this habit and they found extra money stashed in the house, presumably because it was left over each week, as John had not been there to spend it.

The only similarity with his case was that Solomon drew out £50 each Sunday, from the same cash machine and at around the same time. Their leap of thinking leading to the deduction that this money could be a donation for the churches, but again there was no hard evidence to support it.

All three soldiers served in Afghanistan and each had been back in the UK about three or four months. Interviews with fellow combatants and officers told how each soldier had been withdrawn on their return to England, as though badly affected by their tour of duty, but everyone was loath to talk about it. In fact everyone seemed reticent to talk about the possible effects on the men of a tour of duty in Afghanistan.

As Crane sat nursing an overpriced coffee during one of his breaks, he felt it was as if it couldn't be acknowledged that a soldier couldn't cope with war. After all, wasn't going to war the whole purpose of an army? An army couldn't function if the soldiers couldn't cope with the after affects. So the consensus seemed to be, best sweep it all under the carpet and pretend that everything was alright and nothing was wrong.

Crane knew how hard it was to cope with harsh conditions when serving overseas and missing family and friends back home. But somehow you had to cope. Put an invisible shield around your emotions and see it as a job. Maybe Crooks, Sergeant and Fisher hadn't been able to do that. They weren't the first and most certainly wouldn't be the last, Crane decided. The question was, had they turned to a local church to find the answers? Crane was determined to find out, clearing his table and picking up his keys, ready for the remainder of the journey home.

CHAPTER 18

It was a beautiful October morning, the skies light blue and the sun's rays bright if not warm, as Crane drove to work the next day. Light flooded across the playing fields and turned the dull grey granite of Provost Barrack's walls, which were usually dark and foreboding, into an inviting building that sparkled in the sun's rays. Even the kids walking to the local secondary school at the top of North Camp larked about instead of slouching. Everywhere Crane looked, people seemed to have a bit more hope about them. A sense of yes, I could make today count. Unusual for Aldershot, he thought.

Crane breezed into the office and called a meeting in 30 minutes for an update on his weekend in Catterick. They met in Crane's office, after he had returned from his briefing with Captain Edwards. Kim looked smart, but as uptight as ever and Billy seemed relaxed after his weekend off, obviously having spent as much time in the sun as possible, from the fresh crop of freckles on his face.

Crane told them of his findings in Catterick and advised that as a result of these, Captain Edwards had authorised further investigation of the case. Crane wanted to focus their efforts on the Church of Jesus is King.

"What are we going to do then, boss?" Billy wanted to know.

"Well, it's a bit tricky that one. We can't do much, so I want to enlist the help of the Padre again."

"Anything I can do, sir?" asked Kim.

"I want you to go out and about on the garrison, visit the NAFFI, talk to the wives, pop into welfare and ask if anyone knows anything about this Church. See if you can find anyone who attends it. Also I want to know if Solomon ever went to see anyone about his mental health. In Afghanistan, we deploy highly skilled and experienced mental health nurses, to provide the necessary in-theatre care and treatment for all our personnel. See if you could find out if he saw anyone whilst in Afghanistan. Also talk to the local Department of Community Mental Health here."

"Yes, sir," Kim smiled and looked pleased with her assignment. "I'm sure I can come up with something." She began scribbling notes on the pad she kept ready on her lap.

"Yeah right, but you'll have to be a bit more friendly if you want the women to confide in you," sneered Billy.

"I can be perfectly friendly when I want to Staff Sergeant Williams," countered Kim, pausing in her note taking to fix Billy with an icy stare.

"See, that's just what I mean, colder than an arctic wind."

"Oh for God's sake, shut up you two," Crane snapped. "Now, Billy, I want you to get as much background information as you can on the church. How long it's been established, what affiliations it may have, that sort of thing."

"Oh right. Shall I contact the Church Commissioners or whatever organisation looks after evangelic churches, that sort of thing?"

"Contact whoever you like, just not the actual Church, alright?"

"Understood, sir."

"There's an article in the local paper."

Crane and Billy looked at Kim.

"And the relevance of that is?" Billy was quick to ask.

Shaking his head at Billy, Crane said, "Ignore him, Kim. What article?"

"About the Church of Jesus is King. I just thought Billy might want to look at it if he's doing background. It was written by that woman."

"What woman?" Crane asked.

"The one that kept pestering us about Solomon. Diane Chambers."

"Interesting," mused Crane. "Kim, get a copy for Billy and also one for me. Right then, off you both go. I'm going over to see Padre Symonds." Crane got up from behind his desk.

"Do you want me to phone him, sir. Let him know you're coming?" asked Kim.

"No thanks, Kim. Appointments aren't really my style," smiled Crane.

***

Crane was banking on finding the Padre somewhere in the church or in its vicinity and he wasn't disappointed. As Crane walked into the small office, located at the back of the Church, it seemed that tidiness wasn't the Padre's style. This time there was even more paper strewn across the desk, spreading across the small office like large pieces of confetti.

"I see you're hard at it then, sir," said Crane.

"Ah, Sergeant Major Crane, just the person. Come in and sit down. Oh maybe not, standing would be good." The Padre was sitting behind his desk and the other two chairs in the room held towers of papers and books, which were threatening to topple over.

"Sir," agreed Crane suppressing a smile and remaining standing.

"This is all really rather exciting, you know," said the Padre, spreading his hands out to encompass the papers on his desk. "I've learned so much about cults and their ways. There are large organised religious movements, sects and those we would more appropriately describe as cults. Cults are where everyone lives on a commune and works for the good of the organisation."

Crane frowned at this piece of information. "I'm not sure that's what we've got here, Padre," he said.

"No, quite," agreed the Padre, leaning back in his swivel chair. "But there's one interesting fact I came across. Did you know that a cult could comprise just a handful of people? It doesn't need to be a large recognised movement, more of a one man band, as it were."

"Really, sir?" asked Crane, not awfully sure where this was going.

"Oh yes, just one man with a big idea who persuades vulnerable people to his way of thinking. And that's what I think we might have here," the Padre banged his hands down on his desk to accentuate his point.

"You do?" Crane replied, moving backwards to lean against the stone doorway and putting his hands in his trouser pockets. If this was going to take some time, he might as well make himself a bit more comfortable.

"Absolutely."

The Padre was becoming more agitated in his enthusiasm, jiggling up and down in his chair and Crane believed he would roam around the office if there was enough space.

"You see there's no evidence to suggest that the Church of Jesus is King is behind these killings. Especially as they're spread around the country. So I was wondering if it was one man travelling around but using the different churches as a front." By now the Padre was swinging around in his chair like an excited child.

But Crane simply stared at the Padre, a chill creeping across his shoulders, making him shiver.

"Are you alright, Sergeant Major?" the Padre asked, falling still.

"Oh, what? Yes, sir. Sorry. Could you just say that bit again please?"

"What bit?" asked the confused Padre, rifling through the papers on his desk. "Oh you mean the one man travelling around but using the different churches as a front?"

"Exactly, you know you could have hit upon something there, Padre. Although there's no evidence to suggest that yet."

"I know," agreed the Padre. "So I thought I could help with that bit. But the trouble is I don't know how or what I could do," he finished.

"Don't worry, sir." Crane smiled. "I've got an idea about that."

Deciding Crane really needed to sit down, they cleared one of the chairs and, surrounded by books and papers, Crane outlined his idea to the Padre. By the end of the meeting they had a plan. The Padre would instigate an Army Liaison Scheme, aiming to foster relations between all the different churches in Aldershot. This would involve the Padre attending the church services and various groups run by each church and of course he would start with Jesus is King.

Whilst attending these, the hope was that the Padre would come across some information about a visiting preacher, or another Church Elder who only attended occasionally. Also he would have an opportunity to see what regular meetings were held, such as Bible Studies. Crane was mindful of the fact that John Sergeant attended some sort of meeting once a week and wondered if that might have been the case in Aldershot with Corporal Crooks.

The two men agreed that the Padre would set this in motion as soon as possible and Crane again urged caution.

"I can't see any problems with this," said the Padre. "It's just normal ecclesiastical practice, fostering good relations with the local community etc etc," he waved his hand around in a foppish gesture. "Let's just hope something good comes out of it."

"My thoughts exactly," said Crane, not sounding as happy as the Padre, as he was fervently hoping that nothing bad would come of it.

***

Billy wasn't happy about it either, Crane could tell, when he got a chance to talk to him about the plan. They were sitting in the open office area, Billy lounging in a spare chair and Crane sitting on the edge of a desk.

"I'm not so sure about this, with respect, sir." Billy leaned forward his arms on his knees. "What does the Padre know about investigations?"

"Nothing, but then he's not really investigating, just information gathering."

"Exactly, and I think we should be investigating," he pushed a thumb onto his chest to make his point, the tone in his voice bordering on insubordination.

"Do you indeed?" Crane couldn't keep the sarcasm from his voice. "You know we've got nothing on the Church and absolutely no jurisdiction either."

"Sorry, sir," Billy mumbled, but then rallied. "It's just that I've had a thought about an undercover type operation," he blurted sounding like a recalcitrant adolescent.

"Okay, let's hear it," Crane said after a pause, deciding not to dampen all the boy's enthusiasm or willingness to go that extra mile. "In my office."

Crane settled back in his chair while he listened to Billy outline his plan to infiltrate the Church of Jesus is King. His theory was that as the three cases had involved a father and young son, Billy would attend the church with his young nephew posing as his son and see where things went from there.

"There must be some sort of programme or study group focused on fathers. If I can find one and join it, then maybe we'll get somewhere." Billy leaned forward in his chair to emphasise his keenness. "What do you think, sir?" the eagerness shone from Billy's eyes like a beacon.

Pausing for a moment, Crane came out from behind his desk and paced around his office, settling on the corner of the desk, close to Billy.

"That is probably one of the worst and yet best ideas you've ever had, Billy."

"Thank you, sir, I think. Um, which is which? I mean, which is good and which is bad?"

"The infiltration part was good but using your nephew was bad. So because of that, I can't authorise it."

"But, sir!" Billy started to rise in protest.

"Sergeant!" warned Crane.

Billy subsided into his chair, once more mumbling, "Sorry, sir."

"Look, let's be realistic. You can't do anything that would put a civilian at risk, particularly not your nephew. You'd never forgive yourself if anything happened to him and come to that neither would your sister."

"But we really need to do something sir!"

"I know, lad, and we will, just not that. Now get back to your desk and let me have your update on the background of the Church as soon as you can."

"Yes, sir," was the dejected response.

Crane watched Billy move slowly through the office back to his desk. And for the second time that day, hoped things don't turn out as he feared they could.

CHAPTER 19

A couple of weeks later, Crane was in the small
bedroom-cum-office at home, once again wading
through the information that Billy had obtained on
the Church of Jesus is King. He still couldn't find
anything remotely untoward. The church seemed to
be highly respectable, if very evangelical, but that
wasn't a crime in anyone's book. Just a bit too
"happy clappy" for some, including Crane himself.

It seemed that Diane Chambers of the Aldershot
Mail had the same thoughts.

Evangelicism
Alive and well in Aldershot?

*The word is out. Jesus was put on this earth to save us
and died so that we may be redeemed of our sins. Nothing
unusual in that you might think, but think again. For this
is the battle cry of the latest evangelical churches springing up
in our area. And once they get their teeth into you it's
difficult to shake them off.*

*There have been reports of people being overly harassed by
the disciples of these churches wanting to convert local people
to their way of thinking. Refusing to leave the doorstep unless*

they get a commitment from residents to attend their church. And then returning if they don't to find out why not!

Their way of thinking includes giving most of your wages away to the church, whether you can afford it or not. Their opinion is that Christ cared not one jot for money, so why should you? A different story when you have children to clothe, feed and put a roof over their head. Pressure from the churches to give more and more conjures up scenes of harassment by debt collectors.

They preach and practice openness towards all, no matter what their sins. Alcoholics and drug addicts are welcome. One must hope that they are not under any influences whilst attending the church, especially not when there are children around.

There have been many well documented instances of evangelical preachers 'gone bad' in America. Tales of their greed for money, for sex and the abuse of the most innocent and vulnerable in our society. We trust this is one export from America that doesn't reach our shores!

The Mail spoke to one local preacher, Elias, Elder of the Church of Jesus is King who simply gave us this prepared statement: "Our church prides itself in our service of Jesus Christ. We actively promote the word of God in the local area and are an inclusive, not exclusive church."

He refused to answer this reporter's questions, which were prompted by the concerns of local people and simply referred anybody seeking more information to log onto their website: www.jesusisking.org.uk.

As this type of evangelical worship is on the rise in our area, it must surely beg the question - what is lacking in the more traditional churches, to make people gravitate towards evangelicalism? We tried to ask this question of local Church *of England and Catholic ministers but no one was available for comment.*

However, rest assured that this reporter will continue to look into the concerns of local people and if anyone has any personal experience of this and other local evangelical churches they are encouraged to email me at: dianechambers@aldershotmail.co.uk.

Crane thought her article was short on facts and long on supposition. As if she was desperate to become an investigative reporter and failing. Trying too hard. She was probably quite young, definitely eager and not very experienced. Her editor had more than likely reigned in the article, not wanting to be faced with a libel suit. Still, Crane needed to keep her away from a possible connection between Solomon and the Church of Jesus is King.

Whilst not religious, Crane appreciated the pomp and circumstance of the rituals of the Anglican Church on the garrison. He, along with all soldiers, had to attend regular services and march-pasts and found some comfort in the solidarity of the whole thing. An outward display of the sense of belonging. Everyone working together for the common good.

As he glanced up from his papers he saw the photograph taken at his passing out parade, when he first joined the army. With a wry smile he thought back to how young and enthusiastic he was then. Full of eagerness and knowledge, convinced he knew everything there was to know. Only to later realise he knew absolutely nothing and that he was only on the first rung of the ladder towards being a good soldier and investigator. Not wanting to think about the events and situations he had been in that had contributed to the experiences which he now relied on almost every day, he pushed away from his desk and went down to the kitchen in search of a fresh cold beer.

Tina heard him come down and followed him through to the kitchen.

"Don't you think you've done enough for tonight, love?"

"I suppose I have," agreed Crane closing the fridge door and taking the top off his beer. "I don't want to stop just because I'm tired, for if it happens again then I'll never forgive myself."

"I know, I do understand, but remember the more exhausted you become the less effective you are." Tina moved across the kitchen and put her hands on his back and then began to massage his shoulders and neck. "You're very tense," she murmured in his ear.

"Jesus, Tina, stop, I've got work to do."

"Tomorrow, Tom," she persisted continuing to massage, her hands roaming across his back and down towards his waist.

"Please, Tina," he gasped. But before he could add the word 'stop' her hands continued on their downward journey, rendering him speechless.

***

The following morning, Crane had to admit he felt better for his rest and recuperation, à la Tina. The black fog swimming around his head was dissipating and he'd a good night's sleep for the first time in a week. It was just as well, considering what he found waiting for him at the barracks.

The first problem was that Billy seemed to be missing. He hadn't turned in that morning and no one knew why. Crane asked Kim to 'find out where the bloody hell he was' just as the phone rang calling him upstairs to see the Captain. There he found the second problem of the day. Another missing person. But this time far more serious than a young sergeant who had probably just overslept.

"The Padre, sir?" exclaimed Crane. "Padre Symonds?" It was a good job that Crane wasn't standing, as he would have fallen into the nearest chair with shock.

"That's what I said, Sergeant Major. Are you having trouble with your hearing, or did the information simply not compute?"

"No, sir, I mean yes, sir." Crane closed his mouth before he could say anything else and make himself look even more stupid than he had already.

"He wasn't at morning service, which started alarm bells ringing. The RMP have been round to his quarters, but he's not there either. Any idea what might be going on, Sergeant Major?" Edwards peered at Crane down his long haughty nose.

Crane paused before answering, not sure how much information he'd given his Captain about Padre Symonds' involvement in the investigation.

He settled for, "No, sir, why should I?"

"I understand you've been talking to the Padre about the murder suicide investigations."

"Yes, sir, I have, but why would that be relevant?" Crane hedged.

"No idea, Sergeant Major, but you better get on it, just in case there is a connection. We can't have people disappearing on us; this is the army after all. We don't do disappearing. Find him. Dismissed."

"Sir," Crane replied, retreating from the Captain's office as quickly as he could, realising that clearly today, Edwards was not as dumb as he appeared to be on some days. Today he seemed to be capable of joining the dots. As Crane hurried to his office to contact Staff Sergeant Jones, he fervently hoped that nothing awful had befallen the Padre and that the Captain was joining the dots in the wrong order.

As he returned to the office, he saw Billy sitting at his desk looking dazed. His shirt was creased, tie askew and suit crumpled, giving the impression he'd just woken up and put on the same clothes that he wore yesterday in his haste to get to the office.

"Billy, my office," he barked as he passed Billy's desk. "Where the bloody hell have you been?" shouted Crane as Billy entered the office and stood in front of Crane's desk. Crane also remained standing.

"Sorry, sir, appear to have overslept," explained Billy in a monotone, head bent, looking at the floor.

"Overslept! For Christ's sake, SIB don't do oversleeping, Billy," shouted Crane subconsciously echoing the Captain's words. "What have you been up to that warranted an extra hour in bed?"

"Nothing much, sir, I just seem to have overslept. I mustn't have heard the alarm. I feel a bit dazed that's all."

"Dazed?" Crane sat, the fire gone from his temper as he examined Billy's creased face. "Look, son, you've got two options. One is to pull yourself together, stop feeling dazed and get back to work; or the second is to go and see the doctor if you're feeling unwell. Now which is it to be?"

Billy straightened up, "Sorry, sir, I'll pull myself together, sir and get back to work," but his pupils were wide and he seemed to be having trouble focusing on Crane.

"Good thing too and next time you decide to go whoring around until the small hours, do it when you have the next day off. I've got bigger problems than you to deal with. Now get out of my sight."

Billy stood to attention, "Yes, sir, thank you, sir. What other problems?"

"Oh yes, you don't know what's happened do you, as you were late in," Crane couldn't resist one final dig. "It's the Padre. Padre Symonds seems to be missing."

"Padre Symonds? Our Padre?" Billy asked stupidly.

"Yes, Sergeant, our Padre Symonds. I'm just off to see Staff Sergeant Jones for a briefing. So get yourself together while I'm over there as I'll need you later."

"Sir," Billy agreed considerably more alert and half marched, half ran out of Crane's office.

***

Unfortunately Jones couldn't shed any more light on the Padre's disappearance. His lads had been to the Padre's quarters, but there was no sign of him. They took the liberty of entering the house, just in case, but he wasn't there, dead or alive. Frustrated Crane took himself off to the Church.

He approached the closed door of the Padre's office in the gloom, wishing he'd brought a torch. How the Padre worked there Crane couldn't imagine. Toiling away in an environment with high echoing ceilings, cold stone walls and enveloped by shadows and half-light would give him the creeps. As he reached the Padre's thick wooden door, he sensed movement behind him. Before he could turn and greet the person he hoped was the Padre, a whoosh of air alerted his sense of self preservation. His first instinct was to duck his head. That probably saved his life, as the heavy object struck a glancing blow on the back of his skull, instead of caving it in. But he still dropped to the floor like a bag of cement.

Crane's next conscious thought was that something was tickling his nose. He wrinkled it as he breathed in and promptly sneezed. That's when he realises he was lying on the floor, just outside the Padre's office. As he moved his head, spots of light danced before his eyes, so he settled back, closing his eyes. After a few minutes he felt more alert and slowly sat up. Dazed, he thought, definitely dazed. Now he knew how Billy had felt earlier.

As the cobwebs cleared from his brain and his eyesight returned to normal, Crane felt able to stand. Using the wall for support, he inched his way into the Padre's office through the now open door.

CHAPTER 20

The office looked as though it had been through a ticker-tape parade. Even more of a mess than the Padre usually left it in. Papers were strewn everywhere and files pulled off shelves, their contents cascading all over the floor. The functional, rather than comfortable chair the Padre used was overturned and each drawer of the desk had been pulled out and thrown towards the door. There was a panicky feel to the search that someone had made of the office. No doubt due to the fact that the intruder had no way of knowing when Crane would regain consciousness.

He took his mobile phone out of his jacket pocket to call Billy. Peering at the screen in the gloom, he realised he had no signal. The walls of the church were just too thick and the office was located deep in the bowels of the building. Pulling a pair of latex gloves from his pocket, Crane fumbled with them, before managing to get his fingers into the appropriate holes.

Finding the phone hidden under discarded and now empty file boxes, he punched the green call button and put it to his ear. Relieved to hear a dialling tone, he called the office, asking Billy to come at once and arrange for a forensic team to meet them at the Church. In response to the young Sergeant's enquiries about an ambulance, he dismissed the suggestion. He then staggered back into the corridor, gently lowering himself to the ground sitting with his back against the cold stone wall awaiting help.

***

The only solid piece of evidence to come out of the whole debacle was Crane's headache. The only finger prints were those belonging to Padre Symonds and Crane. So the intruder had worn gloves. Without the Padre they had no idea what might be missing. The only obvious thing was a computer. Crane had seen the Padre with a laptop, which presumably he had used for his extensive research on cults. Sergeant Jones sent a couple of lads over to the Padre's house again for a more thorough search but they drew a blank on any computer or laptop.

Crane and Billy sat in Crane's office, both staring out of the window at the car park as if hoping for a bolt from the blue that would make things clearer.

"Come on, Billy, let's get some fresh air," Crane suggested, grabbing his jacket from the back of his chair.

"Not all that fresh I bet," smiled Billy, following Crane out of the office and into the car park.

Fishing his cigarettes and lighter out of his

pocket, Crane turned his back on Billy to shield the flame from the wind. As he turned back he found his young Sergeant had a look of intense concentration on his face.

"We must be missing something, sir," Billy said. "What would be so important in the Padre's office that someone wanted? And anyway, who was that someone?"

"Okay, let's try and be logical," said Crane. Using his fingers to emphasise his points he began. "One, the Padre is missing. Staff Sergeant Jones is working with DI Anderson to try and find him. Two, the Padre was helping us with our enquiries so to speak, with the Church of Jesus is King. The last time we spoke he was going to arrange an Army Liaison Scheme so he could attend their services and meetings. Three, someone obviously feels the Padre has information that could harm them. Four, the logical conclusion is that someone is from the Church of Jesus is King. Five, the last time I talked to the Padre about cults, he was warming to his theory that a lone man could be a cult. A cult doesn't need to constitute a large gathering of people all living together in some sort of commune."

Having run out of fingers, Crane stopped and looked up at Billy. "How are we doing so far?" he asked.

"Good, sir. Let's add to that. Six, one man could be behind the other murder suicides as well, if he was some sort of roving preacher. Seven, if that's the case he's now here in this area. Eight, we haven't got a bloody clue what he looks like or what his name is. Nine…" Billy's voice tailed off. Having finished with his fingers, he pushed his hands into his pockets.

"So where does all this leave us?" mused Crane out loud. "For God's sake, Billy, stop that jangling."

"Sir?" Billy looked at Crane.

"You've got your hands in your pockets and you're jangling your change about. Stop it, I can't think."

"Oh, sorry, sir, it's one of those unconscious habits, it's not money it's my keys, sir," said Billy pulling them out of his pocket.

"Well, it sounds like you've got the keys to the whole bloody garrison there."

"No, look," Billy opened his palm to reveal just three keys and a slim flattish black piece of plastic with a metal surround. "They must be banging against my memory stick."

"Memory stick, did you say?"

"Yes, sir, here it is. They're really small these days and hold loads of info. I know I'm not much good with computers, but I do use them for the reports and stuff and sometimes I save things onto a memory stick just to make sure I have a back up copy if it's something really important or interesting."

Crane was staring at the memory stick in astonishment. "Come on, Billy," he said fishing out his own keys.

"But where are we going, sir?"

"The Padre's quarters," Crane called as he climbed into the car and started up the engine.

***

As they entered the Padre's house Crane was surprised to see how comfortable it was. Being the home of a bachelor, he was expecting it to be furnished in a practical stark style. However, the atmosphere was the complete opposite of Crane's expectations. The lounge was warm and welcoming, antique furniture glowing from loving care, the rugs on the floor thick and colourful and colour co-ordinated cushions on the settees. A fine example of an antique leather winged chair sat near the bay window, with an angle lamp carefully poised for reading. But there was no sign of an office.

"Let's take a look upstairs, Billy," Crane said taking the stairs at a run.

The upper floor had a bathroom and three bedrooms, one of which had been turned into a study.

"Just what I was looking for," said Crane with satisfaction as he slowly looked around the crowded room. A large desk sat under the window, with drawers either side of the centrally placed chair. Along one wall was a large collection of books, covering the whole of the wall, five shelves deep.

"Come on, let's get started."

"What are we looking for, sir?" asked Billy as he looked around the crowded room himself.

"I would have thought that was bloody

obvious," was Crane's sharp reply.

"Anything to do with his research on the Church of Jesus is King and cults?"

"Correct and don't forget to search for a memory stick," Crane commanded.

"Memory stick?" Billy looked confused.

"Yes, lad, something like the one you have on your key ring. The Padre had a laptop, so maybe he had a memory stick as well. You never know we might just get lucky, so let's get to it."

PADRE SYMMONDS

Right, Crane, in the true spirit of detective novels, if you're reading this, something must have happened to me! Ha ha! But seriously, please indulge this flight of fancy of mine. I just thought it might be prudent to do a backup copy of everything I have found out about cults and the Church of Jesus is King in Aldershot in particular.

I must say I have found the whole thing rather exciting - fulfilling even. So first of all I must thank you, Crane, for letting me be part of the investigation. Don't get me wrong I love my job and role of Padre to the garrison community, but every now and then one needs a bit more, don't you think? Something to spice up the humdrum everyday life that each of us leads. Something, that at the end of the day, one could say "I made a difference. I was there when it counted."

Anyway, I digress, as usual. So, down to business. Stored on this memory stick are copies of the emails I have sent you, information on cults that I have downloaded from the internet and a bit of background on the Church of Jesus is King. Most of this you already know.

What has been more interesting is the links I have been building with the church under the guise of the Army Liaison Scheme. As we agreed, I started with the Church of

Jesus is King. The Elder, Elias, was more than happy for me to be involved in the church for a week or so, on the promise that he could shadow me at some future date. Then we could offer the services of both churches to the wider garrison community should the need or opportunities arise. He is a very nice man, I must say. In his late 40's probably, always soberly dressed in a dark suit and well groomed. His enthusiasm and commitment to his church is evident and he cares for his members as a shepherd for his flock. As a result he has tried very hard to cater for their every need.

So, as well as the normal church service every Sunday morning, there are counselling sessions for those in psychological need, those suffering from alcoholism, or drug addiction. No one is turned away, but welcomed into the church community and helped as much as possible. The children are also well catered for with a Sunday school and church led activities in the school holidays. As a result, Elias has managed to draw in a large number of families with small children. His view that most churches do not welcome and nurture children, has struck a chord with the younger generation, who welcome his open door policy.

Now we get to the interesting bit, information I stumbled across whilst in conversation with church members. Apparently, as part of the evangelical church movement, efforts are made to link up with other similar churches across the UK. So at Aldershot, they regularly have guest preachers, sometimes during the normal scheduled services and sometimes as special one off events. These churches include those at Catterick and Colchester! See what I mean about interesting! The speakers range from other Church Elders included in the network, as well as independent speakers, who are recommended.

One such speaker was a man called Zechariah. I asked Elias about him. He said that after being a guest speaker at Aldershot, Zechariah contacted Elias and offered to start workshops for fathers with small children. The problem is that the arrangements are fluid. Zechariah seems to contact participants directly with dates, times and locations of the meetings, so Elias is uncertain as to who attends, how often they take place, or indeed where. I asked for contact details for Zechariah, but Elias had to confess that the mobile phone number he has doesn't seem to work anymore.

As this looked to be the most promising lead there is at the moment, I intend to start making enquiries of likely participants, in the hope that I can attend one of the meetings and find out what is going on. It seems this Zechariah stays in the shadows, but maybe I can throw some light on his secrets.

Don't worry, Sergeant Major, I promise to keep you posted!

CHAPTER 21

"Bloody idiot," was DI Anderson's reaction to Padre Symonds's missive that Crane had printed out and brought to the local police station. Anderson pushed the paper back across his desk towards Crane.

"That may be so, Derek, but this information opens up our missing person's enquiry to encompass Aldershot and the surrounding area. Hence your involvement," Crane said. Fed up with sitting, which was making him feel impotent, Crane stood up and leaned against the wall.

Crane and Anderson had a good working relationship, although they only had irregular contact. The local constabulary did not patrol on an army garrison and equally the RMP didn't patrol outside the garrison. This meant that from time to time joint operations and liaison were required, especially for crimes that would be tried in a civil court. Crane and Anderson had worked hard at fostering mutual respect for each other's expertise and local boundaries.

"Have you had any problems with this church in

the past?" said Crane, looking at Anderson who, as always, was dishevelled. Crane knew that he looked little better himself, with his own suit crumpled and dusty from that morning's encounter with the church floor.

"Not really," shrugged Derek. "Only the usual local stuff. Sometimes they have very large gatherings and the police are on hand to watch the traffic, make sure no one parks outside on the double yellow lines, that sort of thing. But nothing you could call trouble. After all it's a church not a brothel or illegal drinking club, Crane," he smiled.

"I know, I know, but it's the only real lead we have," replied Crane, sitting back down. "I'm sure the Padre's disappearance must have something to do with this church. He talks about a shadowy figure and secret meetings. I can only think that this is the person who felt that the Padre was nosing around too much; ergo he was a danger to this unknown preacher. As a result, he has either kidnapped or killed the Padre." Crane played with his scar.

"And your only evidence of this is the Padre's memo on his memory stick?" asked Anderson lifting his hands from his desk in an unbelieving gesture.

"Gut feeling, intuition, call it what you will. But looking at the broader picture, the other murder suicides, the other local evangelical churches, it seems obvious to me." Crane had just spent the last 20 minutes or so filling in the background of the investigation for Anderson. Whilst the police officer had been sympathetic regarding the murder of three children, he had little to offer. Anderson had not been involved with the investigation in Aldershot, apart from his initial contact with the Solomon murder scene and subsequent attendance at the inquest, where a verdict of murder was recorded for the two victims and suicide for Solomon Crooks. He was therefore surprised to learn about the other two murder/suicides in Catterick and Colchester.

"Can't you get a warrant and search the church premises?"

"No one's going to authorise a search warrant on this evidence, Crane. But what I will do is go and see this Church Elder, interview him and ask him politely if we can have a look around. Okay?"

"Tonight?"

"Tonight, Crane, now go home."

Smiling, Crane thanked Anderson, who promised to phone Crane's mobile as soon as he had any news.

***

Someone else making arrangements was Staff Sergeant Jones. As Crane entered his office, straight from his visit to Aldershot Police Station, Jones was organising a sweep of the large, wooded, military owned land and disused buildings located opposite the garrison on the other side of the Farnborough Road. Near to Farnborough airport and adjacent to large playing fields, the area also doubled as a local beauty spot populated by dog walkers and those who just wanted to enjoy being out of doors. The small empty roads and tracks were also popular with the local driving schools and no one was ever sure whether it was the learner drivers trying to avoid the marching troops or the other way round. Because of the large numbers of soldiers constantly in the area, Crane knew that a search wouldn't cause any raised eyebrows and whispers into the wrong ears, bringing unwanted press interest.

"No sign of him yet then?"

"No sorry," replied Jones. "But we're doing all we can, searching the local military areas."

"I know, Jones." Crane sank into the only other chair in the office, which was small and uncomfortable. "Jesus, this bloody chair, can't you change it Jones? I'm sure you could find a better one in a skip!"

"I'll try to get round to it when we've found the Padre. Look, it's starting to get dark, there's not much more you can do at the moment. You've already sent the information on the memory stick to Harris in Catterick and Brown in Colchester, to see if they can turn up any similar information their end. Have you updated Captain Edwards?"

"Yes, although he was none too pleased. Losing an officer is high up on his list of things not to do. As per usual he wants everything sorted out as quickly as possible, so he can take the glory, whilst ensuring that nothing reflects badly on him. At the moment he's busy trying to soothe the upper echelons in the Officers' Mess, assuring them that the lads are on it and it'll all be sorted out in double quick time. Typical," he added running his hand through his hair, "no investigative insight from him, just an order to get it sorted!"

"Well, no point whinging about it, Crane, you've been in the army long enough. You know how the system works. No luck with any evidence from the Padre's office in the church?"

"No, not a thing. I bet it's the same bastard who hit me over the head that's got the Padre. But the trouble is I've got no evidence to back anything up. I realise that even Anderson is working with his hands tied behind his back trying to persuade anyone to take my allegations seriously. But there must be some solid evidence somewhere tying all this together, Jones."

"I know, Crane, and if there is, between us all we'll find it. Look on the bright side, at least people are listening to you since the Padre disappeared and you got hit over the head!" he laughed.

Crane knew Jones was trying to inject an air of levity into the seriousness of the situation but couldn't raise a smile.

"You look done in," Jones said. "Why don't you go home and keep the mobile by your bed? If I hear anything at all, I'll phone straight away. I'm on duty all night and you'll have to be fresh to take over in the morning."

"You're right. I've got a bitch of a headache as well," Crane admitted, as he massaged the now rather large lump on his scalp. "Perhaps a few hours sleep will help. Thanks, Jones," and Crane left the office to go home.

Once in the car, he phoned the SIB office to let them know where he'd be and drove down Queens Avenue towards home. He saw Billy a few cars ahead of him. As it was nearly 19:00 hours, he expected Billy to turn left at the traffic lights and go towards the garrison sports centre, where he was a frequent visitor to the gym and Olympic sized swimming pool. Keeping fit was Billy's obsession. But it seemed that wasn't his destination that evening, as the car continued to crawl along the avenue in the rush hour traffic, hindered every few yards by interminable sets of traffic lights. Intrigued, Crane followed Billy to the junction at the edge of the garrison with Aldershot town, rather than taking an earlier turning to cut through the back roads towards Ash where he lived. As they reached the junction, Crane saw Billy turn right towards the town centre.

Assuming Billy was on a night out with the lads; Crane turned his mind away from his young sergeant and started looking forward to seeing Tina. But more importantly, to taking a few strong painkillers, unaware that a bad headache would be the least of his painful injuries in the not too distant future.

CHAPTER 22

Crane had reason to be concerned about Billy again the next morning. His young sergeant, usually so full of life, was listless, pale and unkempt. From his open office door he could see Billy trying to concentrate on the papers in front of him, but he kept closing his eyes, as if the effort was just too much.

Deciding that a dressing down wasn't the order of the day today, he got up to go out and as he passed through the office called, "Billy, you're with me."

"Oh, what? Yes, sir." Billy scrambled for his things and ran to catch up with Crane.

Once in the car he asked, "Where are we off to, boss?" whilst rubbing his hands over his face in a washing motion, as if to scrub off whatever malady was plaguing him.

"Aldershot Police Station, to see DI Anderson. I want to talk to him face to face about his meeting with Elias."

"Okay, boss," was Billy's tired reply as his head drooped and his eyes closed.

"Billy," said Crane sharply.

"Sir?" Billy jerked awake, opening his eyes wide and blinking.

"Good night last night was it?" Crane smiled to soften the words.

"Sorry, sir, last night?"

"Yes, lad, last night. A night out with the boys was it, one too many beers eh?"

"Beers, no, sir, no beers last night. Why do you ask?"

"Well, because you look like a man with a raging hangover and I saw you drive off last night towards the town centre, so I assumed you must have had a good night out with the lads." Crane's patience was beginning to wear thin.

"No, not me, sir, just a night in watching the telly." Billy sat up straighter in the car seat, blinking repeatedly.

"Then what's wrong with you this morning, for God's sake?"

"Wrong? Nothing wrong with me. At least nothing that a strong cup of coffee won't sort out." Billy smiled his most engaging smile at Crane.

"Mm, well, the coffee's a good idea. Anything's better than that crap at the police station," said Crane as he pulled into the drive through lane of Burger King and ordered two strong black coffees.

Deciding to pull into the small car park in front of the fast food store instead of driving on, Crane took a coffee from the small cardboard tray Billy was holding and said, "Come on, let's get some fresh air."

The combination of fresh air and coffee seemed to bring Billy round and the coffee and nicotine helped Crane calm down, meaning that both men were in better shape when they met Anderson.

Unfortunately the DI had little to offer from his interview with the Church Elder. He told them that Elias had said that he was troubled to hear of the Padre's disappearance, citing him as a close colleague and that he had seemed happy to show Anderson around the church.

"So what's the place like?" asked Crane.

"Well, being the old cinema, it's on two levels, with the ground floor and then the old stalls above. It's quite ornate and looks like it's been cleaned and restored a little by the church volunteers. Some of the seating has obviously seen better days, but it's clear a good effort has been made to make it clean and welcoming."

"Did Elias show you everywhere?"

"I'd say not. I suspect that Elias only showed me the public rooms. I think there are a number of back room areas as well. You know behind the old screen. But without a search warrant, there's nothing I could do about it."

"Anything else?"

"Anything else? What do you mean?" asked Anderson rifling through his papers as though he had forgotten something, but wasn't sure what.

"Any other avenues of investigation that might help us find the Padre?"

"Oh, yes, sorry. Well, he's been logged as a missing person. The lads on the beat and in the cars have been issued with his description and details of his car and told to keep an eye out. We're taking it very seriously, Crane, and will do everything we can. The top brass are obviously aware of what's going on and anxious to co-operate with the military as much as possible. We're all concerned for the Padre's safety and will do everything we can to help find him."

***

Crane and Billy returned to the office, with Crane turning his head this way and that as he drove down Queen's Avenue, hoping to catch sight of the Padre out for his morning constitutional, even though he knew he wouldn't. After a briefing with Captain Edwards that provided no new insights, Crane sat exhausted in his chair in his office, trying to massage away the headache that still plagued him from yesterday.

Crane looked up at a tentative knock on his door. "Kim? Do you want to see me?"

"Please, sir, if it's convenient."

"Of course, come in and sit down. Any news for me?"

"No, not really, sir, just something that's bothering me."

"Yes?"

"Well, sir, it's Billy, sorry Staff Sergeant Williams..." she tailed off, crossing and then uncrossing her legs.

"It's okay, Kim. Stop looking as though you think you're telling tales out of school. What's the matter?"

"Well, I know you've noticed he seems a bit odd at the moment, a bit vague and not quite with it. I'm really concerned that…"

"That what, Kim?" Crane had to prompt her again.

"Well, this may sound a bit stupid, but I'm wondering if he's disobeyed your order and started going to that church. Or maybe he was already going."

"What, to Jesus is King?"

"Yes, sir, I know how strongly he felt about wanting to infiltrate it. Maybe he decided to go out on his own. Oh I don't know, I've got no evidence, it's just a feeling." By this time Kim was fidgeting with her hands. Kim didn't fidget, so Crane knew it must have taken courage for her to speak out.

"Okay, fair enough," he responded nodding slowly. "In that case, why don't you follow him in your car tonight? I think it would be less obvious if it was you rather than me. Let's see where he goes. But don't do anything stupid, Kim, just follow him, ring me on my mobile and then go home. If he does go to the church on no account are you to try and follow him in there. Understood?"

"Understood, sir," said Kim, a smile breaking through the worry.

Crane pondered Kim's concerns for a while after she had left. Surely Billy wouldn't have been so stupid to have disobeyed a direct order? But then again, Crane had done that himself in the past, mostly to good effect. The trick was not to get caught and then talk your way out of it when you came up with results. But there was definitely something wrong with Billy at the moment and Crane was glad Kim had shared her suspicions.

For the rest of the day he had little opportunity to dwell on the problem of Billy. There was still no sign of the Padre and Jones was extending the search to other areas of military land including Longmoor in Farnborough and also Ash Ranges.

As a result, by the end of the day he had forgotten about the tail on Billy. It was only when Billy was leaving the office and he saw Kim quickly gather her things and nod conspiratorially at him, that he remembered. Deciding to stay on at the office, he paced around the open plan area, holding his mobile in his hand.

CHAPTER 23

The call came after 10 minutes.

"Sir, its Kim. Billy has just driven through the town and out beyond the Industrial area to Ash. He parked up and went into an old Victorian school, St Saviour's on Ash Road. I've sat here for a few minutes and seen other people arriving. No one looks furtive or distressed. Everything seemed perfectly ordinary, but I've no idea what he's doing here."

"Okay, Kim, good work," said Crane as he scribbled down the address. "Go home now. There's nothing we can do. I'll have a word with Billy in the morning."

"Are you sure you don't want me to stay and follow him when he comes out?"

"No, Kim, there's nothing we can do. There's no law that says you couldn't attend a meeting and it could be completely unrelated. Let's just see what Billy says tomorrow."

"Very well, sir."

Crane closed his phone, wondering what approach he'd take with Billy in the morning.

***

By the time Crane got home that night he was late for dinner. He found Tina on the settee watching television with a glass of red wine in her hand, riveted by one of the soap operas.

"Hi," she called over her shoulder. "Your dinner's in the fridge, it just needs heating up in the microwave," and turned her attention back the TV, sipping her wine.

This irritated Crane and without speaking he went through to the kitchen. Looking at the mess of pots, pans and plates, all dirty, strewn around, cranked up that irritation. He started banging things around and running hot water in the sink. He went to throw discarded packaging in the bin, but found it full to the brim. The swing bin lid would barely open and the packaging simply bounced back at him falling on the floor at his feet.

Walking to the kitchen door he called, "For God's sake, Tina, can't you even do the bloody washing up or empty the bin? It looks like a bomb's hit this place!" With that he returned to his banging and crashing, putting ingredients back in the cupboards.

This had the desired effect of disturbing Tina's viewing and she came to the door, standing watching him, the glass of red wine still in her hand.

"Oh so you've decided to come and help then," he growled from the kitchen sink.

"What's got into you, Tom?"

"What's got into me?" he whirled round to face

her. "Every time I come home the place is a bloody mess. There's only two of us, can't you at least keep things tidy!"

"It's only what's left over from cooking dinner. I was going to do it when I'd had a rest."

But Crane wasn't about to be placated. "Have a rest, that's all you ever do! Never mind the drinking. I see you've got a glass of wine as usual."

"Yes, Tom, I needed to have a rest. I've had a busy day and there's nothing wrong with unwinding with a glass of wine every now and again," and with that she turned to go back to the lounge.

"But it's not every now and again is it?" he retorted.

"I'm sorry?" Tina turned back to face him.

"I said it's not every now and again. You seem to unwind with a glass of wine every night."

"So what if I do, Tom? What's the problem?"

"The problem is that you're unwinding with a glass of wine, when you should be doing the housework. I shouldn't have to come home to this shit." He flung the tea towel that he was using to dry his hands onto the kitchen counter.

"Tom, what's the matter?"

But he carried on as though she hadn't spoken. "Dear God and you want children. You can't even cope with just us, never mind a houseful of screaming kids. It would be like a war zone. And when would you get time to unwind with your glass of wine then?"

"Tom, stop it. What's got into you."

But it seemed that whatever she said, it made no difference. He couldn't seem to stop himself. The anger built up in him like a volcano, burning his throat and erupting through his mouth, spewing out hurtful insults.

"I bet you'll be like one of those slovenly mums on the garrison. Kids taking over the house, no order, no discipline. You'll be more interested in having your rest and a glass of wine."

"I don't have to listen to this," Tina replied, retreating to the lounge and this time staying there.

"Oh, but you do," he said, following her into the other room. By now he was looking for more debris to clear up and comment on. He looked around the room, but as he couldn't find anything to tidy up, he walked over to the TV and turned it off.

"Tom, I was watching that," Tina protested.

"Load of shit. Can't you watch anything decent? A documentary or something that teaches you things?"

But Tina refused to answer. Placing the glass of wine on the low coffee table in front of the TV, she curled into herself, legs bent in front of her with her arms around them.

"What's the matter, can't you cope with the truth? I need some support from my wife, not this shit."

"I do support you." Crane could hardly hear her as she bent her head to rest on her knees.

"Yeah, right. Call that support?" Crane flung his arm towards the kitchen door.

"I work as well, Tom," she said defiantly, but kept her head low, as though protecting herself from the stream of criticism.

"Work, you call what you do work?"

"Of course and I had a busy day today," she said, this time lifting her head to look at him.

"Oh I'm sure you did. It must be very pressurised counting bank notes all day." Looking at Tina he could see tears welling in her eyes. "Don't start snivelling," he snarled pacing around the room. "You don't know the first thing about pressure. Shall I tell you about pressure?" he asked standing in front of her, legs apart, hands on his hips. "Pressure is three dead soldiers, three dead children, a missing Padre and a Staff Sergeant who seems to have disobeyed orders. That's bloody pressure, Tina. Not counting sodding bank notes!"

Unable to look at his wife any longer, Crane left the room, grabbed a cold beer from the fridge and retreated to his office where he proceeded to bang around and tidy up before pulling the case files from his briefcase.

After a while Tina came upstairs, went into the bedroom and closed the door behind her. Later on he heard muffled crying through the wall. Ignoring the sound, Crane went over and over the files, pushing his personal problems to one side in his determination to try and find any small piece of information he had missed.

As the print began to swim before his eyes he realised he needed to sleep. But unable to cope with the aftermath of his behaviour, he went back downstairs, lying on the settee in the dark and thinking far into the night before sleep overcame him.

CHAPTER 24

The first thing Crane wanted to do the next morning was to confront Billy. But before he went to the barracks, he did a detour to look at St Saviour's School in Ash. It was still early, around 07:30 hours, so there were no children or staff there. Parking the car, he decided to walk past the building. The board on the front gate proclaimed it to be a primary school, taking ages 5-11. It gave the head teacher's name and that of the caretaker. The gates, which he rattled as he passed, were locked. Behind them he could see a large imposing Victorian building with arched windows. Some of the windows held what he surmised to be children's artwork, although all he could see from the outside was the backs of the pieces of paper and the bits of blue tack used to stick them to the windows. The building was set well back from the gates and in front was a large tarmac area used as a playground, with painted lines, painted feet in different colours and an area set aside with several climbing frames.

Walking back past the school towards his car, Crane decided to stop and make a note of the head teacher's name, in case he needed to make enquiries about people hiring the school for outside activities.

As he drove on towards his barracks, Crane's mind wandered back to his precarious domestic situation. Having spent the night on the settee, he was up and about early, taking a quick shower and managing to get his clothes out of the wardrobe without disturbing Tina. Although she could have been feigning sleep he supposed. Just before he left the house, he once again crept into the bedroom to leave a cup of coffee as a kind of peace offering. He knew he would have to phone her later at work, but was dreading it and as he pulled into the car park outside his office, he pushed aside thoughts of Tina and concentrated on Billy and the Padre.

To Crane's relief Billy was at his desk already and seemed bright and alert.

"My office, Sergeant," he called as he passed Billy's desk.

As Crane settled himself in his chair, he left Billy standing to attention in front of him. An old but regularly used ploy. Crane knew it would make Billy feel uncomfortable, which was just what he wanted.

"Right, Sergeant, I've been thinking of several ways to approach this, but have decided on the blunt one. Where did you go last night after leaving work?"

"Sir?" the confusion in Billy's eyes was apparent.

"It's not a difficult question. But I'll repeat it for you. Where did you go last night after work?"

"Well, sir," began Billy. "It's just that...I mean..."

"For God's sake, Billy, where the hell did you go?" Crane's irritation from last night had not dissipated altogether.

"A parent's evening, sir."

"A what?" Crane's astonishment was genuine. "Are you trying to tell me something, Sergeant?"

"No, sir, nothing like that," Billy smiled. "It's just that my niece, Rosie, was ill, so my sister, Sue, couldn't go to Shaun's parent's evening. Shaun being my nephew, sir. So she asked me to go instead. And after that I went round to Sue's, my sister, to tell her all about it. Actually, he is doing rather well in school, we're all pretty proud of him and—"

"Yes, yes, alright," sighed Crane. "Oh by the way, at ease, Billy, sit yourself down."

"Thank you, sir, but why did you want to know?"

"Oh it's just that, well nothing really, just that you've been acting a bit strange. What with being so tired and being late for work, so I was just um, making sure you were alright." Crane finished with a flourish. "Anyway, off you go, I need to make a few calls now. Oh and by the way," Crane called to Billy's retreating back, "chase up the techies for me would you. Surely they must have got to Solomon's computer by now."

"Right away, sir."

Crane fell back in his chair, feeling rather afraid he'd just sounded like Captain Edwards and made a complete fool of himself into the bargain. Shit. Not a good start to the day. He could only hope it would get better as he reached for the phone to get updates from Jones and Anderson on the search for the Padre. As there was still no sign of him, Crane managed to elicit a promise from DI Anderson to search all abandoned buildings in Aldershot. At first Anderson laughed at the suggestion.

"Do you know how many abandoned buildings we have in Aldershot, Crane? It's not exactly a prosperous area at the moment in case you hadn't noticed. Shops are closing down and half the High Street has been abandoned. I blame Tesco's myself. I swear most of the country is turning into Tescoland!"

"Yes, yes, I understand. I only meant the deserted ones out in the industrial areas for instance. Ones in hidden places that no one really knows about. Maybe something that was abandoned years ago. Come on, Derek, you know what I mean. Surely some of the police on the beat know where to look?"

After that Anderson agreed it was a good idea and promised to set things in motion.

Crane's next task was to phone Sergeant Harris in Catterick and ask about Corporal Fisher's wife.

"What do you want me to ask her?"

"I just need to see if you could jog her memory. Ask about the church meetings her husband attended again. Maybe she'll be a bit more co-operative now. You never know."

"Chance will be a fine thing. Anyway, she's not up here anymore. She's moved down your way, apparently, to be near her sister. So she's now in Reading. Here's her mobile number, call her and see if she'll talk to you."

After confirming the number, Crane thanked Harris and called Mrs Fisher. She agreed to see him, but only later that day and only at her sister's house in Reading. She refused to tell him where she was living and said she wanted 'a witness present' when he interviewed her. Crane realised he would have to turn on the charm to get anything out of her and thought it might be better if Kim or Billy came with him. He was rather lacking in the charm department at the moment.

Crane then thought the interview was just the excuse he needed for calling Tina. He always told her if he would be late home, or not home at all come to that. So taking a deep breath he dialled her mobile. No answer. He called the bank who informed him that Mrs Crane was unavailable. So he called her mobile back to leave a message.

"Hi, Tina, um it's me. Sorry about last night. Anyway I've called to say I've got to go to Reading to interview someone at 19:00 hours tonight, sorry I mean 7pm, so I'll be late home. I'll see you then. Um… bye." Crane punched the red button to finish the call. He hated leaving messages. The words always came out wrong and sounded stilted. Still, it was the best he could do for now.

CHAPTER 25

Crane spent the rest of the day on routine work, interspersed with calls to Sergeant Jones and DI Anderson. He also found himself checking his mobile phone every hour or so to see if Tina had called. She hadn't. By 18:00 hours he called for Kim and they went to Reading to see Mrs Fisher. During the journey he told her about his previous interviews with Mrs Fisher and warned her that this one could be as bad.

"She was very angry, as you would expect. But also angry with the army. I got the sense she felt she had been dumped on from a great height and had not only lost her husband and son, but also her home, friends and everything she felt familiar with," Crane explained.

"Well, that's understandable, sir, the army doesn't seem to have the best track record in the world when it comes to looking after wives of soldiers who have either died or left them. What many wives don't seem to understand is that the army needs to evict them from their army quarter."

"Needs to? Explain."

"Well, for most wives or ex-wives their best option will be for the local authority to re-house them. But that's not possible without an eviction order from the army. The eviction order gives them more points on the housing list and therefore a better chance of getting one of the few houses available. So while it seems harsh, it's actually a necessary evil. Of course having kids helps as well, they give you more points."

"Yes, well, Mrs Fisher doesn't have a child anymore does she?"

"No, sir, sorry, sir."

Glancing sideways at Kim, Crane saw her cheeks redden as she turned to look out of the car window. "So for God's sake don't mention that bit at the interview."

"No, sir. Oh here's the sign for Reading," Kim said pointing to her left.

They managed to navigate their way through the maze of streets running off Oxford Road and pulled up in front of a small Victorian terraced house. The street was quiet, although crammed with cars and at the far end of the road a few children played on bicycles. The door was answered by a large woman with a mass of curly hair and equally messy attire. She seemed swathed in layers of clothes of varying lengths, the longest one ending at her ankles.

Crane introduced himself and Kim and reminded her of their appointment with Mrs Fisher.

"ID please," was the only response.

Crane and Kim both pushed their IDs towards the woman, which in any case were visible, as they were always hanging around their necks.

"Very well, come in," the woman turned her back on them and walked through the house. Crane and Kim followed the swaying skirts to the kitchen. Mrs Fisher was sitting at a table in the centre of the room, nursing a mug of something. She turned her head at their entrance but said nothing.

Crane moved round the table to face her.

"Thank you for seeing us, Mrs Fisher," he began. "This is Sergeant Kim Weston who works with me."

Mrs Fisher inclined her head to the chairs, which Crane took as an invitation to sit down.

"This is my sister, Molly, she'll be staying."

"Of course, no problem," replied Crane looking at Molly who was now leaning against the sink, staring at them with cold eyes.

"Mrs Fisher," Kim began, "I'd first of all like to say how sorry we are for your loss."

"Yes, well, easy to say, hard to live with."

"I'm sure, it must be," continued Kim a soothing cadence to her voice. "And I know our visit is unwelcome, but we are working hard to find out what caused your husband to do what he did."

"Really?" was the reply accompanied by a huff.

"Yes, really, that's why we need a bit of help from you."

Crane and Kim let the silence develop.

Mrs Fisher broke it by sighing, "Oh, I suppose so. What was it you want to know?"

"Thank you, Mrs Fisher," replied Kim and nodded at Crane.

Picking up the lead from Kim, Crane tried to soften his voice and attitude. "Do you remember anything about the church that your husband visited with your son?"

"I never went there."

"No, I understand that. We just wondered if he had ever mentioned any courses that he went on, or preachers that he'd listened to."

Crane struggled to keep calm. He knew he couldn't mention the name the Padre had given him, because if the case ever came to court, the defence barrister would say Crane put words into Mrs Fisher's mouth and led her on. So he kept calm, hoping she would continue to answer his questions. Whilst Mrs Fisher appeared to have gone through the anger stage of grief, Crane realised she could still flare up at any moment if provoked.

"Well, he used to go every Sunday and take my boy with him. But I think that was just the normal Sunday service, you know?" Crane nodded in agreement. "But after a while he started going out in the evenings during the week."

"Really?" Crane tried to keep the sharp pique of interest he felt out of his voice. "Do you know why?"

"Um, he said something about a visiting preacher. He got quite excited at the beginning, went on about it quite a lot, and said something about starting a course."

Mrs Fisher lapsed into silence, looking deep into the contents of her mug.

"Did he start the course?" Kim prompted.

"Oh yes, although it wasn't the same night every week, it varied you know. Sometimes he seemed to know what night it would be and sometimes he got a phone call about 6 o'clock and went out then."

"Did he take your son with him on those nights?"

"No, definitely not and anyway I wouldn't have let him. School the next day and all that." Mrs Fisher's voice was hard.

"No, of course you wouldn't," Kim agreed.

"Is there anything at all you could tell us about this visiting preacher, Mrs Fisher?" Crane asked, fighting the urge to walk around the room and rage at the slowness of the interview. Wanting to shout the name the Padre had given them at Mrs Fisher to see her reaction.

"Um, I'm not sure, but I think his name was something biblical, you know?" Mrs Fisher looked out of the window, past her sister, blinking rapidly.

"I think that's enough now," Molly cut in, pushing her bulk off the sink. "She's getting upset. It's not fair of you lot, dragging all this up again."

"I can assure you, it isn't our intention to upset Mrs Fisher," began Kim.

"That's as may be, but look at her, she's had enough."

Crane saw tears falling into the mug Mrs Fisher was holding up under her chin, although she seemed oblivious to them. She was still gazing out of the kitchen window.

Fighting his frustration, Crane rose. "Thank you for seeing us, Mrs Fisher. If you do think of anything, could you please call? I'll leave my card on the table here."

"What?"

"My card, Mrs Fisher, if you think if anything that may be helpful, anything at all, please phone me."

"No," was the cold reply.

"See I told you," said Molly as she started to bustle Crane and Kim out of the kitchen. "Leave her in peace."

"For God's sake, Molly, shut up!" Crane and Kim stopped at the door to the kitchen and turned back at the sound of Mrs Fisher's voice. "I mean there's no need for me to ring. I can tell you now. His name, the Preacher, was Zechariah. There was a kid down the road called Zach, that's why I remember. He used to play with my Ryan every day after school….." her voice faded as the tears came again, her head falling into her arms as she sobbed.

CHAPTER 26

Crane and Kim were on their way back to Aldershot discussing the lead they had just been given by Mrs Fisher. Crane was rather proud of himself for not punching the air and yelling 'yes!' when she voluntarily gave them the same name as Padre Symonds. They were talking about contacting DI Anderson, when Crane's mobile rang. Crane handed it to Kim, as he hadn't set up his hands free kit, hoping it wasn't Tina as he couldn't speak to her himself. Yet equally hoping it was, as she hadn't been in touch all day.

"Sergeant Major Crane's phone," Kim said into the small black handset. "Oh hello, sir, no sorry he's driving. We're on our way back from Reading."

Crane's disappointment that it was Captain Edwards on the phone and not his wife did nothing to ease the clenching of his gut caused by the hope it was Tina calling.

"Mm...Yes... of course, sir."

Crane kept glancing at Kim, wanting to know what was going on.

"Thank you, sir."

As Kim closed the phone Crane was none the wiser about what had been said.

"Well? What did the Captain want now?"

"Oh, it wasn't the Captain, sir. It was Detective Inspector Anderson."

"And?" Crane risked another look at Kim as he negotiated his way around the large roundabout at the bottom of Camberley, threading his way through the huge volume of traffic streaming out of the Tesco and Marks and Spencer's Superstores. He was on the bypass heading towards Aldershot when Kim next spoke.

"And I think you should take the next turning to Frimley, sir," Kim grinned. "They've found the Padre and he's been taken to Frimley Park Hospital."

"Thank God for that," replied Crane, pushing down hard on the accelerator, forcing Kim to hold onto the hand grip above the passenger door. "Where did they find him? What condition is he in? Has he said anything?" Crane's questions tumbled over one another.

"No info at the moment, sir. DI Anderson just said to meet him at the Accident and Emergency desk as soon as we could."

Glancing at the clock on the dashboard as he changed down two gears in order to accelerate, Crane estimated ten minutes to the hospital.

In fact he made it in six, much to Kim's horror, as he wove in and out of the traffic on the dual carriageway and blasted his horn at anyone unfortunate enough to get in his way. His tyres squealed in protest as Crane slewed into the hospital entrance and then had to brake hard, as an unfortunate pedestrian dared to use the zebra crossing. Crane abandoned the car in a corner by the emergency entrance marked '10 minute pick up only' and sprinted through the sliding doors as though he was racing in the Olympics.

He was looking left and right, when Kim reached him and touched his arm, "Over there, sir."

Following her arm, he saw Derek Anderson standing talking to the Receptionist. "Derek!" he called, running over. "How is he?"

"Ah, Crane, glad you got here...come on, this way."

Crane followed Anderson through the A&E waiting room which was crammed with people waiting to see a doctor. Most were sitting without talking, shrouded in either pain or misery. They follow a corridor at the side of the A&E, through to the lifts.

"He's in intensive care," Anderson said as they waited for the lift, "so don't expect any information from him just yet."

"No, no, of course not," Crane muttered, feeling the opposite. Information was precisely what he did want, but his desire was muted with relief that the Padre was at least alive.

"How is he? Where did you find him? When—"

"All in good time, Crane, when we're alone," Anderson interrupts as the lift doors opened.

The three of them entered the lift and Crane nodded to a porter guarding an empty wheelchair, who was eying them as though their main intent was to take it off him. Ignoring the man, Crane concentrated on the display panel as the lift ground its way upwards, tapping his foot with impatience. The doors opened at last and Crane was just about to push through them, when Anderson held him back. Realising it was not their floor Crane moved away from the doors, allowing the porter and his precious cargo out of the lift.

Derek then briefed Crane and Kim about the Padre. "He was found in an abandoned warehouse on one of the industrial estates."

Crane grinned at this piece of information.

"He's in a bad way, I'm afraid. Let's see if we can find the doctor," Anderson finished as the doors opened onto the corridor near the entrance to the ICU.

Crane paced as Anderson pushed the buzzer outside the ward and waited to be attended to, as the notice on the wall requested. "What's taking them so long?" he growled.

"Patients I expect, sir," was the whispered reply from Kim.

Grunting, Crane continued pacing, as Kim and Anderson sat on the hard plastic chairs running down one side of the wall. At last a nurse came to the door and Anderson had a quiet word with her.

Glancing imperiously at the three of them, the nurse said, "Very well, but only two of you. The doctor is on the ward, but with another patient, so

I'll ask him to come over when he's available."

Motioning to Kim to stay and wait, Crane and Anderson slipped through the door and walked onto the ward, following the nurse. She stopped at a screened cubicle nearest to the nursing station and held back the curtain so they could go in.

Padre Symonds was a mess. His head was shaved on the left hand side, revealing an angry bruise which started at his temple and spread across the side of his head. He was unresponsive, with tubes in the back of his hands and beeping machines crowding his bed. Crane looked at the once vibrant and eager man he had come to like and admire, whose naivety had been his downfall and sent an arrow prayer to the God he didn't really believe in, to save the Padre, insisting to the invisible deity that he should at least have the decency to save one of his own.

Hearing a rustling behind them, Crane and Anderson turned to look at the doctor who was standing at the bottom of the bed.

"He's in a bad way, I'm afraid," said the doctor, who looked young enough to be Crane's son. "Suffered a very bad blow to the side of the head as you can see. At the moment he's in a coma and we're monitoring the pressure on the brain. We think we're going to have to operate tomorrow, as his brain's swelling and we need to relieve the pressure."

"Any other injuries?"

"Not that we're aware of," answered the doctor turning to look at Crane. "But he's also suffering from hypothermia and dehydration. We can handle both of those. It's the brain injury that's bothering us more than anything at the moment. I'll keep DI Anderson informed of any changes."

Crane said, "Do what you can for him won't you, doctor?"

"Of course. Look, if you leave your contact details at the nurse's station, we'll phone you as well if there is any change."

Crane mumbled his thanks as the doctor turned to leave. "Sorry but I think you should go as well. We've only just got him stabilised. We'll know more tomorrow."

Crane managed to squeeze the Padre's fingers as he was leaving, to let him know he was there. Hoping for a responsive squeeze back, but didn't get one.

CHAPTER 27

By the time they emerged from the hospital it was dark. Sodium lights cast a harsh glare around the entrance to A&E and a stationary ambulance stood with the doors open, having already discharged its human cargo. Crane pulled out a packet of cigarettes and put one in his mouth as Anderson touched him on the arm and pointed to a large sign, forbidding smoking in any hospital buildings, grounds or car parks.

"For fuck's sake," grumbled Crane, "what's this country coming to? Never mind, I'll have one in the car."

"Um, the car, sir," called Kim.

Crane turned to find Kim looking at an empty space. Where his car should be.

"For fuck's sake," said Crane again, louder this time, as Kim and Anderson tried to suppress their laughter.

"Anderson," he said menacingly, "I just don't need this right now. Okay?"

"Okay, Crane, let me see what I can do." As Anderson pulled his phone out of his pocket and turned his back on them to make his phone call, Crane could see the policeman's shoulders were still shaking. Lighting up in defiance, he pulled out his own phone and called Tina.

"Hello?"

"Hi, Tina, it's me."

"Tom." Flat voice. No inflection.

Crane ploughed on regardless. "Sorry, love, good news and bad news. The good news is that we've found the Padre."

"Oh, Tom, that is good news," said Tina, her voice softening just a touch. "What's the bad news?" Hardening again.

"I've had my car towed away from Frimley Park Hospital."

"Right." Tina elongated the word.

"So I'm going to be a bit late back."

"A bit late, Tom, you're already a bit late."

"Yeah, sorry. But I did let you know. You got my message?" Crane drew on his cigarette and began wandering in circles around the pavement.

"Yes, I got it."

"Good, look, um…."

"Well, I guess I'll see you in the morning," she cut in. Obviously she wasn't quite ready to forgive him yet. "I'll probably be asleep by the time you get back."

"Oh, yes, sure."

"Night then and, Tom?"

"Yes?"

"Thanks for letting me know."

"Love you," Crane finished the conversation

with their usual endearment, but Tina had already put the phone down. Looking up he saw Anderson striding over.

"Found your car, Crane."

"Thank God for that. Where is it?"

"On its way to the police pound. Got towed away for illegal parking. I've told the lads not to book it in and that we're on our way. Come on I'll give you a lift down there and we can catch up on the way."

As they drove through the quiet back roads from Frimley Park Hospital, through Ash and then onto Aldershot, Anderson told Crane how they'd widened the search to include old and abandoned buildings as he had suggested. A policeman making a tour of the industrial estates had been rather more vigilant that day, because of the information included in the daily briefing and noticed a broken piece of fence. After gingerly climbing through the gap, he found a door ajar that led into a large warehouse and saw what he first thought was a pile of rags in the corner. Not wanting to touch the rags for fear of some disease or other, he poked the pile with his feet. Thankfully not too hard, as it turned out to be a person.

He immediately called in the find without touching anything, apart from the Padre's neck, where he couldn't feel a pulse. However, the ambulance paramedics were better trained and found the Padre had a thin irregular pulse and immediately called the hospital, arranging to have an emergency team ready to receive him.

Anderson told Kim and Crane that his forensics team had gone over the site and found nothing but a few footprints in the dust. They assumed the Padre must have been transported in a car but couldn't find any tyre tracks or any forensic evidence. The Padre's clothes had been taken for evaluation, but Anderson didn't hold out much hope of finding anything useful.

"So it looks like Zechariah left the Padre for dead," said Crane.

"Why do you think it was Zechariah? What have you got?"

Then it was Crane's turn to tell Anderson about their interview with Mrs Fisher. He explained that, due to his restraint, Mrs Fisher came up with the name on her own, without prompting.

"Okay, that's all very well, but had she ever met him? Did you get a description?"

Kim joined in the conversation from the back seat. "No, sir, she hasn't met him, never even been to the Church herself. It was strictly something Fisher did on his own, or with his son."

"So, all we've got at the moment is the name of a visiting preacher who came to Aldershot called Zechariah and a preacher in Catterick also called Zechariah. No description, nothing. It could have been him who attacked the Padre, but the Padre can't give us any information," finished Crane.

"That sounds about right," Anderson agreed with the assessment.

As they drew up at the police pound, Crane could see his car parked by the gates. "Can we meet up tomorrow morning?" he asked, climbing out of Anderson's car.

"Yes, about 10ish?"

"That's fine it'll give me time to brief Captain Edwards first. And thanks for sorting out the car," Crane called, as a young constable approached them and after a nod from Anderson put the keys into Crane's outstretched hand. It was very late when Crane finally got home, after dropping Kim off at the barracks and as he expected, the house was still and quiet. Taking a cold beer from the fridge and falling into a kitchen chair, Crane savoured the drink before going upstairs to bed.

Tina stirred in her sleep as he got into bed, but didn't wake up, or if she did, pretended not to. Crane had no idea either way. He would have to wait until the morning to talk to her.

***

The shrill of the alarm woke Crane from his fitful sleep. He quickly reached out and turned it off. Turning to embrace Tina's back, his hands begin to caress her as she slowly awoke.

"Tom," she mumbled.

"Morning, Tina," he said, against her back and then started kissing the side of her neck.

"I've got to get up," she said and began to struggle against him weakly.

"Soon," replied Crane continuing with his kisses and caresses. When she stopped struggling he murmured, "I want to say sorry first."

CHAPTER 28

Crane's meeting with his Captain wasn't going well. Sitting behind his desk with the files open in front of him, Captain Edwards said he was relieved the Padre had been found, but pointed out rather snootily that Detective Inspector Anderson's men found the Padre, not Crane. As he couldn't be bothered to score points and remind the Captain that the RMP and SIB had no jurisdiction in the town of Aldershot, and that it was Crane himself who insisted empty warehouses be searched, he merely turned to outlining the evidence they had so far.

"So, you've got nothing then," Captain Edwards said as Crane finished.

"Sorry, sir?"

Shrugging, Edwards explained. "No physical evidence, no description. You don't even know if this Zechariah person attacked you and the Padre."

"No, sir," Crane admitted.

"What about the other garrisons?" Edwards leaned forward to point at the files.

"What about them, sir?"

"Any evidence from them about a mysterious preacher?"

"Well, obviously I want Catterick to make enquiries of their Church about a preacher called Zechariah, after the interview last night with Mrs Fisher, and the same with Colchester."

"Well, what are you doing here then? Get on with it, Sergeant Major. Dismissed."

Crane collected his files and left the office swearing under his breath. On the way out he instructed Kim and Billy to do the follow up calls to Colchester and Catterick and then went to his meeting with DI Anderson.

***

He was searching for a parking space when he caught sight of Anderson running after the car, his coat tails flying in sync with his hair and his hands waving in the air. Turning his vehicle around Crane pulled up next to the now puffing DI and wound down the window.

"Did you want me?" he asked smiling at the bedraggled Anderson.

"No, I was running to catch a bloody bus. Of course I do," Anderson reached for the door handle and got into the car. "Just heard from the hospital. Padre Symonds had a good night and is conscious, thank God. So I thought we should get over there, if you promise not to smoke in the car."

"No problem," Crane said as he pumped the accelerator and dropped the clutch, rapidly leaving the car park.

Once at the hospital, Crane parked in the car

park this time. He used the overflow car park due to the large numbers of cars parked in every available space, as if their owners were desperate not to have to walk any further than was absolutely necessary. Grumbling at the amount of money demanded by the health authority for the privilege of parking there, he retrieved his ticket from the machine and put it on his windscreen. As they took the long walk through the car park to the hospital itself, Crane lit up, once again ignoring the no smoking signs. Anderson challenged him, but Crane explained he had no idea what damage his smoke could do to someone in an acre of car park with only sky above them. And anyway he hadn't smoked in the car. Conceding the point Anderson led the way to the ICU.

This time they were buzzed onto the ward straight away and met at the central desk by the young doctor from the night before, who by now looked ill himself, exhaustion hooding his red rimmed eyes.

"Oh hello, Inspector, Sergeant Major. Glad you arrived before I left the ward. Padre Symonds had a good night and the pressure on his brain is easing, meaning he regained consciousness this morning. Obviously we're continuing to monitor him closely but it looks like we won't have to operate and we should be able to transfer him to ITU this afternoon."

"ITU?" asked Crane.

"Oh sorry, Intensive Therapy Unit. It's actually the other half of the Intensive Care Unit. What we have in ICU is a nurse assigned to each patient, but in ITU it's a nurse to between two and four patients. So as a patient recovers and needs less individual constant attention, we are able to move them to free up a much needed ICU bed."

"How long do you think he'll be here?" Anderson asked.

"Well that's a bit more difficult, but I would say if he continues to make good progress, we should have him on a general ward in a few days. Obviously we still need to monitor the head injury, make sure he's hydrated and get him eating."

"Can we see him?" was what Crane really wanted.

"Yes, of course, but only for a few moments, you understand." The doctor pointed to the Padre's bed and then returned to his paperwork.

Crane couldn't see much difference in the Padre's condition from the night before. He was lying very still with his eyes closed, with IV tubes still connected and beeping monitors at the head of his bed. Crane took the Padre's hand and squeezed it. This time there was a response and the Padre opened his eyes.

Crane was relieved to see a smile of recognition. "Hello, Crane," the Padre croaked.

"Hello, sir, glad to see you awake."

"Mmm, head hurts."

"It seems you had a bad blow to the head, Padre. Can you remember anything about what happened?" Crane hated to push, but knew they only had a few minutes.

"Not really," was the slow reply. "In my office, tidying up, someone hit me." The Padre closed his eyes again.

"Did you see him? Padre?"

"Not really. Black, all black."

"The person who hit you was dressed in black?"

But the Padre's hand went limp in Crane's.

"Crane," Anderson indicated they should leave with a jerk of his head.

Having to admit there wasn't going to be any further conversation, Crane followed Anderson out to the central desk. Anderson asked if it would be okay for them to visit again that evening, but the nurse told them to ring first for permission.

With no choice but to agree, the two men left.

"So, at least we know the Padre was attacked in his office, as we suspected," Crane said to Anderson, as the two men leaned over the top of Crane's car on opposite sides. "And by someone dressed in black."

"But nothing to say who it was, or even if it was a man or a woman."

"No. Looks like we'll have to wait a while for more information. If the Padre knows anymore that is."

Crane climbed into the car, taking Anderson back to Aldershot Police Station and then driving on to the garrison.

"Oh, sir, glad you're back," called Kim. "The computer techies have found something on Solomon's computer."

CHAPTER 29

Internal Memorandum

From: Sergeant M. Scraggs

To: Sergeant Major T. Crane, Special Investigations Branch, Aldershot Garrison

After a full investigation of Lance Corporal Crooks' computer (Dell Laptop Model No HD50 Serial No 325TN000554AB144), several documents that may be of interest were partially recovered from the hard drive. These were emails that had been deleted. Unfortunately it was not possible to determine the sender, nor the sender's IP address. Dots have been inserted where the software was unable to recover the words.

Email No 1

…..June…..

Solomon

Welcome…………group………..consisting ……………fathers………..I know……faith…….Jesus……show……way……
.next……meeting…….at……

………name………..Lord………Christ……Z

<u>Email No 2</u>

2…..July

Dear ………..

Your……..faith……..Christ……rewarded……time……..near……baptised..blood.

Jesus……with   you. Soon……..ascend………..heaven.

In the…………..of………Jesus……..Z

<u>Email No 3</u>

…….August..

………..time   draws   near let……love…….Christ…..fortify………..steps……heaven.

A   fountain………..   blood…….the sins……who come………..Him…….. salvation.

…………..time…………..16…hrs………..August.

Drench   …………….blood   ………..son ……………….all   ………saved…. you……...soldier….Christ……Z

This represents everything we could find relating to religion or having any religious connotation. All other material appears to refer to normal mundane matters and the usual amount of spam email.

I apologise for the delay in obtaining this information, due to a backlog of work and relocation to new premises. Please do not hesitate to contact me if you have any queries or wish to know more about the retrieval system.

M. Scraggs

Crane asked Kim to make several copies of the memo for him to first take to Captain Edwards and then DI Anderson. But before contacting his Captain, he sat reading the contents over and over. The words, 'blood' 'rivers' 'Heaven' cycling round in his head without a destination. He decided to take a walk around the playing fields. The sun was shining and only a light breeze occasionally ruffled his hair. As he strode along the touch line of the rugby pitch he remembered his meeting with the Padre a few weeks ago, whilst he was taking his morning constitutional. Contrasting the Padre's vitality that day, with the broken man now lying in Frimley Park Hospital.

***

Edwards was putting the finishing touches to some report or other and made Crane wait, sitting in front of his desk. Once the papers had been whisked away by an aide, he turned to Crane.

"So," he began. "I take it you must have news from the other garrisons."

"Not at the moment, sir, although it's in hand. I wanted to see you about this," Crane said as he pushed the memo across the desk.

"What is it?"

"The report from the computer people. They've got some snippets of deleted emails from Lance Corporal Crooks' computer."

Edwards read the memo in silence. Several times.

"So, it looks like you were right, Crane," he eventually said.

"Unfortunately yes, sir. The first email seems to welcome Solomon into the group. If you notice there is a reference to fathers and what appears to be details of the next meeting. The second one looks like a kind of reassurance, keep the faith and that sort of thing. And the third one..."

"Yes?"

Clearing his throat, Crane continued, "The third one seems to be confirmation of the date when Solomon was to carry out the killings."

"Jesus Christ."

"Exactly, sir. It all seems to be done in the name of Jesus Christ."

"And Z? Is that who I think it is?"

"I believe so, sir, Zechariah."

Captain Edwards stared off into the distance for a moment. Finally he shook his head and turned back to Crane. "So, what's your next move?"

"Well, with your permission, sir, I would like to share this with DI Anderson, so he can put more pressure on the Church of Jesus is King. I hope that by showing this to the Church Elder we can persuade him to help us. I also intend to send it to Catterick and Colchester to see if they can find anything similar. As you know, we've already had confirmation from Mrs Fisher about a preacher named Zechariah."

"Very well," the Captain agreed. "At least we've got some good news about the Padre."

To raise their spirits, they discussed the health and positive prognosis of Padre Symonds. As Crane left the Captain's office, he pulled out his mobile phone to let Anderson know he was on his way. He popped into his office to tell Kim where he was going, instructing her to send the email to the other garrisons and to see if she could have a go at filling in the blank words. Turning to leave, he noticed Billy was not at his desk. He asked Kim where he was, but she seemed vague, mumbling about Billy pursuing something and they could get him on his mobile if he was needed.

As Crane walked to his car, he tried Billy's mobile, which went straight to voice mail. Leaving a message asking for a return call, Crane closed the phone and drove to Aldershot Police Station.

***

Anderson was in an ebullient mood. Finding Padre Symonds, he confided, had done him no end of good with 'them upstairs', the words accompanied by a nod at the ceiling. Indeed his whole demeanour was brighter and sharper, including his white shirt. Crane felt sorry for him, as he was about to burst his bubble of happiness. After sliding the piece of paper across Anderson's desk, Crane waited in silence as the policeman read it.

"Jesus Christ."

"My Captain's thoughts exactly," grimaced Crane. "So, what shall we do about it?"

"Do? What can we do?" Anderson waved the piece of paper at Crane. "There's still nothing here that can help us catch this Z character."

"I think we should go and see the Church Elder."

"We?"

"Yes, we. I'm not being pushed out of this one again, Derek," Crane leaned forward and pointed at the memo. "This is major evidence to show Solomon was attending a group headed by a person called Zechariah, who had been a visiting preacher at the Church in Aldershot. What's more, the tone of the emails is zealous to say the least."

"Zealous?" Anderson spoke as though he had never heard the word before.

"Yes, over the top, fanatical, obsessive, fervent, ardent."

"All right, Crane, stop talking like a thesaurus. I get the picture."

Crane pressed on, building his case. "So, Elias needs to know how serious this is. I think Solomon was hypnotised, brainwashed if you like, into killing his family and then himself. And what's more, I bet you so were the others in Catterick and Colchester. And I think Zechariah is here, in Aldershot. For God's sake, Derek, how many more reasons do you need?" Crane pushed out of his seat and stood by the office door.

"But Elias said the contact number he had doesn't work anymore," Anderson protested.

"I know that. So now we need to lean on him, get him to make further enquiries of his flock, or whatever he calls them. Someone in that Church knows what's going on and we've got to find them." Crane gave up on standing and moved to sit resolutely in front of Anderson.

"I don't really do leaning, Crane," replied Derek.

"Not on a Church Elder."

"No, I know," said Crane folding his arms and leaning back in his chair, "but I do."

CHAPTER 30

Crane was amazed at the number of people filing into the Church of Jesus is King. Curiosity had got the better of him and as the Church Elder couldn't see them until after the Sunday service, he'd decided to turn up early. Crane was standing on the opposite side of the street to the Church, lounging in the doorway of the Blockbuster DVD rental store. Looking at his watch he saw it was 10:45 hours, nearly fifteen minutes to go before the start of the service and people were still arriving.

"Oh, what the hell," he said, flicking his cigarette away and going to join the queue.

As the throng inched slowly forwards, he could see that on either side of the church door (or cinema door to be completely factual Crane thought) people were stationed, welcoming each individual.

"Welcome, welcome.......so lovely to see you again........Praise the Lord...."

Crane shook off the platitudes like the soap suds in his shower that morning, and peered into the gloom of the building. He saw what seemed like hundreds of people milling around, searching for seats, greeting friends, to the accompaniment of piped gospel music. Looking up, those in the ornately decorated stalls were leaning over the balcony, excitedly waving to people they recognised below.

A shrill bell caused Crane to jump. Although it meant nothing to him, it had an effect on the congregation, as everyone sat down, picked up books and song sheets and turned expectantly towards the stage. Realising it was probably a five minute bell, left over from the cinema era, he suppressed a grin and slipped into a seat at the end of a row near the back.

Within a few minutes the lights in the auditorium dimmed and those on the stage brightened. Elias the Church Elder, dressed in a sober dark suit, but no dog collar or robes, strode onto the stage to loud clapping and cheering. Raising his hand for silence, he spoke in a deep basso voice that reminded Crane of James Earl Jones. Not so much Darth Vader, more Vice Admiral James Greer in 'The Hunt for Red October'.

"Then David and all the House of Israel played music before the Lord on all kinds of instruments of fir wood, on harps, on stringed instruments, on tambourines, on sistrums and on cymbals."

As the opening chords of a catchy tune rung out from an invisible organ, a choir swaggered onto the stage, clapping or beating tambourines and swaying with the music. Their robes were simple and black, with their Sunday best clothes visible underneath. Then the congregation rose as one and begin to lustily sing and clap.

"Shine, Jesus Shine, fill this land with the father's glory."

As the hymn went on, arms were raised in praise for the Lord, hands opened, palms outwards, reaching towards some unseen force.

At the conclusion, which was applauded with enthusiasm, Elias welcomed everyone, especially new visitors and requested that everyone 'pass the peace'. Crane was alarmed to see that this meant turning to your neighbour, hugging and kissing them and murmuring, "Peace be with you."

He was enveloped with alacrity in the strong arms of the woman next to him and pulled into her bosom. After mumbling, "Peace be with you," into her cleavage, he was set free, to be immediately set upon by the person in front and the whole process started again. A man clasped him close, ramming Crane's nose into his neck. Crane's nostrils immediately filled with the overpowering smell of a cheap pungent aftershave. After a few minutes of being knocked into one person and then another, to Crane's relief the experience was over and the service continued.

By the time the sermon started, Crane was glad of the rest, expecting everyone to sit quietly and listen to the words of wisdom from Elias. But oh no, not in this church it seemed. Elias' words were frequently punctuated by cries from the congregation. People rose to their feet, swaying, hands aloft, shouting out, "Praise the Lord……..Amen…..Hallelujah!" A few gathered in front of the stage, or in the aisles, to more freely express their emotions. Crane was glad the children had been sent out to what they called 'junior church' before the sermon began, as he saw one supplicant writhing on the floor and spouting gibberish. Expecting people to rush to aid the stricken worshiper who was clearly having an epileptic fit, he was stunned to find it only seemed to encourage more of them to join in and soon there were several people on the floor, clearly in need of medical help.

Turning to the woman whose cleavage he had been intimate with earlier, he whispered, "Are they okay?" pointing towards the stage. "Isn't anyone going to help them?"

"They are overcome by the Holy Spirit," she explained. "They have been saved by the love of Jesus Christ our Lord and the Holy Spirit now lives in them."

Crane noticed his companion was glassy eyed, with a sheen of moisture on her upper lip.

"Feel it," she urged. "Let yourself go, let Jesus Christ save you too."

And then Crane was saved. Not by Jesus Christ, but by the organ which struck up another rousing tune, causing his neighbour to pick up her song sheet and join in the chorus.

At the end of the service Crane managed to extract himself from a large number of the congregation who wanted to talk to him, find out all about him and persuade him to attend the church again. Or maybe sign up for Bible classes, prayer circles and family groups. Crane escaped from the cinema into the bright sunlight. Stopping and putting his hand up to shield his eyes, he spotted Derek Anderson across the street and walked over to join him.

"Hello, Crane, are you alright? Don't tell me you've been converted?" he grinned.

"Bloody hell, what an experience that was," exclaimed Crane lighting a cigarette and drawing on it as if it was the last one he would ever smoke. "Bunch of evangelical crackpots, if you ask me. The Padre was wrong when he said it was a bit over the top. It was a lot over the top. Thank God that's over." Looking at his watch he cried, "Jesus, I've been in there nearly two hours, no wonder I'm exhausted."

The two men stood for a while, watching the worshipers leave the building. At one point Crane caught a glimpse of the back of a man with blond hair and a broad muscular back which seemed familiar, holding the hand of a small boy. As the High Street returned to its normal ghostly Sunday afternoon state, it was time to go and see Elias.

They caught him as he was closing the main doors. After the introductions they retired to a large office just inside the building to the left of the doors. As well as the Elder's desk, phone and usual office paraphernalia, there was room for a large circular table with at least 12 chairs around it. The carpet was red, yet old and faded, obviously the same vintage as the carpet in the main auditorium.

After inviting Crane and Anderson to sit, Elias rounded his desk to sit in a large, yet worn leather chair. Placing his clasped hands on the desk, he smiled benignly and expressed his pleasure that the Padre had been found and would make a full recovery.

Crane, however, was not much interested in pleasantries and wanted to get straight to the point. "When did you last see Padre Symonds, sir?"

"Oh, let me see, sometime last week, I think."

"Could you try to be more specific?"

"Umm," Elias said as if considering his reply, "Oh yes, at our Bible class last Tuesday. He joined us as part of an Army Liaison Scheme. Do you know about that, Sergeant Major? It's a wonderful concept I think."

"Yes, yes, I know all about that," said Crane, becoming impatient and not about to tell the Elder that it was his idea in the first place. Anderson laid a warning hand on his arm, which Crane ignored. "He was making enquiries about the visiting preacher, Zechariah, I believe."

"Was he?" asked Elias.

"You know damn well he was."

"It appears more evidence has come to light about Zechariah, sir," Anderson quickly interrupted, handing over a copy of the memo.

After a few minutes silence, during which Crane stewed, Anderson asked, "Now do you see the seriousness of the situation, sir?"

"Well, I'm not sure what this has to do with my

CHAPTER 31

Crane had no idea whether the threat he made to Elias would work and for now he had to back off, as Anderson put it. They had left the church the previous afternoon with Anderson promising to follow up and keep the pressure on Elias. Crane had to remember that he had no jurisdiction in the town and was only present at the interview at Anderson's invitation. As he needed to keep Anderson on his side, he had no choice but to leave it in his hands.

After the usual Monday morning briefing with his Captain, Crane sat in his office chewing over the evidence so far and trying to think of anything he may have missed. Coming to a decision, he went over to Kim, who was sitting ramrod straight at her desk and typing on the computer.

"Can I help you, sir?"

"Kim, did you send the memo from the computer boffins to Catterick and Colchester?" Crane sat on the side of her desk.

"Of course, sir," was her confident reply.

"And?"

"And, sir?" came the not so confident question.

"And have they responded?"

"Oh, well no, I don't think so, sir. Do you want me to chase them up?"

"No, I'll do it."

In his office he reached for the phone and called Sergeant Major Brown in Colchester. Brown had heard nothing back from his technical department and promised to hurry them along. Sergeant Harris in Catterick, however, said they had no computer to check.

"No computer? But everyone has one these days!" Crane was taken aback and sat upright in his chair.

"Well, sir, we don't have a record of taking one from the premises."

"Hmm," Crane pondered. "Do you even know if there was one there at the time?"

Crane could hear papers rustling in the background.

"Negative, sir. I haven't got an inventory of the contents of the house."

"Bloody hell, so there could have been one but no one thought to look for it."

"Well, it's always possible, sir. But, as I am sure you remember, I wasn't in charge of the investigation at the time."

"Alright, alright, Harris. Point taken. I suppose I'll have to check with Mrs Fisher."

Crane replaced the receiver none too gently and decided to delegate that job to Billy. The last thing he needed was another meeting with the woman and thought that perhaps Billy could charm her. Calling Billy into his office, he asked him to contact Mrs Fisher and to go and collect the computer, if there was one.

Once the business side of the discussion was done, they chatted for a few minutes about the weekend and Crane regaled Billy with tales of his visit to the Church of Jesus is King. Crane thought it strange that Billy looked uncomfortable and started to fidget, so he changed the subject and asked how Billy's weekend was.

"Oh, you know, sir. Just pottered around. Went to the gym, had a run, that sort of thing. Anyway if there's nothing else, sir?"

"No, no, off you go, Billy. Thanks."

Crane watched his young Staff Sergeant walk out of the office, noting his blond hair and broad well-muscled back. The syntaxes in his brain start to pop, but Crane couldn't quite make the connection.

As there was nothing else to do that couldn't wait, Crane decided to call Tina and ask if she wanted to meet for a sandwich lunch and then he would go from there to see Padre Symonds. She seemed pleased to hear from him and was free for lunch, so Tom took himself off to the arcade in Aldershot town centre.

***

It was their usual location for occasional lunches as it was opposite the branch of Barclays bank that Tina worked in. The arcade was stunning, but also stunningly empty. An attempt by local planners to replicate the original 1920's arcade and turn it into a shopping centre, had failed spectacularly. But the place was clean and quiet with light filtering through the high glass dome and plants cascading over the balustrade, reaching down towards the empty shops.

They sat at metal tables and chairs, shaded by incongruous parasols at a health food café located in the centre of the 90 degree walkway and chatted. Crane chewed on a baguette that tasted as dry as it looked and drunk a cup of coffee which consisted mostly of foam.

"This was a lovely surprise, Tom," Tina said. She was dressed in her blue bank regulation suit, which brought out the colour of her eyes.

"Well, I thought it was about time we spent some time together. I know I've been a bit caught up with work lately."

"Maybe just a bit," she smiled.

"Look, Tina, I…" Crane tailed off, clearing his throat and searching through his pockets for his cigarettes.

"Don't say anything, Tom." Tina put her hand on his arm. "Let's just enjoy our lunch. Okay? Oh, and you can't smoke in here."

Smiling, Crane relaxed. Even though he knew he couldn't keep brushing under the carpet his bad behaviour, or the fact that they were still clashing over the decision to have children, Crane was heartened by her attitude over lunch. At least she seemed to understand and anyway he was confident there would be plenty of time to sort everything out after the case was closed. After giving her a long and lingering kiss outside the Bank, he dragged himself away and went to Frimley Park Hospital.

***

Crane arrived to see the Padre in the early afternoon and the staff agreed to let him in for a short while. He had been moved to the ITU and the nurse looking after him strongly suggested the Padre would be able to go on a general ward shortly.

Crane shared this piece of good news with the Padre as he sat down, who didn't seem all that impressed. "I quite like it here though, Crane," he said lying back on several pillows in a pristine bed that had been slightly raised at the head. "Don't think I want to go on a general ward. I enjoy the fuss of the ITU I expect."

"Or the scenery, sir?" Crane looked round at the attractive nurses and got a complicit smile from the Padre. "Anyway, sir, if you could, I just wanted a chat about what happened."

"But I can't remember anything, Crane," the Padre protested.

"No, sir," explained Crane, to stop the Padre becoming anxious. "I want to talk about your last contact with the Church before the attack happened."

Relaxing back on his pillows the Padre smiled, "Oh, I see, well I had started attending some classes. The last one was the Bible Class if I recall."

"Yes, that's what Elias thought too."

"Oh, you've met him have you, Sergeant Major?

Such a nice man, don't you think? So devoted to his flock."

"Quite. Can you tell me what happened at the meeting, sir?"

"Nothing unusual. There was quite a stimulating debate about a particular bible passage and then we had coffee before leaving."

"Did you ask anyone about a visiting preacher?"

"Oh," the Padre thought for a moment. "Now you mention it, yes I did. I was asking one of the longer term members of the Church about visiting preachers. In fact she's the Church Secretary, Mrs Morrison, so I thought she may know."

"And what did she say?" Crane leaned forward.

"Nothing much. She said she wasn't always there when there was a visiting preacher, but she had the church diary which would tell me who they were and when they preached."

"That's excellent, sir. Did you get it?"

"No, sorry, Sergeant Major, I was supposed to go and see her, but got rather unavoidably detained," he grinned and then winced with pain.

"Don't worry, sir, I'll follow that up. Looks like you need a rest now. Just one last question. Who was at this bible meeting?"

"Oh, about six members of the congregation, Mrs Morrison and Elias was there, of course."

"Of course," Crane agreed.

CHAPTER 32

Anderson was not best pleased to see Crane and was immediately defensive. "Look, Crane, I haven't had time to chase up Elias yet," he said gesturing to his overflowing desk. "I was planning to go and see him at home after work tonight. I thought a more softly softly approach would be better this time."

"Not too softly though eh, Derek? We don't want to waste all the good work I did yesterday."

"Don't worry, I won't let him forget we need the information. So was that it?"

"Actually, no. In fact that's not even why I came. I went to see Padre Symonds this afternoon."

Anderson's face brightened. "Oh good, how is he? Making good progress?"

"Yes, thanks." Crane sat down and told Anderson about the Padre's progress, mentioning that he remembered questioning the Church Secretary, who volunteered to let him have a copy of the diary giving them the dates of visiting preachers and hopefully details of who they were. "So I just thought I would let you know that

I'm off to collect it," he finished.

"You?"

"Yes, Derek, me. She promised it to the Padre after all, so I thought I would call in and let her know that the Padre is safe and well and that I'm just following up on a senior officer's request."

"Oh for God's sake, you do know how to manipulate, Crane," said Anderson, shaking his head in disbelief. "Have you her details?" he asked, scrabbling about in a desk drawer.

"Yes, thanks. Billy came up with them whilst he was doing his background research on the Church."

"Okay, but try not to upset her, will you? Remember she's not a suspect."

"Of course not, Derek," Crane replied. "What do you take me for?" he asked, leaving before Derek could throw something at him.

***

Crane decided not to call ahead to warn Adele Morrison of his visit. The address Billy had given him was in a complex of assisted living houses and flats for over 55's opposite the large Tesco supermarket at the top of Aldershot.

After wandering through several manicured lawns, he figured he had the right ground floor flat, as gospel music was pouring out of a downstairs window that appeared to be a kitchen. Finding the buzzers located by a central door, he pushed the one marked Morrison.

Soon afterwards the sound of the music faded and a tinny voice called out, "Yes?"

Crane introduced himself as a messenger from Padre Symonds and Mrs Morrison buzzed him into the apartment block.

Mrs Morrison stood just inside her front door. Crane realised that in making assumptions of the type of person who listens to gospel music, he was way off the mark with Mrs Morrison. Instead of the large, friendly, laughing black woman he envisaged, Mrs Morrison was white, slim, upright and even a bit uptight. He couldn't seem to put her together with the type of worship at the Church of Jesus is King at all.

"Sergeant Major Crane," she said, "may I just see your credentials?"

After Crane showed her the plastic coated ID card around his neck, she nodded and let him in.

The flat was bright, airy and modern, with stylish, simplistic furniture bordering on minimalistic. No fluffy cushions or cluttered souvenirs from a bygone age here. After inviting him to sit down, but unfortunately not asking if he wanted a cup of tea, she asked him to repeat why he was there. He explained he had come to collect a copy of the diary for the Padre.

"You say Padre Symonds asked you to come," she said. "May I ask why he didn't come himself?"

Realising Mrs Morrison didn't know what had happened, Crane decided to tell her, in the hope of eliciting some sympathy and assistance. Luckily it worked.

"Oh dear, how dreadful," her expression softened, but not her posture, which was as rigid as ever. "Why do you need the diary though?"

So once again Crane had to go through explanations. He kept his reasons as vague as possible, telling her he was investigating a murder suicide on the garrison and that it appeared the young man in question had been attending the Church of Jesus is King.

"So, Mrs Morrison," he concluded, "we're trying to find out why a young soldier would have done such a thing. Trying to trace people he may have met, listened to, or been influenced by."

"Yes, yes, I see. Wait one moment please, Sergeant Major."

Mrs Morrison disappeared into another room and came back with several pamphlets in her hand. "These are for the past year or so. I hope they help. Although I do hope no one from our church was involved."

Standing Crane took them from her outstretched hand and made to leave. Turning to face her once he reached the door he said, "Forgive me for saying so, Mrs Morrison, but you don't look ready for assisted living just yet."

"Well, thank you for the compliment, Sergeant Major," she smiled for the first time since Crane entered the flat. "Just a bit of forward planning."

As he drove home that night, he pondered Mrs Morrison's words. Perhaps he needed to do a bit of forward planning as well, but first he needed to check into the past.

CHAPTER 33

Checking dates against the church diary and those in Lance Corporal Crooks' service record was the type of job Crane would normally give to a junior member of staff. But not this time. Working from when Solomon arrived back from Afghanistan (around May) he looked through the pamphlets carefully. Checking for themed study groups or visiting preachers with the name of Zechariah. He eventually found what he was looking for. Zechariah had preached at Jesus is King on the 2nd June and then hosted the first meeting of 'How to walk the steps to Heaven' later that week.

After that, though, Crane could find no mention of any other similarly entitled meetings. But, the dates fitted and the timing fitted. Solomon would have had exposure to Zechariah for just over two months, before he turned on his family and then killed himself.

Crane wanted to do a high five with someone to celebrate, but he was on his own, in his small office at home, Tina having already gone to bed. Instead he decided to ring Sergeant Major Brown in

Colchester and Sergeant Harris in Catterick. Neither man was particularly pleased at being woken by Crane after midnight, although Harris, being of a lesser rank, had to be rather more deferential. Crane managed to elicit a promise from both men that they would do a similar check at their respective ends, first thing in the morning.

***

Crane's own mission, first thing the next morning, was to phone Anderson and bring him up to date.

"Well done, Crane."

"It was nothing really, just standard detective work."

"No, Crane, I mean well done for not antagonising Mrs Morrison."

Ignoring the sarcasm, Crane asked Anderson if Elias had ever given them a description of Zechariah.

"No. Apparently, when there are visiting preachers at the church, the standard practice is for the preacher from the host church to go and preach at the other one. A sort of religious tit for tat. You scratch my back and I'll scratch yours, kind of thing. So they've never met."

"No problem," said Crane.

"No problem, of course it's a problem. We don't have a reliable witness with a description. You know what that lot are like, carried away with the service, off their heads most of the time. And we can't get anyone to admit to attending a course or study group with Zechariah."

"As I said no problem. Not with this member of the congregation," Crane replied and put down the receiver.

***

Mrs Morrison didn't ask to see his identification this time, offering him a seat, but still no cup of tea.

"Did the information I gave you yesterday help, Sergeant Major?" she asked, settling herself on the settee opposite Crane's easy chair.

"Yes, it did, thank you. I hope you don't mind but I wanted to ask for your help again."

"I will if I can."

Crane then told Mrs Morrison about the dates matching for Solomon's return to Aldershot and the visiting Preacher Zechariah.

"So, I wondered if you remembered him."

"Who, your dead soldier? I'm sorry but I don't."

"No, Mrs Morrison, you misunderstood me. Do you remember the visiting preacher?"

"Oh yes, very well indeed."

Crane stopped himself from falling down on his knees in front of the glacial Mrs Morrison in grovelling thanks. Instead he cleared his throat and asked, "Do you think you may be able to give us a detailed description?"

"Most certainly. I welcomed him into the church in the absence of our Elder and stayed with him until he took the service."

A swift phone call to Derek Anderson confirmed that he could be with them in 15 minutes, with a police artist, if they didn't mind waiting - at which point Crane got his cup of tea.

It turned out that Mrs Morrison was a retired head teacher (no surprise there then) and that she had been a leading member of the Church of Jesus is King since its inception several years ago (a big surprise). She wanted to know if Crane had ever joined them for a Sunday service and he said he was there last Sunday.

"I don't remember seeing you, but then we are lucky enough to get a large but fluctuating congregation. What did you think of the service?" she asked, putting her cup and saucer on the coffee table in between them.

"Well, shall we say it's rather different than I'm used to? Army church services aren't normally that expressive."

"No, I suspect not. I expect you think it's strange that I like it."

"No, not at all," Crane lied, hiding his face behind his cup of tea.

"Now, Sergeant Major, stop being polite. I can let my hair down too, you know. I suspect I still retain some of that childlike wonder of the world that I used to see so much of in my pupils. To be a good teacher, you know, you have to have a childlike view of the world yourself at times. I just get so much pleasure from experiencing the exuberance of people who love expressing their faith."

Crane was relieved when Anderson arrived saving him from further religious or educational conversation.

The session with the police artist went well and

in the end they had a reasonable likeness, according to Mrs Morrison. The picture she painted in words was one of a black man, of medium height put at just under six feet (she even got Crane, Anderson and the police artist to stand up against her to judge it), with flared nostrils and bulging cheeks. He had long Rastafarian type hair although no woolly hat holding it in place. In complete contrast to Elias, Zechariah wore green and gold robes with a long matching stole, making him a very striking figure when on stage. His voice was deep and musical with a Jamaican twang. Mrs Morrison accompanied him while he was chatting with members of the congregation before the service, but not afterwards. She said she'd looked for him after the service to give her thanks for his uplifting sermon, but had been unable to get near him for the crush of people surrounding him. All in all, the visit seemed to have been very popular.

Crane wanted to know about the meeting called 'Steps to Heaven' but Mrs Morrison was unable to help on that one. Apparently Elias asked her to include it in the diary but she hadn't attended herself.

"To be honest, Sergeant Major," she said, "I don't really know who did attend or what it was about. Obviously I don't go to every group otherwise I'd never get anything else done and anyway some aren't suitable."

"Suitable?"

"Yes, those for alcoholics or drug users. I'm sure you understand why I don't go to those," she said smiling. "Also, there are other groups for families with children, so I don't go to them either."

"And you say you don't have any contact details for the elusive Zechariah?"

"No, sorry, Sergeant Major. Elias made all the arrangements and the only thing I had to do was to include him in the church diary and welcome him on his arrival."

"How did he arrive?" Anderson asked.

"Do you know, I have no idea." Mrs Morrison frowned in concentration. "He simply seemed to appear at the front door of the church. And I can't tell you how he left either. I was tidying up after the service and suddenly noticed he was gone. I'm so sorry."

"No need to apologise, Mrs Morrison. You've helped us tremendously already. Just one last question if you don't mind?"

"Not at all," Mrs Morrison inclined her head in a regal gesture.

"Do you think you would recognise him if you saw him again?"

"Oh certainly, Inspector," came the confident reply.

"Even without his robes?" Crane asked.

"Even without his robes."

CHAPTER 34

After collecting several copies of the artist's impression from Anderson at the police station, Crane was anxious to get back to the barracks, to find out if Harris and Brown had come up with anything and to email them a copy of the picture of Zechariah.

Once there he called in Kim and Billy.

"So what do you think?" he asked them with obvious satisfaction in his voice.

"Very good work, sir!" enthused Kim. "I'm sure we'll get somewhere now we have this."

"Billy?"

Billy was staring at the pictures in his hand. One was a full length version of Zechariah in his robes and the other an enlarged one of his head and shoulders.

"Sergeant!"

"Sir?" Billy came out of his daze and slowly met Crane's eyes.

"What do you think?"

"Think? About what?"

"About the description?"

Swallowing, Billy replied, "Well it's certainly detailed," and threw the picture down onto Crane's desk.

"Isn't it just," Crane agreed. "Good old Mrs Morrison."

"Do you think it's accurate?"

"Sorry?"

"Well, she is getting on a bit, sir."

Crane stared at Billy, "If you'd met her, which you would have, if you hadn't been 'unavailable' at the time, then you would know that her age is totally irrelevant. I've never had a more reliable witness."

If anything those words seem to make Billy blanch more than ever.

"Oh, sorry, sir."

"Are you alright, Staff Sergeant?" asked Kim.

Whirling around, Billy snapped, "Of course, what's it to you anyway?"

Kim recoiled from his anger, pressing herself back into her chair.

"Tell you what, Billy, why don't you scan those pictures into the computer and then email them to Harris and Brown for me," the authority in Crane's voice was clear.

Standing Billy mumbled, "Yes, sir, of course, sir," and left the office.

Kim made to follow, but Crane held her back with a shake of his head. Once Billy had closed the office door behind him, Crane asked, "How many times has Billy been out of the office lately on other investigations?"

Still startled by the force of Billy's attack, she said vaguely, "Oh I'm not sure sir."

"Well, look in the office log will you please and give me a list of the dates and times he was off on his own. Go back, let's say two months."

"Sir?" Kim looked at Crane and then out through Crane's office window to where Billy was busy with the scanner and back again.

"Just do it please, Kim, but don't tell anyone. Okay?"

"Yes, sir. Of course, sir."

"Thank you, Kim, dismissed."

Pushing Billy's strange attitude out of his head for the time being, Crane grabbed the phone and called Harris and Brown. He soon had the three of them on a conference call, so they could hear each other.

Crane firstly wanted to know about the timing of Zechariah's visit to both Catterick and Colchester but neither man had any answers for him.

"Sorry, sir," said Harris. "We've looked again through all the information we have but there's nothing in there that gives dates of events or preachers. I've contacted the local Church Elder and arranged to meet him at 14:00 hours today to pick up copies of all the church notices."

"Okay, what about you, Brown?"

"Similar story here, Crane, but I can't see our Church Elder until tomorrow morning at 10:00 hours."

Hiding his frustration, Crane pressed on, "Well I

suppose that's not too bad under the circumstances," and told them about the sketches Billy was emailing over. "So take them with you and see if you can get a witness who might be able to confirm that was the Preacher they know as Zechariah."

Crane urged both men to get back to him as soon as they had any news.

Grabbing a copy of the pictures, Crane then drove to the hospital to see the Padre, who was sitting up in bed when he arrived.

"It's good to see you looking so well, sir." Crane smiled.

"It's good to be feeling so much better, I can tell you, Crane. It seems there was someone up there looking after me."

"No more than you deserve, sir," Crane said with feeling. Changing the subject and sitting in the visitor's chair, he brought the Padre up to date with developments.

"So," he finished, "I was hoping these artist's impressions of Zechariah would jog your memory. Maybe you recognise him as the one who hit you?"

Padre Symonds stared at the pictures for a while.

"Sorry, Crane," he said, putting them down on the bed covers. "I just can't seem to remember anything."

"No problem, sir, it was just on the off chance."

"Yes, yes, I see. I'll tell you what, leave these with me, Sergeant Major."

"Sir?"

"Well, you never know, they might just jog my

memory. I don't know, there's something there, I'm just not sure what."

"Don't worry about it, sir, just concentrate on getting better."

As Crane left the ward, he turned to take a last look at the Padre, who was still staring at the pictures in his hand.

***

The rest of the day was spent in briefings with Derek Anderson and Captain Edwards. On his return to his office he found Billy gone and Kim waiting for him.

"What are you still doing here, Kim?"

"I was waiting for you, sir. I wanted to hand this to you rather than just leaving it on your desk."

Crane glanced through the papers and saw they were details of when Billy had been out of the office on his own for the past two months.

"Thank you, Kim, you can leave this with me now."

"I think you'll find it interesting reading, sir," she said as she gathered up her bag and coat.

"I was afraid you'd say that," replied Crane.

BILLY

Standing at the door of a house in the middle of Aldershot, Billy tried to shake the fog from his brain. He was still dressed in his dark suit with his ID round his neck, having just finished work. He looked at the house with fascination, but it was just an old Victorian terrace which looked dilapidated, as did the rest of the houses on the street. The small front gardens were crammed with bins and spindly plants struggled to survive in the face of continued neglect.

On one level he knew he shouldn't be there, but on another couldn't make his legs turn and walk away. There was something in his head, trying to take over. It felt like a spider was encasing him in its web. Its legs reaching and probing into his brain as it moved deeper and deeper into his head.

He was contacted after his first visit to the Church of Jesus is King. He'd taken his young nephew with him then and they had been going regularly every Sunday since. But for the life of him, he couldn't remember why he went in the first place, let alone taken Shaun with him. Maybe it had just seemed a good idea at the time. Still, Shaun seemed to enjoy himself, especially the junior church sessions and his sister welcomed the break.

Since that first Sunday, each week he got a text message to go to a meeting, sometimes once a week, sometimes twice. Always on different days of the week, at different times and different locations.

But he couldn't remember what happened at the meetings. Nothing at all. It was just a blank. He only knew that he went and that he couldn't stop going. He also knew he couldn't tell anyone about the meetings. But again didn't know why.

He shook his head in confusion once more. Sometimes he felt like he was going mad. At other times he knew with absolute certainty that he was doing the right thing by continuing to go to the meetings and not telling anyone about them.

As he raised his hand to knock, the door opened as if by itself. Billy peered into the gloom but couldn't see anyone there. Then a voice spoke.

"Welcome. Do you want to climb the steps to Heaven?"

"With the help of Jesus Christ the Lord," Billy replied.

All doubt was gone now. He knew with absolute certainty that he was in the right place and doing the right thing. He was drawn into the house by invisible hands and went to take his rightful place with the others.

"Follow the will of the Lord," they chanted in unison, "Follow the steps to Heaven."

CHAPTER 35

The next morning Crane found time for a quiet word with Kim. After eliciting her co-operation, he met with Captain Edwards. They discussed the updated information about Zechariah and his request of the two SIB men in Catterick and Colchester. Edwards then turned his attention to the team.

"So tell me, Sergeant Major," he began, relaxing back in his chair. "How's Kim working out?"

"Very well, sir," Crane answered truthfully. "Solid, reliable, punctual." Crane put his files on the corner of Edward's desk as it was clear he wasn't going anywhere for a while.

"And in terms of initiative?"

"Definitely getting there, sir." Crane relaxed and crossed his legs. "She's beginning to overcome her reserve and speak out. It's something I've been encouraging."

"Excellent. And Staff Sergeant Williams?"

"Equally as good," Crane replied.

"Any problems?" Edwards was still relaxing back in his chair, but his gaze had hardened.

"No, sir. Why do you ask?" Crane uncrossed his legs and crossed his arms to stop him fiddling with the files on the desk.

"It's just that I've noticed he's out of the office quite a lot at the moment. Is there a good reason for that?"

"Yes, sir," Crane responded, resisting the temptation to cross his fingers as the lie slid easily from his lips. "He's being extremely helpful at the moment, especially during this difficult investigation and following up leads on other on-going investigations for me as well."

"Very well. As long as you're sure?" Edwards raised his eyebrows.

"Absolutely, sir."

Damn, Crane thought as he left the office. So it wasn't just Kim that had noticed Billy's absences. The last thing he needed right now was interference from Edwards, so he'd have to hope that Kim complied with his request.

However, his first priority was to find out what was happening with the other SIB investigators, so he placed a call to Harris in Catterick, who had seen his local Church Elder that morning.

"Bingo!" was Harris' answer to Crane's question about any visits by Zechariah to the Church.

"That's good then I take it?"

"Oh, yes, sir, sorry, sir. I've found out that Zechariah visited our Church on the 9th of August, which was about 2 months before Fisher killed his son. He couldn't identify him though, as the he was away when Zechariah preached here."

"Excellent, Harris, well done."

While he was waiting for Brown to have his meeting later that afternoon, he called Billy into the office as he wanted a report on Mrs Fisher's computer.

"Computer, sir?"

"Yes, Billy, her bloody computer. Does she have one? Have you got it?"

"Sir?" Billy's eyes were darting from one side of his head to the other.

"Don't you remember, lad? I asked you a couple of days ago to ring Mrs Fisher to see if she had a computer or laptop. If she did you were to go and collect it. I wanted you to go so I didn't have to meet her again."

Billy's eyes were still unfocused and it was clear he didn't recollect the request. Deciding to leave it at that, Crane told him in no uncertain terms to get out of his bloody office and get onto it right away.

Once on his own he consulted the copy of the office log Kim printed off for him. Clearly marked for two afternoons ago was an entry logging Billy out of the office, visiting Mrs Fisher in Reading.

Feeling the need for a cigarette, Crane went outside and leaned against his car, gazing over the playing fields where an inter-services rugby match was being played. Although he was too far away to see the actual action, the cheering of the crowds told him that the army were doing well. Either that or the navy had brought along coach loads of supporters, outnumbering those who had bothered to turn out from the camp. Pride dictated the decision that the army were winning and so he turned his attention to the traffic passing up and down Queens Avenue.

A learner driver was stationary in front of him in a queue of traffic and he could see the young man's knuckles whitening as he gripped the steering wheel, as a drowning man would grip a life ring. Without warning the traffic started to move again, startling the driver, who kangarooed his way down the road. Crane likened the car's progress to this investigation. Stop, start, stop, start. The whole thing seemed so drawn out, with spurts of action and activity, followed by times when the investigation seemed becalmed. But Crane thought that at last he was getting somewhere. His determination to keep the investigation alive had paid off in the end and they were closing in on Zechariah.

He wondered whether his prey had any idea that he was being circled, could feel their closeness and was worried. He decided not. Zechariah was too egotistical to think that anyone could stop him. At least he hoped not. For he needed the action to play out. Hopefully not to the end. But close enough to it for a result. But it all hinged on Billy playing his part unwittingly. Pushing aside his fears that things may go too far before he could stop them, he reminded himself that manipulation was what he was good at. Grinding out his cigarette underfoot, he marched back into the office.

CHAPTER 36

The next trip Billy made out of the office really was to Mrs Fisher in Reading. She agreed to give the laptop computer to him, on the promise that she got it back and nothing relating to her son would be destroyed. In fact, charmed by Billy as she was, she even gave them the passwords to all the email addresses she knew about. So Crane was able to pass the machine to Kim to have a look at first, instead of sending it to the IT Department. Crane stayed while she started up the machine.

"Just be careful, for God's sake, Kim. I know we're trying to save time but the last thing I want is anything vital being deleted by mistake."

"Don't worry, sir, that's why I'm doing it not Billy," she grinned and Crane was glad to see her saying that with a smile on her face, instead of with her usual antagonistic attitude towards her colleague.

The first thing they saw when the machine booted up was a large picture of Mrs Fisher's son on the desktop. They both stared at the photograph. The boy was looking directly into the camera, grinning widely. He had an ice cream in his hand, with most of it plastered around his face. His hair was ruffled from the breeze and he was wearing a pair of swimming trunks. Crane dragged his gaze from the heart-breaking picture, to see Kim looking at him with haunted eyes that held an unspoken question he just couldn't answer. Clearing his throat he motioned Kim to carry on.

They worked together on the computer for more than an hour, at one point loading their printer software onto it, so they could print off various pages. Crane took these into his office and left Kim searching for anything else she could find of interest. It seemed that Corporal Fisher had been less paranoid than Solomon and hadn't deleted some of the emails from Zechariah. Attached to one was the following piece of rhetoric.

STEPS TO HEAVEN

Remember how the Lord our God sent his only son Jesus to die for us on the cross? Jesus is the saviour, a fountain whose blood covers and cleanses the sins of all who come to Him for salvation.

Do you want to live in eternal damnation for your sins? Do you want your sins to be passed onto your sons? No. But the question is how can you save their innocent lives and ensure their salvation?

I can show you the way. "I am the light," said Jesus. And I, as his prophet can shine that light and show you the steps you can take to reach Heaven.

There is no time to lose; the day of salvation is nearly

upon us. There will be rivers of blood. But at the same time, there will be rivers of healing blood. Blood that brings salvation to the true followers of Jesus.

Are you ready to be redeemed in a fountain of blood, covering your sins and the sins of your children? This is the only way to eternal salvation. Drench yourself in the blood and drench your sons too, so that you may all be saved.

***

As Crane sat in Derek Anderson's office, and reread the rhetoric, the words had lost none of their horror. He slumped in the chair opposite Anderson and watched the policeman's ruddy face drain of colour.

"And you think this lunatic is here in Aldershot?" he demanded of Crane.

"Yes, there's definitely something going on here. We've got to find this man, Derek."

"Well, Crane, it's not for the want of trying. Every copper in Aldershot has been briefed on what's going on. They've all got the description and there are copies in every police car."

"Do you think it's time to go public? Put out a call to the press. I know none of us wants them involved, but I think we need more help here. Let's just say he was wanted in connection with an attack on Padre Symonds."

"Okay, Crane, I think you're right. I'll get approval from above and you get it from Captain Edwards and then I'll set up a press conference."

***

The following morning they were ready to meet the press. They called it a joint public appeal for information by the Aldershot Police and Aldershot Royal Military Police. The wording of the press statement having been thrashed out the previous afternoon.

Crane and Anderson walked into the room together and took their places. They shared a single desk with two chairs placed behind it. In the room were six people and that included some police officers. Not exactly big news then. Not even a TV crew, as BBC South Today and ITV Meridian News had declined to attend, simply requesting a copy of the statement and artist's impression by email.

A lot different to the all-day news channels when there was a large breaking story, Crane thought. Then, hundreds of journalists and several TV crews hung on the police's every word, all shouting questions at once afterwards, demanding to be heard, desperate to ask that key searching question that gives an illuminating reply. Realising he was grinning, Crane quickly composed himself and listened to Derek read the statement.

"We are appealing to members of the public for their help in finding this man. We believe he is still in the Aldershot area, following an attack on Padre Symonds from Aldershot Garrison nearly two weeks ago. The attack took place in the Padre's office in the Royal Garrison Church of All Saints. The Padre is currently in Frimley Park Hospital, suffering from head wounds but recovering well. We would ask that members of the public do not approach the man themselves but instead contact the police at Aldershot Police Station on 01252 645103. Thank you."

On a screen behind Derek flashed the head and shoulders picture the police artist had drawn of Zechariah. They had decided not to use the one where he was dressed in robes, as they didn't want to draw attention to the religious connection, nor alarm any innocent members of the Church of Jesus is King.

Nobody seemed to have any questions and the bored looking members of the press were gathering up their papers when the door to the room opened, slamming against the wall. Looking up in annoyance, Crane saw a young woman rush into the room and grab a press pack as the door banged closed behind her.

"Sorry," she apologised, pulling the statement out of the folder. "Have I missed anything?"

"Missed anything? Diane you've missed the whole thing!" Anderson shook his head, a grin on his face.

"Diane?" whispered Crane leaning towards Anderson.

"Diane is the local crime reporter from the Aldershot Mail, aren't you, Diane?" Anderson said as he stood up. Crane did the same and they gathered their papers and prepared to leave.

"Hang on a minute, Derek," she called, "So what's the story behind this then?"

"No story, Diane, just what's in the statement."

Around them the other members of the press were leaving and the police were packing up.

"Sergeant Major Crane," she called. Approaching the table she held out her hand. "I don't believe we've met. Diane Chambers, Aldershot Mail. I've tried to speak to you several times in the past, but you never seem to be available."

Crane shook her hand, expecting it to be hot and clammy as she should have been flustered about arriving late, but it was surprisingly cool and dry.

"Miss Chambers," he acknowledged. Looking at her properly for the first time, he saw she was dressed in jeans and trainers with a checked tailored shirt partially unbuttoned to show a white tee shirt underneath. Her dark curly hair was cut short and framed her face.

"So why are you here, Sergeant Major?"

"Because the investigation involves Padre Symonds, a member of the army." Crane held his papers to his chest.

"Isn't it unusual for the police and army to work together?"

"Not at all, Miss Chambers, we work together more than people realise."

"So in that case it's unusual for you to make a joint investigation public?" It seemed Diane Chambers was determined to ask that key question. As Crane refused to be drawn and remained silent, she turned her attention to Anderson, "Don't you think so, Derek?"

"There's nothing here, Diane, other than the need to find this un-named person who we believe attacked the Padre. So stop looking for things that aren't there."

Crane and Anderson turned to leave again and this time got as far as the door before she called out, "Who gave you the description? Was it Padre Symonds? Did he see his attacker? Is it possible to interview him?"

Sighing, Anderson turned to face her, "Diane, he's still in hospital. You won't be able to interview him I'm afraid. Stop acting as though you're an investigative reporter on a tabloid newspaper. You're just making a fool of yourself."

"No, Derek, I'm not," she replied with a confident tone, her head held high. "I'm just doing my job. Don't worry, I'll be in touch."

Crane watched the exchange in silence, which he believed to be the better part of valour under the circumstances. As he and Derek left the room, he realised he would have to be careful of Diane Chambers, if she was as good as her implied threat.

CHAPTER 37

When Crane got home that evening, he asked Tina if they had a copy of the Aldershot Mail.

"Sure, somewhere here, I think," she replied. "Go and drink your beer in the front room and I'll bring it in."

Just as he settled down with his beer, his slippered feet propped up on the coffee table, she returned.

"Here you are, love. Why do you want it?"

Crane sat up and spread the paper on the table. Whilst he was skimming through it he told Tina about the press conference and Diane Chambers.

"I just wanted to see what sort of stories she writes and how well she writes them. She did a piece a while back on local evangelical churches," he finished.

"What have you found?" Tina asked looking over his shoulder.

"Only local crime, her reports on cases heard in the local courts, stuff like that."

"Well, let's face it," laughed Tina, "Aldershot isn't usually the crime Mecca of the South East.

"Oh but it is, Tina, it's just that we don't tell anyone about it!"

They smiled at each other and then over dinner Crane brought Tina up to date with the investigation, all thoughts of Diane Chambers pushed to the back of his mind for now. But, she didn't go away as Crane had hoped.

***

The following morning Crane had just finished a call to Sergeant Major Brown in Colchester, who confirmed that Zechariah had also preached at his local evangelical church. Crane was feeling pretty pleased with himself, when Kim popped her head around the door.

"Sorry to bother you, sir," she said, "but Diane Chambers is on the phone. She won't tell me what the call is about and insists that she met you yesterday and may be able to help your investigation into the attack on Padre Symonds."

Smiling, Crane realised he had half been expecting such a call.

"Put her through, Kim, let's see what she wants."

Diane started with an apology.

"I'm sorry, Sergeant Major, but I could only persuade the editor to put the picture of your un-named suspect in the middle of the paper."

Crane feigned disappointment. "Oh dear, Diane, is there nothing you could do about that?"

He could hear her tapping a pen or pencil on her desk. "Well....I've tried everything I can think of. But there may be a way we could persuade him to treat it a bit more seriously."

"What's that?"

"Look, it's probably better to talk about this face to face," she suggested.

Smiling, Crane agreed to meet her at the health food cafe in the Arcade.

***

"Really, Sergeant Major," Diane Chambers grimaced as she took a sip of her coffee. "Couldn't we have met at Starbucks? Their coffee's a damn sight better."

"I'm sure it is, but it's quieter here, Diane. And by the way, call me Crane, most people do." Crane looked at her across the small metal table. She was still dressed in jeans and trainers, but this time complemented by a small t-shirt that emphasised her breasts and slim waist.

"Tell me about your problem with your editor."

Diane launched into an account of her discussion with the editor, who felt that he couldn't put the story on the front page because there was a distinct lack of information.

"So?"

"So, I did a bit of homework. I looked through back issues of the paper for stories about the garrison and wondered if this un-named suspect was connected with the murder/suicide of Lance Corporal Crooks?"

Crane looked at her but refused to speak.

"Shall I take your silence as a yes, Crane?"

He still refused to speak. She pushed her coffee away, half finished.

"So," she continued, "if it did, I could possibly persuade my editor that there's more to this than meets the eye. And, if I could convince him that our co-operation with an un-named source at the garrison, would ensure further information in the future that no other paper would get..." she paused for dramatic effect, "then I am sure I could persuade him that this is worthy of the front page."

Unable to contain himself any longer, Crane burst out laughing.

But he hadn't rattled Diane, who continued to stare at him.

"Diane, how old are you?" Crane pushed back his chair, stretched his legs and put his hands in his trouser pockets.

"What's that got to do with anything?"

"How old are you?" he persisted.

"22."

"And how long have you worked at the Mail?"

"Six months. It's my first job since leaving University, where I got a degree in Journalism. Look, I—"

"So you're a bit green to say the least," Crane cut in.

At that remark Diane had the grace to blush. "Maybe I am," she said recovering and sitting up straight in the metal chair, "but it doesn't mean I'm not good at my job."

"No, it doesn't," Crane conceded. "You're just a bit over enthusiastic. Look, Diane," Crane leaned across the small space between them, "this isn't some American work of fiction, where a femme fatal of a journalist gets a scoop by co-operating with a maverick detective. This is real life. Aldershot, for God's sake. Stop reading things into things. There isn't a conspiracy in everything you know." He sat back to see her reaction.

"I know that, Crane. I'm merely trying to foster good relations between the garrison and my paper."

"Okay," he said drawing out the word. "Then in that case, foster good relations and stop trying to blackmail me with things that aren't true. Get your editor to print my artist's impression on the front page, leave the Crooks case alone and I promise to keep you abreast of developments. How's that?"

"Not 'abreast of developments', I want exclusive interviews."

"Excuse me?"

"I'll accept your proposal if you give me exclusive interviews."

"You drive a hard bargain, Diane. But you've got yourself a deal," said Crane, stretching his hand across the table to shake hers.

Crane watched Diane Chambers leave the café as happy as if she'd just won the lottery and shook his head at the naivety of some people. He had no more intention of giving her an exclusive interview than he had of buying a luxury yacht.

CHAPTER 38

On Friday and Saturday, Crane and Anderson hovered by the telephones as various constables and junior detectives took calls from concerned members of the public – concerned with getting their five minutes of fame, that was. Crane had met his fair share of weirdoes in the past, but the civilian population of Aldershot were a breed unto themselves.

They watched the appeals on the local TV stations in Anderson's cramped office. BBC and ITV aired the artist's impression of Zechariah for about 10 seconds, with a grave warning by the announcer not to approach the man but to call the Aldershot Police hotline.

"Oh well," sighed Anderson, zapping the TV mounted on the wall with the remote control. "Short and sweet. At least they did the piece."

"Don't they normally?"

"Depends on what else is happening at the time. A good murder or something will take most of the slot available for local crime. Let's see if we've done any better in the local papers," he finished as a constable entered the office, staggering under the weight of the Aldershot Mail, Aldershot News, Evening Post, Farnham Herald, Surrey Chronicle and all the subsidiary editions.

By the time Crane and Anderson had poured over them, the local papers were strewn all over the desk in Anderson's office. All the newspapers had included the item somewhere in their pages, but the Aldershot Mail, courtesy of Diane Chambers had, as usual, gone completely overboard. There was a large picture of the photo fit on the front page with a lurid warning that this man could be armed and dangerous. Her piece then went on to speculate about the local drugs trade and a spate of burglaries in the area. Could this man be involved? Who knew? Certainly not Diane Chambers, Crane and Anderson decided.

As a result of this extended publicity, there were many calls from police informants, or those wishing to be police informants, saying that they thought the mystery man was involved in the local drug's trade. They wanted paying for the information, of course, which in all cases turned out to be false, saving Anderson a great deal of money.

Other calls came from concerned citizens who had witnessed a man running away from houses that had recently been burgled. Is there a reward, they wanted to know?

All in all it added up to a big fat zero.

CHAPTER 39

On Monday morning, after a Sunday when Crane managed to resist the temptation to go to another service at the Church of Jesus is King, he was just leaving to go to the garrison, when Tina walked into the kitchen.

"Morning love," he called cheerfully, draining the last of his coffee. Putting it down on the kitchen table, he moved to kiss her. "I'm just off now, see you tonight." He carried on talking while he gathered his briefcase and coat and tied his shoe laces. "We've got a big divisional meeting this morning. Something about 'setting parameters for co-ordinating effort between Special Investigation Branches', or some such bollocks. I seem to have been co-opted by Edwards, supposedly because I have actual hands on experience of this stuff. More like because he doesn't want to get involved. It's going to be as boring as hell, but there you go, I mustn't be late."

"Tom," her voice stopped him as he got to the front door.

"Yes, love?" he turned to face her, hoping the

wariness in his eyes wasn't evident.

"I've been meaning to talk to you…" her voice trailed off.

"About?"

"You know what about, Tom," she said turning away from him and going to fill the sink with water.

Walking back into the kitchen he put his hands on her shoulders and turned her to face him. "Sweetheart, why didn't you say anything earlier? We've had all weekend when we could have talked."

"All weekend?" she glared at him.

"Alright, I know I worked on Saturday following up leads from the hotline, but we had Sunday."

Turning back to the sink she said, "I suppose I didn't want to spoil the one day we had of our weekend. Do you think we could talk tonight please?" her voice had dropped to a whisper, so he had to strain to hear her.

"Of course," he agreed planting a kiss on the back of her head, not wanting to argue first thing in the morning. "I promise I won't be late," he called as he left the house.

***

The meeting went on much longer than it should, as these things always do. Crane was coerced into staying for lunch, rather than returning to barracks in the break and so it was almost 16:00 hours when he eventually arrived at the SIB office.

He found a flustered Kim waiting for him.

"Thank God you're back, sir," she said following

him into his office at a run. "I was just about to get them to interrupt the meeting."

"What on earth for, Kim?" he said as he put his stuff away and hung up his coat. As he turned to look at her, he saw she was looking worried. "Sit down, Kim, take a deep breath and tell me all about it."

"It's Billy, sir, or rather Billy's sister, or rather his nephew. Oh God, it's coming out all wrong!"

Crane had never seen her so upset, gone was the cool calm exterior that he knew so well. Whatever had happened was causing not just chinks, but major cracks in her professional armour. She was alternating between wringing her hands together and running them through her hair, which was no longer neatly tied up, but falling around her face and shoulders.

In between more false starts and gulps, the problem became clear. Billy's sister Sue had telephoned Kim, asking if Billy was there. Kim looked around the office and realised he was missing. She quickly checked the log to find that he'd left the office at lunch time and not returned. Having to admit that to Sue produced an almighty wail. It appeared that she'd gone to school to pick Shaun up at 3.30pm as usual but Shaun wasn't there. He'd gone off with Billy.

"I'm sorry, sir, I know I was supposed to keep tabs on Billy and follow him if he went out, but he just seems to have given me the slip. He said he was going to get a sandwich for lunch and wouldn't be long. He was even going to bring me one back! I couldn't go with him because Captain Edwards needed some figures collating for this afternoon and I was so engrossed in them I didn't notice Billy hadn't come back."

"Don't worry, Kim, it's not your fault. What's Sue's number?"

Getting Sue's mobile phone number from Kim, Crane immediately called her. Sue answered at the first ring.

"Billy?"

"No, Sue, sorry it's Sergeant Major Crane, from the Special Investigations Branch. Where are you now please?"

"Oh God, I'm at home. I left Rosie with a friend and ran all the way back. But he's not here!" Crane held the phone away from his ear. Sue's voice had risen so much, she was screaming.

"Sue, please calm down." He heard gulping sobs at the other end of the phone. "Sue please," he continued, "I can't help you unless you tell me exactly what happened."

"I......I went to St Saviour's School in Ash as usual at 3.30 to pick Shaun up. But he didn't come out with his other classmates. I stood in line as one by one the children filed past Mrs Hale, the teacher. They're not allowed to leave the classroom until their parent is present."

"That's better, Sue," he encouraged. "What happened then?"

Taking a deep breath Sue continued, "As the last child left Mrs Hale looked surprised to see me and turned to go back into the classroom. I called out and grabbed her by the arm, demanding to know where Shaun was. She told me that he was with Billy." Sue began to quietly cry. After a few moments she continued. "Apparently Billy had gone to the school at lunch time, as I was supposedly unwell and had been taken to hospital. Billy was going to take Shaun to see me. That's when we realised something was seriously wrong and went straight to the headmistress. I telephoned the barracks from the school and spoke to Kim."

By now Sue was sobbing loudly again and Crane had to shout to be heard. "Sue! Sue!"

"Yes?"

"Sue, I'm going to put Kim on the phone while I get this sorted out. Just talk to her until you've calmed down." Without waiting for a reply, he covered the receiver. "Just keep her talking and occupied. See if she can get someone to sit with her. I'm going to ring Anderson and then get over there."

"Over where, sir?"

"The Church of Jesus is our bloody King!"

CHAPTER 40

As Kim talked to Sue, Crane rung Derek Anderson. He explained what had happened and Anderson agreed to send someone round to Sue's house immediately. Crane particularly wanted to know if Billy had been attending the Church of Jesus is King and taking Shaun with him, so asked that the attending police officers find that out as quickly as possible and for Derek to ring him on his mobile with the information.

"What are you going to do, Crane?"

"Go to that bloody Church."

"What the hell for?"

"Because I have a feeling whatever is going down is happening there and sooner rather than later."

"I'm warning you, Crane, don't cause any trouble and—"

Crane put down the phone cutting off Anderson's diatribe and ran for his car.

In the five minutes or so that it took for Crane to arrive at the church, turning left out of the barracks, along Queens Avenue and then right into

Aldershot at the bottom of the hill, Anderson had walked from the police station and was waiting for Crane in the car park.

"Thought I'd join you, Crane," he explained, leaning against the car. "You seemed in too much of a hurry before to explain what the hell you're doing, so I thought I'd give you the opportunity to do it now."

Realising that he needed help and back up, Crane ran through the events that caused him to think Billy and Shaun were in the church.

"Firstly, some mornings Billy's been dazed and sleepy. Not with it. One day he actually overslept, which is unheard of for him."

"He's a young lad, Crane. Maybe it was just the after effects of being out with the lads?"

Ignoring the question, Crane continued, "Secondly, he's been missing from the office on a couple of afternoons. Logging out with a fictitious reason and not returning to the office until the next day. I've covered for him with Captain Edwards, but I think it's suspicious."

"Fair enough. Anything else?"

Giving up on counting Crane continued, "I'm sure I saw him when we went to the church the other Sunday. As I was watching the crowds leave, I caught a glimpse of the back of someone that reminded me of Billy and he was leading a young boy by the hand."

"That's not much to go on, Crane, anything else?" Anderson asked, still lounging against Crane's car.

Before imparting the next reason, Crane lit a cigarette with trembling hands. "Billy wanted to go undercover at the church, posing as a father with Shaun as his son."

"Bloody hell!" Anderson stood up straight.

"I know, Derek," agreed Crane, drawing deeply. As he exhaled, he carried on speaking. "I warned him off and gave him strict orders not to do that. But…" Crane shrugged, "well now I'm not so sure. I had him followed by Kim one night but he only went to a parent's evening as his sister Sue couldn't go. Which made me feel a bit stupid at the time." Crane paused for another drag. "Honestly, Derek, I still think he's been going to this bloody church," he emphasised the point by raising his arm and gesturing towards the nearby building.

Just then Anderson's mobile rang. Looking at the caller ID he said, "Hang on a minute, Crane, it's the officers reporting in from Sue's house." After a few grunts and then a groan, Anderson closed the phone. "Looks like you could be right," he had to admit. "Billy's been taking Shaun to the church for a few weeks now. Apparently Shaun really loves going to the junior church and Sue couldn't see any harm in it so-"

Derek didn't finish his sentence as he was interrupted by Crane's mobile.

"Kim?" Her voice was high pitched and tinny in Crane's ear, the words jumbling and falling over each other. "Calm down, Kim, I can't understand a word you're saying. Take a deep breath and start again."

"Sorry, sir." Kim paused for breath and Crane waited. "I'm alright now. I've been looking at the incident board," she began.

"Haven't we all, Kim, time after time, what's new about that?" Crane was restless, pacing backwards and forwards.

"It's the dates and times, sir."

"The dates and times of what? Sorry, Kim, you've lost me."

"All the murder suicides. Just listen, sir."

"Wait a moment, Kim," Crane paused to put the phone on speaker. "Okay Derek can hear now. Carry on,"

"If we look at the dates and times of the murder suicides, Solomon at 16:00 hours on the 16th of August. John Sergeant at 23:00 hours on the 23rd September. Peter Fisher at 09:00 hours on the 9th October…"

"Oh sweet Jesus." Crane stopped pacing and stared in horror at Anderson.

"Exactly, sir, it's the 18th of November."

"That means it could be happening at 18:00 hours today." Crane looked at his watch. "That gives me an hour. Thanks Kim." Crane cut the call and put the phone back in his pocket.

"Right, that does it for me. I've got to get inside that building." Crane threw his cigarette down and ground it out with his shoe.

"But why the church, Crane?" Anderson held Crane back. "Why not Billy's place? All the other murders were done at home."

"Because Billy lives in single men's quarters on

the garrison. He can't take anyone there without permission and certainly not a child. So he has to have brought him here."

The two men ran down the street until they came to the converted cinema. From the front, the only way in was the large doors, which were closed. Crane marched up to them and tried the handle. Locked. He rattled it and was about to put his shoulder to the door to try and force it open, when Anderson put his hand out to stop him.

"What the hell are you doing, Crane?"

"Trying to get in, Derek, what do you think I'm doing?"

"Trying to break your shoulder. You'll never force a door like that, Crane. Look at the bloody size of it."

Crane took a step back and admitted Anderson was right. The door towered above him and was probably about eight feet high and double the width of a normal door. It was made of polished oak.

"Alright then, what do you suggest?"

"Let's have a look around the back. Come on this way."

Crane followed Anderson back towards the car park but his friend veered off to the right before he reached it. He ran down an alley, full of empty cardboard boxes and crates from the pub and supermarket on the main street opposite the alley and an odd collection of filthy blankets and quilts.

"One of the favourite haunts of the local homeless," Anderson explained.

The alley opened onto the back of the buildings where the cinema was located. As they rounded the corner, the cinema loomed above them and Crane had a sense of what a formidable building it was. Solid, strong and seemingly impenetrable. The ground floor windows on this side were covered with wire mesh and bars and the fire exit was a metal door clearly barred from the inside. There was not so much as a handle on the outside.

After spending a few moments looking up at the sheer walls, Crane came to a decision and raced back towards the alley. "Come on, Derek, give me a hand!"

"What the hell?"

"Come on," Crane cried from the corner of the alleyway. Not bothering to wait for Anderson, Crane ran into the alley and began collecting the beer crates. As Anderson rounded the corner he shouted, "Grab as many of these as you can."

With an armful of crates Crane stumbled round to the back of the cinema. He was stacking the crates when Anderson caught up with him.

"Quick, put them here on top of each other, against this drain pipe. Look up there." Crane was pointing to a casement window set in the middle of and higher than the ground floor ones. The glass was frosted and the top half of the window was ajar on a stay. "I reckon that's the toilets. If I grab this drain pipe and use the beer crates to help, I could climb up the wall and get in through the window." Crane was ripping off his jacket and rolling up his shirt sleeves as he spoke. "I've got to get in there,

Derek. I think Billy and Shaun, but more importantly Zechariah, are in there.

"What makes you think Zechariah is here?"

"Because this is a church, Derek, a holy sanctified place. Where better to stage the finale?"

"What finale?"

"I think Zechariah could be instigating a mass murder suicide. Right here. This afternoon. With all the members of the father and son group." With that he grabbed the drain pipe and began to climb, using the crates as purchase for his feet.

CHAPTER 41

Of course, breaking in wasn't as easy as Crane hoped. He stretched out his right hand to the window, grasping and unfastening the stay, locking it into place so it wouldn't rip down his back, and then held the window open. He considered trying to get in feet first, but then again gymnastics had never been his thing, so his only option was to go in head first.

Letting go of the window, Crane decided to climb further up the drain pipe, so his middle was in line with the bottom of the opening. The old iron drain pipe creaked and moved under his weight. He wiped his hands one by one on his trousers. Pieces of gritty burnt ochre rust covered his hands, making it difficult to get a firm grip, a testament to the drainpipe's age. Crane could only hope it would hold out long enough for him to push off against, as he propelled himself towards the window.

"I'm calling for back up!" Anderson shouted.

Crane put his thumb up and took a deep breath. He reached for and grasped the bottom of the open window with his right hand and pushed with his feet. The iron drainpipe, weakened by many years of rain and sun held for a moment, then crumbled. Pieces of rust and metal fell to the floor below. Knowing there was now no way back, Crane's left hand reached for the bottom of the open window as he clung on with his right. But he couldn't seem to get his hand through, grazing knuckles and breaking finger nails as he tried to get his hand inside. By now he was dangling precariously by one hand, ten feet from the ground.

He scrabbled around the wall with his feet, at last finding the narrow window sill. Balancing as best he could on his toes and ignoring the burning pain in the muscles of his right arm, he lifted the window open with his left hand and finally got his head through. Placing both hands firmly on the bottom of the window he pushed upwards and forwards, forcing his body inside, coming to rest half in and half out of the window.

Taking a few seconds to get his breath back, he looked at the inside of the room. He found his assumption was correct and he was in the toilets. Or rather hanging around in the open window of the toilets. But he was not in a cubicle, where he could have used a cistern or toilet bowl to break his fall. He was in the middle of the room, with stalls at one side and sinks on the other. There was nothing for five feet below him.

"Oh shit," he exclaimed dropping forwards, landing on his hands and executing a parachute roll.

As Crane stood and brushed himself down, his

hands left streaks of rust and grime on his once pristine white shirt. But he seemed unhurt, apart from a few bruises. Shaking his right arm to try and loosen the damaged muscles, he looked around, but the toilets were empty. So far so good.

The exit was opposite the window and he crossed to it, opening the door just a crack. He could neither hear nor see any movement outside, so he slipped through it and took a few moments to consider his position.

He was in an empty corridor. He knew he was more or less in the middle of the building, so really it didn't matter which way he went. Being right handed, he naturally gravitated to that side and moved forward, hugging the wall as he went. After a few yards he came to an opening on his left. A sign screwed to the wall said 'Stalls' with an arrow indicating up the stairs. The entrance was covered by a dark coloured curtain.

As Crane touched it, he felt thick heavy velvet and the disturbance caused a musty smell, which tickled his nose and threatened to make him sneeze. Holding his breath he pushed the curtain completely to one side and climbed the stairs. But his nose had been irritated by the dust motes released from the curtain and try as he might, he couldn't stop the sneeze. He put his hands around his nose and mouth and turned his head away, back towards the stairs, muffling the sound as best he could. Praying he hadn't been heard. He then turned to look into the cinema.

From his elevated position at the top of the

stalls, he could see rows of seats stretching down below him to a barrier resplendent in red velvet with a brass rail on top. It had obviously been lovingly polished, as the lights in the auditorium roof reflected off it.

A murmuring lilt rose up from the bowels of the building. He moved one step at a time, down the stairs towards the sound. As he reached the barrier, he crouched down, placed his hands on the rail and slowly raised his head, looking under the brass rail, like a sniper surveying the landscape.

The scene below took his breath away. A blow to the head took his sight away.

CHAPTER 42

Crane had always hated wasps and bees. Probably because he'd trodden on a queen bee when he was a boy, walking through a field in bare feet. He'd ended up with paralysed toes and an equally paralyzing fear of the small stinging insects. It didn't matter if it was a bee or wasp. Either one was equally feared.

Now there was a wasp trapped in the pocket of his trousers. The bloody thing wouldn't go away. It was buzzing and vibrating against his leg, clearly trapped in his trouser pocket. Convinced he was about to be stung at any moment, he lifted his hand to try and liberate the bug from the fabric. But there was no response. His hand remained firmly clamped against the arm of the chair he was sitting in. He willed his hand to move once again, but it disobeyed the instruction from his brain.

"What the hell?" Or at least that was what he tried to say. It actually came out as "Ot uugh el?" Had he already been stung and this time been paralyzed all over?

When he looked down to see why his hand

wouldn't work, he realised he was sitting in semi darkness. As his eyes adjusted to the dim light, Crane remembered where he was. In the converted cinema belonging to the Church of Jesus is King He closed his eyes as the memory of what he'd seen over the railing of the stalls came back to him. Men and boys, sat huddled together on the auditorium floor, swaying and chanting in unison. The men all holding knives.

Desperate to get up and save them, he tried to get out of the seat, but this time his back seemed glued in place. Clenching his fists in frustration he looked down again. This time, he could make out that his wrists were bound to the arm of the seat by duct tape. Lifting his legs showed him that they were bound together. Struggling to free his body he surmised the tape had also been placed around his shoulders and chest, running around him and the seat. There was more duct tape around his mouth, the adhesive tasting foul as he ran his tongue along the inside of his partially open lips.

Shit, Crane thought, this stuff was going to be a bastard to get off, but get it off he must. He guessed the easiest to remove, would be the tape around his wrists, so he started pushing his arms backwards and forwards, as far as they would go. Which wasn't far enough. In fact, not far at all. The hairs on his arms and backs of his hands seemed to scream as they were wrenched backwards and forwards. They stuck firmly to the adhesive and pulled free of his skin with each movement. Once the hairs were off his skin, the adhesive rubbed like sandpaper across his hands and wrists. After a while it became agony, but he bit the inside of his cheek and carried on struggling to break free.

Then the bloody wasp started up again. Crane grinned when he realised it was his mobile phone. He'd put it on vibrate just before he climbed through the window into the cinema. Someone needed to get hold of him. Probably Anderson, but there was nothing he could do at the moment and even if he could, he couldn't risk talking. Not after a sneeze had clearly given him away.

He wondered if he squirmed in his seat enough he could loosen the tape around his body, but gave that idea up as the rattling of the old seats would alert his attacker to the fact that he was conscious.

Taking a short break from pushing his hands backwards and forwards, he lifted his head to look over the railing. It was difficult to see the floor of the auditorium from this angle, but he could see a figure on the stage and he could still hear the chanting from the assembled men and boys.

He continued rubbing away at the duct tape, but now in time with the chanting from below. He couldn't quite hear the words, but could follow the beat and that spurred him on. If they could keep chanting, he could keep rubbing. Luckily it was dim where he was sitting, so he couldn't see if there was any blood seeping from the back of his hands. Still if there was, he reckoned that would help loosen the adhesive.

Crane became lost in the rhythm himself. Backwards and forwards, backwards and forwards.

He focused his mind on the fact that he needed to help the innocent children, in an effort to ignore the growing pain.

After a while, he realised his right hand was moving further forwards than the left. Looking down he saw the tape had bunched up and stretched so much, his hand was now loose under the binding. He pulled it free and grabbed at the tape tying his left hand to the seat. Once he had both hands free he tore at the tape around his chest and shoulders. Soon he'd ripped it from his legs and then turned his attention to the strip at his mouth.

This was going to be a bastard. It was taped across his face, which meant it was taped across his beard. Oh well, he never liked the beard much anyway, he thought, as he gritted his teeth and pulled.

CHAPTER 43

As soon as he was free, Crane once more crouched by the barrier in the stalls and peered through the gap, under the brass railing. Now he had an uninterrupted view.

The man on the stage was dressed in beautiful gold and green robes. His black skin gleamed in the lights and his deep bass voice had a lyrical quality. He had long Rastafarian dreadlocks. Zechariah. The men were set out in lines, sitting on the floor of the auditorium, facing Zechariah. Each had a small boy next to him. There must be over twenty pairs of men and boys Crane calculated.

As he watched, each boy moved to sit in front of their parent. The men's legs opened and the boys settled themselves in the gap leaning back against the chest of their father. Neither child nor man made any sound and no one appeared to be frightened. There was no frantic struggling, just calm. Each man had a knife in his hand, the blades glinting in the lights of the auditorium.

Zechariah's voice rose as he began delivering his rhetoric. Now Crane could hear him clearly.

"Jesus is the saviour, a fountain, whose blood covers the sins of all who come to Him for salvation."

Bloody hell, here we go, thought Crane.

"Do you want to live in eternal damnation for your sins?" Zechariah paused and looked at his followers. Locking his eyes with theirs. "Do you want your sins to be passed onto your sons?" he demanded.

Crane looked at the backs of the men. Then he saw what he was looking for. The familiar shape of Billy's broad muscular back and his short, blond hair.

"I can show you the way. 'I am the light,' said Jesus. And I, as his prophet can shed that light and show you the steps you can take to reach Heaven," Zechariah continued, his voice rising and falling, mesmerising in its depth and cadence.

"There is no time to lose. There will be rivers of blood. But at the same time, there will be rivers of healing blood, blood that brought salvation to the true followers of Jesus." Zechariah was cranking it up now and the loud voice rang out strong and true in the auditorium.

Crane realised what Zechariah was leading up to. Fuck. Rivers of blood. Jesus Christ they're going to kill the children and them themselves. Crane turned and ran up the steps of the stalls, not caring this time if anyone saw or heard him.

"Are you ready to be redeemed in a fountain of blood, covering your sins and the sins of your children?" Zechariah's voice followed him, taunting

Crane as he tried to think of a way to stop this horror. He needed to break the trance, hypnosis, or whatever it was. As Crane reached the top of the stairs he was grateful that Zechariah was relishing this part. His speech had slowed, giving emphasis to each word.

"This is the only way to eternal salvation!" he screamed.

Crane practically pulled down the velvet curtain as he grabbed it to help stop his fall and scanned the corridor.

"Drench yourself in the blood!"

Crane knew what was coming next from the emails they retrieved from the computers and needed a major, never mind minor miracle, to stop it. Sending up one of the arrow prayers that Padre Symonds told him about during one of their frequent conversations, Crane called upon God for help. He turned left and ran around the corridor.

"And drench your sons too…"

Crane knew he couldn't let Zechariah finish his sentence. And that's when he saw it. A fire alarm, as old as the cinema. In the cabinet was a fire axe. Fumbling with the catch, Crane opened the glass door, grabbed the axe and smashed the fire alarm glass.

"So that we all may be saved." Zechariah finished his hypnotic rhetoric, but it was too late. His final words were drowned out by the shrill fire alarm.

Running back up the stairs to the stalls, still with the axe in his hand, Crane this time leaned over the edge of the balcony. A wonderful sight met his eyes. The men and boys were now standing up, looking around, shaking their heads as if to clear the fog in their brain. Some were looking at the knives in their hands as if they were alien objects and clearly had no idea why they are holding them.

Crane searched the crowd looking for Billy. He found him in the centre of the crowd and screamed his name. Standing up and waving his hands, now empty of the threatening axe, Crane tried to get Billy's attention. Finally Billy looked up and saw Crane. His eyes cleared with recognition.

"Get everyone out, Billy," Crane gestured wildly to the front of the building. "Out. Now!"

Billy waved in response and grabbed Shaun's hand, moving towards the exit, encouraging those around him to follow.

"Hello, Sergeant Major Crane."

Crane whirled round at the sound of his name, expecting to meet the mad man called Zechariah face to face. Instead he found himself looking at Elias.

"Thank God. Am I glad to see you," Crane shouted above the noise of the fire alarm. "We need to go downstairs and get these people out. Then I'm going to look for Zechariah."

CHAPTER 44

The fire alarm suddenly stopped its insane clamour and Crane fell back against the brass rail. The ringing in his ears still making hearing difficult. He could see Elias' mouth moving but couldn't hear the words. He looked up at the Church Elder, who was standing on the steps leading to the back of the stalls and the exit and shook his head to clear his ears.

"I said, I don't think so, Sergeant Major."

"Don't think so, why the hell not, man?" Crane pushed himself upright in his indignation.

"Because you've caused me quite enough trouble as it is. I don't intend to let you cause me anymore."

The words and the deep basso voice caught Crane's attention and he looked closely at Elias' face. As he examined it in silence, he saw plumped up cheek bones and wide nostrils. But no Rastafarian hair, just a bald pate. No robes, just a sober black suit. Crane's eyes travelled downwards and saw the gun in the Church Elder's hand.

"How could I have been so stupid?" Crane

questioned himself rather than Elias.

"Understandable, my dear Sergeant Major. Did you like my disguise?" Elias put his hand in his mouth and removed two large plastic wedges from his cheeks. He then put a finger up each nostril in turn and poked out a piece of plastic.

"Latex," explained Elias. "Works rather well. I particularly like the hair and robes though, don't you?"

Crane actually nodded before he realised what he was doing. Agreeing with this madman. "Was it you who hit me over the head?"

"Yes, rather stupid of me not to kill you then."

"Why didn't you?"

Keeping the gun pointed at Crane's chest, Elias explained, "I suppose I wanted an audience. A witness to my total control, my triumph. Then I was going to kill you."

"Weren't you going to kill yourself when your 'followers' or whatever you want to call them, killed the children and then themselves. Your contribution to the 'rivers of blood?'"

"Oh no, Sergeant Major. I need to continue God's work."

"God's work? Is that what you call killing innocent men and children?"

"But I didn't kill them!" Elias shouted, the gun wavering in his hand. "They sacrificed themselves and their children, so they could enter the Kingdom of Heaven."

"But this lot haven't." Crane nodded towards the auditorium.

"No," Elias's deep bass voice became a growl, "but your soldiers did."

Crane said nothing. He was incapable of speech.

Elias broke into a grin. "I was rather proud of them, actually. A simple phone call and the control words, 'Steps to Heaven' was all it took to trigger the inevitable."

"Why my soldiers?" Crane demanded, shaking with rage.

"That's simple. Because they were easy to manipulate, Sergeant Major. How could you ever hope to keep men sane after what you and your precious army put them through? Day after day thinking they were going to be the next one to die, lose a limb or their eyesight. Watching their friends being blown to smithereens before their very eyes. Not really understanding why they were there, or what they were trying to achieve. Oh yes, Sergeant Major, you and your superiors contrived to give me the perfect subjects. The only slight flaw was Peter Fisher. He was supposed to kill his wife as well, but the stupid man decided on his own that she wasn't to be part of it. If he hadn't hated her so much, maybe we wouldn't be in this position now. But still, there's no point worrying over spilt milk, wouldn't you agree?"

"I'll make you pay for this." Crane had never hated anyone as much as he did this righteous, religious, madman.

"I don't think so. I'm the one with the gun remember."

As Crane stared at Elias, desperately thinking

how to get out of this situation, his mobile phone began buzzing. In the split second that it took for Elias to glance down at his leg, Crane threw himself to the ground and went for the axe.

The gunshot echoed through the old cinema as Crane's fingers grasped the axe and threw it at Elias. There wasn't enough power in the throw to do much damage, but it had the desired effect of startling the Church Elder. Crane saw Elias look at his leg in horror, as blood began to seep from the glancing blow from the axe head. Looking back at Crane, he fired a second shot and then turned and ran up the stairs.

CHAPTER 45

Crane sat on the floor of the stalls, stunned for a moment, both by the revelation that Elias was Zechariah and by the fact that he'd been shot. The bullet had caught him high up on the left shoulder so there were no vital organs for it to hit and he was right handed, so that was an advantage as well. But he was bleeding profusely. He could feel, rather than see, the warm, sticky blood seeping from the wound like warm honey. Not having anything to put against it as a pressure pad, Crane just had to hope for the best. He got to his feet, feeling as unsteady as a toddler taking his first steps.

He turned and looked over the railing again. It seemed the auditorium was still full of men and boys, milling around. The floor was littered with knives, all of which were now ignored by the men who just a few minutes ago were going to use them to slit their son's throats. Crane wondered why they hadn't left, taking the children to safety.

He saw Billy in the middle of the throng, looking up at the stalls, his head turning this way and that as if trying to catch sight of someone.

Then he stopped, stooped down and picked up a knife from the floor. Placing Shaun's hand firmly into that of the man closest to him, Billy disappeared from Crane's limited view. Crane realised Billy must have heard the gunshots and was either coming for Crane or going after Zechariah.

Holding the axe in his dangling left hand and pressing his right against his wound, Crane turned and slowly took the steps up the stalls to the exit. By the time he got to the red curtain, he was sweating and his hand was doing as good a job as a sieve trying to staunch the bleeding. Giving up, he wiped the blood off his hand the best he could on his trousers and took the axe in his right hand.

He found the stairs leading down to the auditorium and half ran half fell down them, ending up ignominiously on his bottom. Climbing to his feet, he circled the room, keeping to the shadows as much as he could. For one thing he didn't want to alarm the men and boys. But neither did he want to alert Zechariah to his presence.

He saw Zechariah, sat on the edge of the staging. The gun wasn't in sight, but his hands were in the pockets of his suit jacket. None of the congregation seemed scared of him. But then they wouldn't, Crane thought. To them he was Elias. He also realised they may have very little memory of the hypnotic Zechariah.

As he looked across the crowd, he saw Billy opposite him. Circling the room, as he was. He saw the knife grasped in his hand. They nodded in agreement and Crane motioned with his head for

Billy to continue. So, a knife and an axe against a gun. Not such good odds. Crane let the axe hang by his leg and stepped into the space before the stage.

"Good afternoon, Elias," he called, raising his voice only slightly, so as not to alarm those near him.

"Ah, Sergeant Major. We meet again. How nice."

Crane took a few steps towards Elias.

"That's far enough, I think. Don't you?" the Elder said. Crane was on one side of Elias, close enough for the two men to converse without raising their voices. Elias had a clear view in front of him.

"Elias, this has to stop."

"Oh, not just yet. I'm in quite a good position, don't you think? Consider how many of these faithful souls I could shoot before you reach me." Elias slowly took the gun from his pocket and placed it in his lap, the fold of his suit jacket hiding it from any curious eyes.

"The police will be here soon, Elias, give yourself up now." Crane kept his voice low but insistent.

"Oh you mean the good Detective Inspector Anderson." A deep chuckle followed the words. "Such a nice man. Luckily for me, he was very respectful of our church and didn't investigate me as vigorously as he should have done."

"Well, he's vigorously investigating now," Crane countered. "He knows I'm in here and I'm sure backup will have arrived by now."

"That may be so, but he's going to have trouble getting in. Why do you think they are all still in here?" Elias nodded at his followers. "I've locked and barred the main door."

"So why aren't they panicking and trying to get out?"

"I've spread the word that the old locks have become stuck. We've been meaning to replace them for a long time, but never seemed to get around to it. They're just waiting for someone to come and rescue us."

Crane followed Elias' gaze towards the front of the cinema and as he did so, took a quick look to check Billy's position.

Billy was level with Crane and Elias now, on the other side of them, continuing his slow, silent journey towards the back of the staging.

"You surely don't think you can get away with this?" Crane knew the question was a stupid one, but he had to keep the man talking, whilst Billy continued his stalking.

"Get away with what, Sergeant Major? I am merely Elias, the Church Elder. When I speak to Anderson, I'll regretfully inform him of your death, claiming that Zechariah killed you and then escaped."

"Not a bad plan, I guess," Crane went along with the theory, glancing up to check on Billy's progress. "But what about your fingerprints on the gun?"

Elias lifted his hands and plucked at the latex

gloves encasing them. "What finger prints?"

"Well, it does seem that you've thought of everything. What about witnesses?"

"Witnesses?"

"Yes, what if one of these faithful folk sees you killing me?" Crane's eyes swept around the room as if to make his point, noticing that Billy was no longer in sight.

"No chance of that, Sergeant Major, I shall make sure they're out before I kill you. I'll call out to them to go first. The police won't be able to get in through 40 people all trying to get out at once. And of course, they'll have to let them through. They won't risk children getting hurt."

"Oh, so now you're concerned about the children? Not 10 minutes ago, you were hoping they would all be killed."

"Not killed, Sergeant Major," Elias growled. "Saved. Haven't you listened to a word I've been saying? I was going to save them all from the sins of this world. Ensure the children kept their innocence forever." Elias continued, his voice low, reminding Crane of a growling dog, aware of a threat but not wanting to pounce just yet.

"But surely murder and suicide are sins? How do you reconcile that with your theory of saving their souls?"

"What an imbecile you are, Sergeant Major. Don't you know that Jesus forgives all our sins and the sins of our fathers? The men confess their sins before they kill themselves and then cover their children with their healing blood."

"You're nothing but a cold blooded murderer," the words spewing from Crane's mouth before he could stop them, "hiding behind your religious rhetoric."

"How dare you!" roared Elias, leaping to his feet and aiming the gun at Crane's stomach.

CHAPTER 46

The force of the explosion knocked Crane off his feet. He staggered backwards but as there was nothing to break his fall he toppled over, knocking the air out of his lungs as he landed. On his way down, he saw vague images shimmering in front of him as if lost in a heat haze. Billy was grappling with Elias, both men trying to wrench control of the gun and the knife. Then the images slid away and all Crane could see was the ceiling.

The noise of a second explosion caused him to turn his head towards the sound which, seemed to come from the front entrance. Through a mass of legs that were constantly moving, obscuring his view, Crane saw army boots swim in and out of his line of sight. His last conscious thought was, 'thank God the lads are here.' The last thing he saw was Anderson leaning over him, before the darkness took him. The light fading, like an eclipse.

"Tina," he managed to mumble through parched lips. But there was no reply.

Crane floated away once again.

"Sergeant Major," a voice calls urgently. "Can

you hear me?" Crane wanted to say that he could, but his mouth wouldn't work. His head wouldn't work either. He couldn't seem to turn it to look at the speaker. The darkness of the eclipse claimed him once again.

"Damn it, Crane, hang on."

This time Crane recognised Anderson's voice. But he couldn't seem to understand the words. He managed to open his eyes, but seemed to have trouble focusing. It must be that damn heat haze again he thought. Never realised it got this hot in Aldershot. Or maybe he wasn't in Aldershot. Maybe he was in Iraq or Afghanistan. It was bloody hot there. He was thirsty as well. Maybe that's why his tongue felt so thick and immobile. Must be dehydration. And he was tired, so very tired. His eyelids fluttered as he fought the tiredness.

Through the heat haze a figure appeared, walking towards him, her dark hair shining in the sunlight, bobbing up and down with each bounce of her step.

"Tina," he croaked, the word splitting like brittle wood, dried out in the heat of the desert.

"Tom," he heard her call. "Tom, can you hear me?"

He tried to warn her about the heat, frustration building as he struggled to form the words. He saw the eclipse starting again, threatening to engulf the world in blackness, taking him and Tina with it.

"Tom, no!"

Her voice broke over him, pieces of refreshing ice amid the searing heat. He had so much he wanted to tell her. Gathering all his strength he called, "Tina!" screaming her name over and over again. He struggled against the draining effect of the heat, forcing his limbs to work, struggling to sit, but he was held down by the flowing white robe he seemed to be wearing.

"It's alright, Tom, I'm here." Tina's voice once more soothed and refreshed him, bathing him in coolness, forcing the heat away.

"The fever's broken," another voice said. "He'll be alright now."

Crane didn't know who had spoken, or what they were talking about, but he believed them and gave himself up to the cooling ministrations of his wife.

CHAPTER 47

"Ah, Sergeant Major, glad to see you're awake." The efficient sounding voice was complemented by efficiency of movement, as the nurse began the routine of noting Crane's blood pressure and taking his temperature.

"Well, if I wasn't I certainly am now, sister."

Ignoring the sarcasm, she continued as if he hadn't spoken. "You've got a visitor."

"Tina?"

"No, I've sent the poor woman home for some rest. She's been here constantly for the last week, refusing to leave your side." She lifted Crane's hand and felt for his pulse, her other hand holding her watch as she timed the beats. "How are you feeling? Any pain?"

Crane moved slightly in his bed and wasn't sure which hurt more, the pain in his shoulder, or the pain in his stomach. "Nothing I can't handle," he assured her, fed up of being dosed up to the eyeballs with morphine. At least this way he could think straight, even if he could feel the pain.

"Very well. Just push this button if it gets too

much, won't you? You can self-medicate whenever you need it. Don't worry, you can't overdose, the machine monitors how much you've taken."

The morphine wasn't the only thing monitoring him. He had a heart monitor on, which beeped away in the background. A blood pressure machine that woke him every hour with the automatic constriction on his arm. A catheter snaked its way through the sheets and under the bed and a drip attached to his hand that fed him all sorts of stuff that he couldn't remember the names of.

Satisfied that she had done her job, sister adjusted Crane's pillows after raising the head of the bed and walked back to the nurses' station.

A few moments later, Anderson entered the ITU at Frimley Park Hospital.

"Ah, Crane, they got you ready for me then?"

"I was asleep," grumbled Crane.

"Oh well, never mind. The long arm of the law and all that." His joviality seemed forced. "Anyway," Anderson cleared his throat, "it's much better to see you in here, than down there." He indicated with his head to the ICU.

"How long was I there? Nobody's telling me much at the moment."

"Long enough," Anderson's voice dropped. "We, um, thought we'd lost you at one point. Well, several times actually." This small speech was accompanied by much clearing of the throat.

"Maybe someone was looking down on me," Crane joked to lift the mood. He'd never seen Anderson with tears in his eyes before.

"Well, if anything, I reckon love and faith got you through."

Crane frowned at Anderson, not understanding.

"Tina and Padre Symonds. Neither of them hardly ever left your bedside. If they had to, they took it in turns, so one or the other was always here."

Crane took a few moments. "I don't remember much," he admitted. "I remember you and Tina and being very, very hot."

"That was the fever. The wound in your shoulder became infected. The bullet was lodged in there for quite some time and caused serious infection. The one in your gut was better though," Anderson smiled. "A clean through and through."

"Oh joy. Pass me a drink would you and then you could tell me the rest of the good news."

As Crane sipped the water through a straw, Anderson explained what had happened after Crane was shot for the second time. The black boots Crane thought belonged to the army were worn by the Armed Response Unit of Hampshire Police. Anderson and his team had realised the cinema door was barricaded and were planning to storm the building when they heard the faint sound of the first gunshot.

After a hurried conference, it was decided to risk taking a battering ram to the front doors and everyone was ready when they heard the second shot. The local commander lost no time in ordering his men to force their way in immediately. The explosion Crane heard were the old oak doors falling to the floor. The wood had been stronger than the hinges, which gave way under the unaccustomed force.

"I must admit we were lucky there was no one standing in front of them, but the risk to anyone trapped in there was too great to wait."

"Thank God for that," was all Crane managed to say. Not wanting to relive those moments again he encouraged Anderson to continue. "What about Billy?"

Anderson then regaled him with the tale of Billy's bravery. He reminded Crane that Billy crept up on Elias, armed only with a knife against a gun. After Crane had bitten a bullet, so to speak, Billy pounced from behind. But the door falling in distracted him and Elias managed to escape through to the back of the stage.

Calling to the officers that entered the cinema first, Billy directed them to Crane, shouting that Elias was Zechariah and then ran off in pursuit. Anderson followed the armed officers inside, making sure the paramedics had been called for Crane and then pursued Billy.

"How did you know where he'd gone?" Crane asked as he handed Anderson back the cup of water.

"Simple. I followed the blood."

"Blood?" Crane's eyes widen. He sat up, winced with pain and settled back against the pillows.

Anderson explained that at the time he hadn't known whose blood it was. Billy's or Elias'. Nor, to be fair, did he really understand the message that

Elias was Zechariah. That bit hadn't computed.

The trail of blood led him to the back of the auditorium. Once Anderson was through the curtains which hung at either side of the stage, darkness had enfolded him. The main room was blocked by the old cinema screen. Anderson could still hear the shouts from the other side. Officers directing the men and boys out of the building. Paramedics working on Crane. As he moved deeper into the bowels of the building, those sounds became muffled and eventually faded altogether.

Something had clattered on the floor to his left and he quickly followed the sound. Not daring to speculate what had caused it. Feeling his way through the gloom across the back of the screen, Anderson had failed to see the two figures at his feet, until he fell over them. Landing on something soft, which grunted under his weight, Anderson had screamed for someone to put the lights on. Luckily his foray to the back of the auditorium hadn't gone unnoticed and he was being followed by armed officers, who immediately put on their torches.

In the sweeping beams, Anderson had seen a gun on the floor. Immediately picking it up he had swung it at what appeared to be two bodies intertwined. One black male. One white male.

"Billy," croaked Crane.

Anderson nodded, poured more water into the beaker and handed it back to Crane.

CHAPTER 48

Anderson opened his mouth to continue his story but Crane put his arm out to stop him.

"No, I mean Billy's here. Now."

Crane drunk in the sight of him instead of the water, which lay forgotten in his hand. A sight more refreshing than any drink. The blond hair was still as unruly as ever. A sling bound his left arm tightly to his body. He was dressed in a hospital gown, sitting in a wheelchair, being pushed by the same formidable sister who looked after Crane.

"Hello, sir," the boyish grin lit up his eyes. "Just needed to see for myself that you were okay. They told me you were. But I didn't believe them."

"No, he kicked up a bit of a fuss down on the ward and managed to charm a young inexperienced nurse into bringing him up here." Sister sniffed to show her disapproval. "Now, Staff Sergeant Williams, you've seen your Sergeant Major. So back to bed for you." As she turned and wheeled Billy away, she called over her shoulder, "And rest time for you, Sergeant Major Crane. If you don't press that morphine button right now, I'll do it for you!"

"Must admit you are looking a bit rough now, Crane."

Crane could feel sweat breaking out on his forehead from the pain. Derek took the beaker which was slipping out of Crane's hand and put it back on the locker by the side of the bed.

"Feeling it too Derek." Crane fumbled for his morphine feed and his thumb presses the button. "Second instalment later?" But he'd drifted away and didn't hear the answer.

***

The muted sound of a television woke him and he lay there for a while listening to the beeps of his hated monitors. He was beginning to concentrate on them too much, listening to see if there was a skip of his heartbeat and constantly checking his blood pressure.

He struggled to sit up, a movement which sent searing pain through his shoulder and he collapsed back with a groan. But he tried to get up again, damned if the pain was going to stop him. His efforts were seen by the nurses, who came straight over, raising the head of the bed and making him more comfortable.

"If you don't stop doing that," one of them admonished, "you'll open the stitches. As it is you're aggravating the wound. Next time you want to sit up, just push the call button."

Crane groaned again, this time with frustration and looked around for something to distract him.

"When's Tina coming in?" he called after them.

One of the nurses returned to his bedside. "You

know we sent her home for at least a day and a night. She had to get some rest otherwise…" her voice tailed off.

"Otherwise?"

Refusing to look him in the eye she continued, "Otherwise she'll end up being as sick as you. Now stop fussing. Oh look," she said brightly, "here's Detective Inspector Anderson to see you," and almost ran from his bedside.

"Derek," Crane asked without preamble, "have you seen Tina?"

"Not since last night. Should I have done?"

"How did she seem?"

"Knackered. Now do you want the second instalment of the story or not?" Clearly Anderson was refusing to discuss Tina, so acquiescing, Crane leaned back on his pillows.

"As I was saying this morning, we found Billy and Elias in a tangle on the floor. Elias had a graze on his head, but otherwise seemed uninjured, although he was struggling to breathe. Billy had a knife sticking out of his arm. I arrested Elias for the attempted murder of Billy, which was the best I could think of at the time and then they were both carted off by the paramedics. Elias was briefly examined outside and pronounced fit to interview, so we hauled him off to Aldershot nick. Billy was brought here by ambulance, where he underwent emergency surgery for the damage to his arm."

"Will it be okay?" Crane asked, worried about Billy's future career.

"So they say. He'll need some recuperation and

physiotherapy, but in time will be back to normal."

"Good old Billy," Crane grinned. "Always was a brave soldier."

"Yeah well, he nearly throttled Elias." Anderson didn't seem to share Crane's enthusiasm for Billy's actions. "Why are you so concerned about Billy anyway?"

"Well, you know," Crane hedged, "he's one of my men."

Anderson's eyes narrowed in suspicion, "Are you sure there's not more to it than that?"

"Of course not, Derek." Crane changed the subject, "Where's Elias now? Locked up somewhere I hope?"

"Yep, Broadmoor. Bloke's as mad as a hatter. Spouting religious rhetoric, threatening everyone in sight with eternal damnation, that sort of thing."

"You know he told me he was responsible for my three soldiers?"

"Yes, he confessed to those to me as well. Very proudly in fact. Bastard. When I think of those kids…"

Crane asked for a drink.

"So, I think that's pretty much brought you up to date. Oh, by the way the powers that be, or upper echelons, as you call them, are all very happy. They think you're quite the hero of the hour, albeit a bit unconventional. So that's one less thing to worry about. Better leave you to rest now, otherwise I'll get my head chewed off by sister over there."

"Just one more thing before you go," Crane put

out his hand to stop Derek. "Who the hell kept ringing my mobile when I was in the cinema? Was it you?" Crane feigned anger.

"No, not me."

"Then tell me who it was, Derek. They won't let me have my mobile phone so I can check. Because of all the monitors or something. If you don't tell me now, I'll find out later anyway."

"Well, the first two times were the Padre and the third time was Mrs Morrison. Why does it matter?"

"Because they saved my life and the lives of the poor idiots trapped in the church with me." Crane could clearly remember the times when his mobile had vibrated. "What did they want?"

"Would you believe they'd both realised why the police artist's image of Zechariah looked familiar. They'd worked out it was Elias and had phoned to warn you."

"Well, they were a bit too late for that, but their intervention did the trick. Will you pass on my thanks to them?"

"Sure," Anderson patted Crane's arm. "But you'll be able to thank them for yourself soon when you're transferred to a general ward. Both of them want to come and see you. Although they might change their minds if you carry on being so grumpy and demanding. Oh by the way, Crane, talking about people being grumpy and demanding, Diane Chambers keeps turning up saying she needs to urgently interview you for her paper. Apparently she's been given the promise of an exclusive."

Smiling Crane said, "I think that'll have to wait

for now, don't you Derek? Get her off my back and I'll owe you one." Falling back against the pillows, Crane let Derek leave and pushed his morphine button once more.

As he drifted off, he was pleased that Anderson hadn't rumbled him. He must make sure no one ever found out that he set Billy up. When he realised Billy had disobeyed a direct order and was going to the church, he should have stopped him, but had decided not to. Wanted to let things play out, used Billy and his nephew as bait, hoping he could cover their backs. He'd have to make sure Billy's career didn't suffer too much. It was the least he could do.

CHAPTER 49

Crane opened his eyes to the most welcome sight he had ever seen. Tina.

"Hello, Tom," she said softly, the anxiety of the past few days written in the new lines on her face and the paleness of her skin. "How are you feeling?"

For a moment Crane couldn't speak. He squeezed her hand and took in every contour, every shadow. Coughing to hide his emotion, he then said more gruffly than he meant to, "I'd be better if I could sit up."

Tina held him by his good arm as he leaned forward and then deftly raised the top of the bed and rearranged the pillows one handed. As he sunk back, he joked, "You're pretty good at that, I bet you could get a job here." But somehow the joke fell flat and he ended up spluttering, "Not that you're not good at your job, I didn't mean that."

"Tom, it's alright. I knew you were only joking," she replied, taking his hand once more.

"Tina," he began then stopped again.

"Tom, we've got to talk."

"I know," he agreed.

"I've got something I want to say to you," she paused and looked down at her lap.

"No," he said finding his voice. "Let me go first. I've been thinking a lot about this and rehearsing it."

"Tom, it's not a presentation," she laughed.

"No, I know," he said, "but I want to make sure the words come out right."

"Okay."

But Crane had seen the small, sharp, involuntary, widening of her pupils. She was scared of what he was going to say. Well, so was he.

"First of all, sorry I didn't make it home for dinner. The last time we spoke I promised I wouldn't be late," Crane had copped out and he knew it.

Tina laughed, "Apology accepted, but I don't think that's what you really want to talk about."

"No you're right. It's, it's, this business of having children," he faltered. Tina squeezed his hand in encouragement. "Well, I know I've been pretty reluctant to make a decision. Refusing to talk about it when you needed to. Putting obstacles in the way. Need I go on?"

She shook her head. A small movement that caused her hair to hang over her face.

"Well I want to explain why. I don't think I even knew at the time. But I've had time to go over it." Tina kept her head down. "It was because of the case I was working on. Those children getting killed. Killed by their own fathers. It was more than

I could bear really. And I got to thinking that how could anyone bring a child into a world such as this. Where people can be manipulated into doing something so terrible."

"I see," Tina whispered, continuing to hide behind her hair.

"So I came to the conclusion that I couldn't have children. Understandable don't you think?"

Tina nodded, the movement making the tears fall from her face and drop into her lap.

Crane struggled to compose himself, tears pricking the back of his own eyes. "But lying here, at least in my more lucid moments, I realised I felt like that because I cared so much about children. I've had to accept that it's part and parcel of being a parent, wanting to do the best for them and protect them as much as you can. So my thinking was a bit skewed really. Tina?"

He got no response, so raising his tube infested hand, he touched her under the chin and lifted her face to his.

"Tina, do you understand? I'm trying to tell you I want us to have a child. Hell, more than one if you like!"

Tina gulped back her sobs.

"For God's sake say something!" he pleaded.

"I'm pregnant," she said, smiling through her tears.

****

ABOUT THE AUTHOR

Wendy Cartmell has a BA (Hons) degree in English and Education and is a former teacher, PR manager and editor of a large corporate newspaper. She has always written, either for work, or stories for her children. Recently she turned her hand to crime writing, resulting in a new crime series featuring Sgt Major Crane of the Special Investigations Branch, drawing on her husband's 22 years' service in the British Army. Wendy is lucky enough to live on the Costa del Sol with her husband and two dogs.

Website: www.wendycartmell.webs.com

40 Days 40 Nights

Someone wants to kill the Olympic athletes.
He'll stop at nothing to achieve his goal.
An SIB detective determined to catch the terrorists.

A soldier is found dead under the Olympic-sized swimming pool. His neck is broken and his weapon stolen. When Team GB descends on Aldershot Garrison in the run up to the 2012 Olympics, there is a terrorist determined to kill them. Sergeant Major Crane, a Branch detective with the Royal Military Police must keep the athletes safe through 40 Days and 40 Nights of accidents, thefts and murders. Can Crane pull it off? Or will the terrorists win?

DAY 1

They found the body at 04:00 hours. As he drove to the scene Sergeant Major Crane's hands gripped the steering wheel, his vision sharpened and his breathing rapid. Excitement that he had something to investigate overlaid, as always, with guilt. For his good fortune was at the expense of another man's life. He parked his car in front of the Aldershot Garrison Sports Centre, a squat grey lump surrounded by green and rushed to the scene. It was 04:45 hours.

He slowly walked around the remains, wearing protective clothing over his dark suit and white shirt, keeping well clear of the corpse, whilst he waited for the pathologist, Major Martin. As Crane crouched down to get a clearer view of the dead man, voices overhead interrupted his study.

Rising, he called, "We're down here, Major. The body is at the bottom of the steps." Crane's words echoed around the large underground cavern that was the underbelly of the huge Olympic sized swimming pool. The Major emerged, ducking his head under large grey pipes as he picked his way to the bottom of the stairs, encumbered by his medical case and the protective overalls he was wearing.

"I thought I recognised your voice, Crane. Right, what have we got?" The Major placed his case some way from the body and turned to look at it.

Crane called Sergeant Billy Williams from out of the shadows.

"Well, sir," Billy said, "as members of Team GB are on the garrison as part of their preparations for the Olympic Games, routine security patrols are made of the swimming pool every hour during the night. The soldiers keeping in touch by radio whilst they are separated. Corporal Simms failed to meet the others at the front door of the complex and did not answer urgent calls on his radio. So," Billy consulted his notes, "Lance Corporal Fielding went to find him. He saw Simmons crumpled at the bottom of the stairs that lead underneath the swimming pool. Unable to find a pulse, he swept the area, which he found to be empty and retreated. He then called the Royal Military Police as per procedure."

"So, the question is," Crane took over from Billy, "did the lad fall or was he killed?"

"For God's sake, Crane, at the moment I have no idea." Major Martin rose from his examination. "His neck appears to have been broken. It could be from a fall, possibly accidental, or he could have had some help. Another option is that someone surprised him and broke his neck here at the bottom of the stairs. I won't know anything until I get him on the table." The Major snapped off his gloves.

"Which will be?"

"Later this morning."

"I don't need to remind you…"

"No, Sergeant Major, you do not," the Major's voice was as taut as the latex he had just peeled from his hands. "I am well aware of the sensitivity of the situation at the moment, as no doubt Captain Edwards will also be happy to make clear to me. Including the Commanding Officer and anyone else who feels they have a right to put in their two pennies worth." Glancing at his watch, he continued. "It's nearly 05:30 hours. I'll do the post mortem at 10:00 hours. You can come if you want."

"I will… sir." Crane eventually finishing with the acknowledgement that Major Martin was an ex-officer. Even though Crane was a Sergeant Major, his position within the Special Investigations Branch enabled him to cut across the rank system when on an active investigation. Making the Branch as feared as it was respected. But officers, even ex-ones such as Major Martin, who was an accredited Home Office Pathologist whilst in the army, still expected the deference their rank deserved.

***

Crane decided to attend the post mortem later that morning, meeting the Major in the morgue at Frimley Park Hospital. Not out of ghoulish curiosity, nor because he enjoyed seeing corpses reduced to a pile of organs and empty cavities, but

317

simply because it was the quickest way to find out how Corporal Simms died. Actually, Crane hated everything about the morgue. The sterility, the smell, the noises. An incongruous operating theatre, where instead of opening up a living human being to heal them, doctors cut open a dead body to find out what had gone wrong. Once he was suitably kitted out and standing beside the metal trolley that held Corporal Simms in its icy embrace, Crane asked Major Martin to start on the neck first.

"I hope you aren't trying to tell me how to do my job, Crane?" the Major shouted over the noise of the grinding electric saw he was holding in his hand, which loomed perilously close to Crane's head instead of the corpse's.

"Not at all," said Crane, only just managing to duck out of the way in time. "It's the quickest way to get me out of your hair." A bizarre comment as the Major was practically bald under his protective headgear. "Figuratively speaking, of course," Crane finished lamely, adding, "sir."

"Very well, Crane." The Major turned off and put down the saw, then manipulated the young Corporal's neck. "Definitely broken. Feels like the spinal cord is ripped as well." Turning the head backwards and forwards, and peering at the face, he continued, "No obvious sign of trauma."

"Any sign of trauma to the neck itself? Bruising from fingers, or a garrotte of some kind?"

"No nothing. Here give me a hand to flip him over," the diminutive Major asked Crane. Crane helped to turn Corporal Simms over onto his front. A young man reduced to an ignominious naked body. Even through latex gloves the grey flesh felt rubbery and unyielding, reminding Crane of the texture of squid he once ate and hated. He waited whilst the Major cut through and then peeled back the defensive skin covering the young soldier's neck, exposing the bones and spinal cord.

"There!" the Major exclaimed with some satisfaction. "Broken between C3 and C4 and here are the loose ends of the spinal cord, see?"

Crane didn't want to, but glanced at the neck anyway, seeing mangled flesh and bones that meant nothing to him. Straightening up he said, "So now we definitely know what killed him."

"Certainly. Broken neck and spinal cord."

"But not how it happened."

"No evidence to suggest foul play at this stage. I would say it was most likely an accident."

"Most likely or definitely?" Crane wanted the distinction clarified.

"Most likely," confirmed the Major turning back to get on with the rest of the Post Mortem. "Now get out of my hair, Crane!"

By 11:00 hours Crane was reporting the findings to Captain Edwards.

"Excellent news," was Captain Edward's verdict as he smiled at Crane.

"Excellent sir? A soldier s dead!" Crane looked at Edwards, unable to mask the horror that must be etched on his face. Not wanting to believe what he had just heard.

"Oh for goodness sake, Crane. You know what I mean. Excellent news that it was an accident." Edwards went on, "I'll draw up a press release immediately to say that there has been an unfortunate accident, that has resulted in the death of a soldier on the garrison and, of course, confirm that to the family." Edwards gathered up his papers. A clear indication the meeting was over.

"But, sir, are you sure you shouldn't err on the side of caution and treat it as murder? There could be a potential threat to the athletes here. Someone could have been staking out the swimming pool and been surprised by Corporal Simms." Crane leaned forwards, his elbows on his knees.

"Crane, as I see it I am 'erring on the side of caution' as you put it. I am not about to spread panic throughout the Olympic community and the local community, by calling an accident a murder. Imagine the implications." Captain Edwards shuddered. "No. Sorry, Crane, accidental death it is."

"But -"

"No buts, Sergeant Major." Edwards rose from behind his desk, as was his habit, showing Crane that he was not only superior in rank, but superior in height.

Crane stood, but didn't leave the office. "Major Martin said 'most likely' not 'definitely'. I specifically queried that point."

"Crane, that's enough. I really think you are splitting hairs. I'm going with accidental death." Edwards moved from behind the desk and opened the door. "That will be all."

"Sir," Crane moved towards the open door. Then stopped. "You don't think?"

"I don't think anything, Crane!" Edward's voice rang out, causing a passing soldier to stop and look round. "And neither should you. Dismissed."

As Crane stalked off he tried to rein in his temper by reminding himself his special assignment was only for just over a month. As of today he was responsible for security on the garrison for forty days and forty nights whilst Team GB and then the Paralympians were on the garrison - so he better get on with it.

40 Days 40 Nights is now available from Amazon or by order from other bookstores.

21594001R00195

Printed in Poland
by Amazon Fulfillment
Poland Sp. z o.o., Wrocław